Murder at a London Finishing School

Books by Jessica Ellicott

MURDER IN AN ENGLISH VILLAGE

MURDER FLIES THE COOP

MURDER CUTS THE MUSTARD

MURDER COMES TO CALL

MURDER IN AN ENGLISH GLADE

MURDER THROUGH THE ENGLISH POST

MURDER AT A LONDON FINISHING SCHOOL

Published by Kensington Publishing Corp.

Murder at a London Finishing School

Jessica Ellicott

KENSINGTON
PUBLISHING CORP.
www.kensingtonbooks.com

KENSINGTON BOOKS are published by

Kensington Publishing Corp.
119 West 40th Street
New York, NY 10018

Library of Congress Card Catalogue Number: 2023934457

ISBN-13: 978-1-4967-4014-4
First Kensington Hardcover Edition: August 2023

ISBN-13: 978-1-4967-4015-1 (ebook)

10 9 8 7 6 5 4 3 2 1

Printed in the United States of America

Murder at a London Finishing School

Chapter 1

The day was just exactly the sort Edwina Davenport most loved. The air was fresh and a rose-scented breeze floated in through a pair of windows opened onto the back garden. She had nothing marked down in her diary for the day and had decided to allow herself the pleasure of a few hours spent working on her novel.

When she had last left her cowboy hero, he had just been bitten by a rattlesnake slipped into his saddlebag by his archnemesis, the leader of an outlaw gang, and she itched to extricate him from his difficulties. As she considered the most thrilling ways she might do so, a discreet knock landed on the office door. Beddoes, her perfect paragon of a housekeeper, entered bearing a thick stack of envelopes and placed it on the edge of the desk, withdrawing without a word.

Edwina tried to turn her attention to her typewriter once more but try as she might, the top envelope would not be ignored. The crest on the letterhead was exactly as it had been all those years ago when the first missive had arrived from Miss DuPont's Finishing School for Young Ladies, addressed to her mother. Unable to resist, she plucked the letter from the stack and neatly slit open the envelope.

She read through the letter carefully. It was an invitation to the prospective students' week. She heaved an assuredly unladylike sigh of relief. Neither she nor Beryl had a daughter in need of finishing. Neither had any children at all. While Edwina often felt this misfortune acutely, it was an undeniably legitimate reason to decline the invitation. She would not even have to broach what would surely be an unwelcome topic with Beryl.

She reached for the envelope once more with the intention of tucking the letter back inside, when she noticed it was heavier than it ought to be if it were empty. She tipped it up and a half-sheet of thick, creamy stationery slid onto her desk blotter. She picked it up and recognized the firm and beautiful handwriting of Miss DuPont herself.

> *Dear Edwina,*
>
> *Although you may not be aware of it, since graduating my first class of young ladies I have made a point to keep myself acquainted with their progress in life. As a result of that policy I am aware of Davenport and Helliwell, Private Enquiry Agency and it is in connection with the same that I am writing to you.*
>
> *Some matters at the school have arisen of late and I am in need of assistance from someone in your field of endeavor. I would not like for anyone to know that I have contacted you in a professional capacity and so hoped that I might convince you to attend the prospective students' week with what I believe is referred to in detective novels as a cover story. I regret the last-minute nature of*

my request and would not have considered inconveniencing you if it were not a matter of some urgency. I thought if you are willing, you could say that you have a second cousin or a goddaughter overseas whom you are interested in enrolling, but that you wished to be sure the school was as you remembered before you did so.

Please send a reply posthaste and do give my regards to Beryl.

Faithfully,
Miss Ermentrude DuPont

Edwina felt her relief slink away like a dog who has been caught with his mistress's carpet slipper in his mouth. There was no way she could avoid discussing it with Beryl now. A shiver of worry slipped between her shoulder blades.

Miss DuPont was not the sort to ask for favors of any kind. Nor was she one inclined to baseless drama. If she had penned this note, the matter was one of real urgency. The only thing that would have shocked her more would have been if the elderly lady had made the request by telephone, a practice that even to Edwina's far younger mind was tinged with vulgarity.

She was still deciding whether it would be best to break the news to Beryl by preparing one of her favorite meals and suggesting a round of her dear friend's favored American-style cocktails or if she ought to simply come out with it, when the object of her pondering appeared in the doorway.

"I'm not disturbing you in the middle of something, am I?" she asked, not waiting for an answer before entering the room and dropping into a chair opposite the desk from Edwina. That settled it. She might as well get it over with.

"No indeed. I was just attending to my correspondence," Edwina said.

"Anything interesting?" Beryl asked.

"As a matter of fact, we have received a joint invitation that I am inclined to accept."

"Has Charles finally decided to host us for bridge at his place rather than leaving it to you to proffer an invitation?" Beryl asked, leaning forward and winking extravagantly.

Beryl had somehow become convinced that the local solicitor, Charles Jarvis, not-so-secretly pined for Edwina. Until very recently she would have vehemently disagreed. If only she could congratulate Beryl on her guess. She shook her head.

"As pleasant as that surely would be, I am afraid not. The invitation comes from further afield. Just outside London, in fact." Edwina held her breath and fixed her gaze on Beryl's face, wondering if her friend would start to put the puzzle together.

"London! I adore London. But you are rarely keen to pry yourself away from Walmsley Parva. What on earth could have tempted you? We haven't been asked to attend the opening of some high-end millinery shop, have we?"

Edwina allowed herself a thought as to how much she would love to attend the opening of a new hat shop. There was little she loved more than the careful consideration of a new piece of headwear, especially if she was doing so by trying on a myriad of them. With another unladylike sigh, she shook her head.

"As you so often prefer to go about bareheaded, I cannot see encouraging you to make the trip to London for something in that line," Edwina said. "We have received an invitation to pay a visit to Miss DuPont's."

Edwina paused and waited for her words to sink in. Beryl's mouth popped open in a perfect "O" of surprise. Then, her mouth snapped shut and the corners of her lips lifted in a smile.

"It must be a clerical error. Miss DuPont is far too well connected to not be well aware that neither of us has a daughter who requires finishing. And she has the good sense to realize that even if I did, I would be the last woman on earth to hold with such an old-fashioned practice."

Edwina truly hated to be the bearer of bad news and to be responsible for returning that look of dread to Beryl's face, but there was simply nothing else to be done.

"She wishes to hire us for a job, and one to be attended to discreetly at that, which is why she is inviting us to come to her at the school claiming to be there to evaluate the school for a goddaughter or a young cousin."

"A job? You mean to say she requires a private enquiry of some sort?"

Edwina slid the letter across the desk and Beryl eyed it for a moment before condescending to pick it up and read it for herself. She did so with her usual speed and dropped the half sheet back on the desk as though it were a live electrical wire.

"Surely there are plenty of agencies in London she could hire rather than ask us to make such a trek."

"Have you ever known Miss DuPont to make a request that she did not think the very best option?"

"Historically she was very exacting in her standards," Beryl said, her usually rosy complexion blanching at what Edwina guessed was the memory of Miss DuPont's critical evaluations. In her mind's eye Edwina could see Miss DuPont leaning over Beryl's shoulder and tut-tutting at her young charge's clumsy attempts at embroidering a handkerchief.

"I expect that is why she has requested us. She believes we are the exact right agency for the job."

"But, Ed, can't you go without me? You know how much I have been looking forward to my getaway," Beryl said.

Indeed, Edwina did know. After all, Beryl had made more mention of her plans to spend the next few days at a nearby hotel complete with golf course, in the company of a man she referred to as her favorite Viking, than Edwina preferred to hear. Edwina had heard her friend moving about her bedroom, humming to herself far earlier than was her habit. She had even already loaded her valise into the boot of her motorcar and planned to set out directly after lunch.

"I know that it matters a great deal to you, but I cannot see how we can refuse. In fact, I think it best if we leave today."

"Maybe it is some sort of a hoax. The idea that Miss DuPont is in any actual difficulty simply boggles the mind." Beryl widened her eyes at Edwina in much the same way her small dog Crumpet did when he wished to communicate the desire for a tasty morsel from the tea tray.

Edwina was no more likely to fall for such nonsense from her human companion than she was from her canine one. In her opinion, begging could simply not be rewarded no matter how pitiful the beggar. Besides, Beryl ceaselessly admonished and cajoled her into setting her entirely reasonable fears aside in order to tackle new challenges and to have new adventures. Turnabout was fair play.

"You put your finger on the heart of the matter precisely. To imagine Miss DuPont is so worried about something that she is compelled to contact private enquiry agents, is almost inconceivable. Which is why I feel we must accept the invitation and why you surely could not expect me to attend to this matter on my own. If it is a problem beyond Miss DuPont's abilities, it will absolutely require the both of us."

Edwina kept her eyes focused on Beryl's face. She watched as a range of emotions, from fear to irritation to resignation flit across it with hummingbird-like speed. Then, Beryl shrugged her shoulders back down away from her ears and gave the briefest of nods.

"Since you put it that way, I suppose the Viking will have to wait."

"That's the spirit," Edwina said as Beryl hoisted herself from her chair and headed for the door.

Beryl paused at the threshold. "That said, I did cheer myself up on occasion behind enemy lines, reminding myself that at least I wasn't still at finishing school. I suggest you start your own packing as I am already packed. If we leave fairly soon, we can be there in time for tea."

Edwina's stomach clenched. "I consulted the timetable and then next train isn't until late this afternoon. The earliest we could possibly arrive would be in time for dinner," she said.

"If you will insist upon me canceling my well-deserved and long overdue romantic getaway, that's one thing, but I refuse to miss out on taking the old bus out for a good long ramble. It's been simply ages since she has had a real run out on the open road." Beryl drew herself up to her full height and tapped her foot impatiently on the polished wood floor.

"You don't mean to say you wish to drive us," Edwina said.

"Those are my terms. If you want me to accompany you, I insist that I be allowed to drive," Beryl said. Edwina appeared to hesitate on the knife-edge of a decision. After a few heartbeats she bobbed her head in acquiescence.

Edwina ran through a mental list of all that she would need to make ready in order to leave with confidence. "I shall be ready in two hours' time at most."

"Whatever do you need so much time for? You aren't planning to torture yourself about the packing, are you?" Beryl asked.

"Not everyone is as blasé about throwing a few items haphazardly into a rucksack and calling it good. Besides, I need to take Crumpet for a walk and consult with Beddoes about running the household whilst we are away. Unless you would like to speak with her?" Edwina asked, knowing full well what the answer would be. Beryl had learned to leave any necessary communication with their most excellent housekeeper to her.

"I would not think of interfering. Besides, I must telephone to my Viking to let him know that I am obligated to cancel our getaway."

"While you're at it, would you please place a call to the school to tell Miss DuPont to expect us, that is if we manage to make it there alive."

Chapter 2

Edwina chided herself for ever having doubted that Beryl would be willing to cancel her plans in order to accompany her to Miss DuPont's. Although her friend had enthused almost constantly about her upcoming visit with Ralph ever since he had telephoned her with an invitation two days prior, she could not imagine Beryl leaving her to handle a case all on her own, especially not one that took her to London. Well, the outskirts of it at least.

For one thing, Beryl absolutely adored the verve of city life. She positively thrived on it. But for another, she was well aware that Edwina most assuredly did not. The noise, the smells and the endless crush of strangers made Edwina's skin feel clammy just thinking of it. She had somehow managed to survive her time at Miss DuPont's in her youth but had not felt particularly desirous of returning to London, or any other city for that matter. She thought of her roses once more and her heart sank.

Still, she was a professional working woman now, and as such, sacrifices would need to be made. While she had not considered that their cases might take them farther afield than the outskirts of her beloved Walmsley Parva, she realized with a slight thrill that although she thought of herself as a resolute homebody, the notion of becoming a successful enough private investigator to be called out on cases as far away as London provided her a shiver of delight. And to think, Miss DuPont was the first such far-off client to request them. There was something truly remarkable about the idea of her conservative and respectable headmistress esteeming them this way. Not everyone was modern enough in their views to consider that women could perform as private enquiry agents, and Edwina was somewhat surprised to consider that Miss DuPont might be amongst them.

She tugged her thoughts back to the task at hand. While Beryl was incredibly adept at tossing a few things into a bag and feeling confident that she would find herself suitably attired for any and all occasions, Edwina despaired of ever developing such a skill. She invariably over-packed and ended up feeling as though she planned to move in permanently to any location where she merely intended to spend the night. Perhaps it was one of the reasons she did not particularly care to travel.

Surely there must be a system that would allow her to select the appropriate number of garments, shoes, and unmentionables for a set number of days. Her mind drifted off again as she thought of how such a handy guide for ladies might become a best-selling book, especially at train stations. Her stomach gave a lurch once more as she imagined what she was sure would prove a harrowing journey between Walmsley Parva and London. How she longed for the comfort of even a second-class coach on the train. But, she supposed, if Beryl could be a good sport about missing her golfing getaway, Edwina could make the best of a trip in the motorcar.

She resolved to take a knitting project with her in order to give her hands something better to do than to clutch at the dashboard in front of her. With a sigh she flung open the wardrobe door and peered inside. Crumpet nervously shadowed her every step as she placed armloads of clothing onto the bed. She wished there was some way he could accompany her to London, but did not think that would be for the best.

Within a mere fifteen minutes' time she had packed and unpacked then packed the suitcase once again, absolutely certain she would arrive at Miss DuPont's with nothing whatsoever to wear. Just as she was about to despair, her stomach tied in a queasy knot; she heard the stomping of Simpkins's boots passing along the upstairs hallway. She turned to see him framed in her doorway, a look of concern on his face.

"What's this I hear about you heading up to the city?" Simpkins asked.

Although Simpkins had recently come into a large fortune as the sole proprietor of Colonel Kimberly's Condiment Company, headquartered in London, he had not yet come to feel entirely comfortable with the role or with the place. In fact, Edwina had a hard time imagining him with his gardener's boots and slow gait keeping pace with city folk as they rushed through the streets past towering buildings.

"You've spoken with Beryl, I see," she said.

"Indeed, I have. I assume this must be for a case; otherwise I can't imagine you leaving the Beeches just as your roses are coming into their last flush of bloom for the season," he said.

Edwina felt a lump forming in her throat. For as much as Simpkins could be set in his ways and inclined to contradict her about almost anything under the sun, she was touched by how well he knew her. No one else shared her passion for the grounds at the Beeches like Simpkins did.

He had invested considerable quantities of his own recently acquired fortune into renovating the gardens throughout the property and bringing them back to the condition they had enjoyed before Edwina's own finances had taken such a turn for the worse. It was just like him to realize how much she had been looking forward to those last glorious days of scent and bloom the garden put forth as a final display of glory, before the cool weather laid branches bare and the landscape dreary for months on end.

"The trip is for a case, and one I'm afraid we cannot refuse. Both Beryl and I wish the timing were different, but alas, these things happen sometimes. You shall have to enjoy the roses enough for the both of us and hope that we are able to wrap up the case with sufficient speed that I may return before they are finished blooming."

"If you can wrap it up in only a few days, that should leave you at least a bit of time to get back and enjoy them. What do you plan to do with Crumpet?" Simpkins nodded toward the little dog, who looked up at the sound of his name.

"I was meaning to seek you out and speak to you about him. I hardly think it professional to take him along on a case, and I can't imagine he would enjoy being subjected to the ravages of Beryl's driving any more than I. Would you be willing to keep a close eye on him while I'm gone? Beddoes is excellent at her duties, but I don't think she considers dog sitting to be amongst them," Edwina said.

"The poor little fellow and I will cheer each other up while you're gone. I'll make sure he gets out for a ramble now and again and I'll see to it that he manages to eat something from time to time. You know how he pines whenever you're away," Simpkins said, shaking his head dolefully as he bent down and scratched the dog behind his right ear.

As if Edwina did not feel guilty enough about missing out on the last of the roses, she felt absolutely heartsick at the notion of leaving poor Crumpet behind. Simpkins was right to say that the little terrier did poorly in her absence. Generally speaking, he lay down in front of the hall tree where she kept her collection of hats and refused to budge until her return. When she had been away for a few days at a nearby country house on a case weeks before, he had only been persuaded to leave his spot long enough to take a few sips from his water bowl.

She felt a sudden surge of gratitude for Simpkins and his willingness to tend out on her little dog. If she were the demonstrative sort, she was sure she would be tempted to throw her arms about him in a grateful embrace. As she was not, she simply nodded and turned back to the piles strewn across the surface of the bed. The sooner she left, the sooner she would return.

She felt a knot gathering at the base of her skull and forced her shoulders to draw back down from around her ears. There was no way she could manage the task of packing, not even in a vulgarly overblown way, until she cleared her head. She needed a walk. And if she were to be London-bound, the least she could do was to take her dear little terrier out for an extra-long romp.

She patted Simpkins on his boney shoulder and made her way out to the landing at the top of the stairs. She whistled for Crumpet as she descended, and found him awaiting her as she reached the bottom step, his tail thumping against the carpet with anticipation. Despite her downturned mood, she spared a thought for the devoted ministrations of her new housekeeper, Beddoes.

The paragon of domesticity had arrived some weeks ago at Simpkins's behest and had promptly set about giving the entire house a thorough bottoming out. In the few years between her mother's death and Beddoes's arrival, Edwina could not have truthfully said she had ever taken the carpets out to a line strung between a pair of the property's eponymous beeches. Crumpet's tail had done the majority of any beatings the carpets had received in those bleak days.

She plucked her third-best hat and Crumpet's lead from the hall tree. She gave his ears an affectionate rub as she clipped it to his collar before tugging her hat onto her head. She stepped out into the sunshine and made for the shady lane beyond the drive. She turned left and meandered in the direction of the open fields on the outskirts of the village. She was in no mood for company, besides Crumpet's.

The September sun was warm on her head, even through the protection of her hat, and she thought of how glorious the gardens at Miss DuPont's had been at this time of the year when she was a girl. She would be delighted to see them once again; that is, if she managed to arrive in the outskirts of London in one piece and with her wits intact.

Many things had changed since Beryl had arrived the previous autumn. Edwina was no longer beset by loneliness, she had secured a place for herself in the world as a working woman, she had bobbed her hair. But one thing she had not done was to become an enthusiast of motorcars, particularly those driven by Beryl. While her friend had a generous store of fine qualities, an apparent value of her own life, or those of her passengers, when finding herself behind a steering wheel was not one of them.

Edwina vastly preferred to travel by train. It was safe, it was civilized, and it arrived where it promised vaguely on time with no unexpected detours for interesting side roads or because of tire punctures. Unlike so many of her trips with Beryl, great clouds of smoke were a sign of things functioning properly when on a train, not a harbinger of hours spent sidelined on a grassy verge whilst her friend yanked on hoses and muttered darkly under her breath. Still, if Beryl had condescended to join her at Miss DuPont's despite her qualms, the least she could do was to bear the mode of travel with good grace.

Up ahead she spotted a dense patch of shade spreading beneath a towering oak. It was the perfect place to rest for a moment and she urged Crumpet to leave off his sniffing and to trot along. As she leaned against the trunk of the sturdy tree, she took in the view of the sweeping pasture in front of her that rolled down toward the bank of the river.

She held a small hand over her eyes as she caught sight of a tall, trim figure making his way along the river's edge, some sort of box tucked under his arm. The figure stopped abruptly and knelt to fiddle with the box. With a few deft maneuvers of his hands, the box unfolded and transformed into an easel. Crumpet tugged determinedly on his lead. She quickened her pace at his urging and hurried forward to greet her dear friend Charles Jarvis.

While Charles was best known as the local solicitor, he was known to his intimates as an enthusiastic and dedicated amateur watercolorist. As Edwina made her way across the field, she was startled by the colors she could see even from a distance on the canvas Charles propped up on his easel. They were far more vivid than those he usually employed.

The painting was less representational than his usual work as well. From a distance she could only discern swirls of color upon the canvas, but as she drew closer, she could tell from the direction of the brushstrokes and the energy of the movement that Charles had captured the essence of the scene in front of them.

Edwina felt her breath catch in her throat. She had encouraged Charles to pursue his interest in painting, of course she had. But truth be told, she had not felt particularly moved by any of it. Certainly, she had found his mild watercolors of village houses and rather twee scenes of her garden endearing, but none of them had provoked in her more than an almost maternal approval.

He had turned his hand to a credible likeness of herself and Beryl that she had happily hung in a place of pride across from her desk in her office at the Beeches, and she had been particularly surprised at the boldness of a painting he had made of her during a recent stay at an artists' colony. But this was something altogether different. It was as if Charles had captured the spirit of the river and all that surrounded it. She looked from the canvas to the river to her friend, in awe.

Crumpet let out a sharp bark of greeting and Charles turned. He stepped in front of his canvas, as if to shield it from Edwina's view. Her heart went out to him. From her own experience with her novel, she understood completely the urge to create something in complete privacy and to wish to keep it secret from the glare of the world until one was entirely sure of its merit.

She continued to keep her eyes firmly fixed on his face as she slowed her pace. She lifted an eyebrow questioningly and laid a hand on the cuff of his rolled-up sleeve as she stopped at his side. He gave the barest of nods and stepped away from his easel, providing an unobstructed view of his work in progress.

Up close, the painting was even more vibrant, more moving than it had been from afar. The swirl and swoop of the various shades of blues and greens indicating the river left Edwina feeling as if she were seeing the body of water as a sentient being. The deeper greens and golds bending gracefully toward the current reminded her of a dance from India that Beryl had once demonstrated after imbibing an unadvised number of cocktails. Her breath caught in her throat once more and she shook her head in amazement as she tugged her gaze from the painting and turned it instead on Charles.

"I must commend you on your creation of something so absolutely stirring," she said. "I am utterly beguiled by it."

Charles stepped back a pace to stand beside her and to share her vantage point. "You are?"

"I am. Somehow you have captured the sense of the river and its banks without providing any exacting detail. However have you done this?" she asked, tilting her head back to look at him as he towered above her.

The motion slid her hat precariously away from its perch

and Charles caught it before it reached the ground. He handed it back to her with a slight bow then turned to the painting as if to consider her question.

"I realized that what matters to me most is the heart of things, the feeling of them rather than the specifics. Odd, I know, for a solicitor to be so frivolous with details, but I find it much more interesting than fiddling with the act of replication. With so many excellent and portable bits of photographic equipment about these days, I am not sure my efforts to accurately capture an image are worth the paint required."

"But this has nothing whatsoever to do with replication. It is more like you have melded into the scene. It is as if you have entered the consciousness, if such a thing could be, of the river and the trees and then placed them here for others to understand." Edwina leaned even closer. "Charles, you have astonished me. I think you have come into your own with this new direction."

Despite a decidedly red tinge to his cheeks, he held her gaze for a long moment. "I have had a very encouraging source of inspiration. If it were not for your own bold attempts at trying new things, I am not sure I would have challenged myself to do likewise."

Edwina was not sure how to respond. Fortunately, Crumpet began to bark and to rear up on his hind legs, placing his forepaws on Charles's trouser legs, insisting attention be paid to him as well as his mistress. The way that her dog begged to be noticed put her in mind of the solution to something that had troubled her ever since Simpkins agreed to take Crumpet out for his daily walks.

"While I am delighted to have happened upon you since it meant viewing your new work, I have another reason to be pleased. I should like to beg a favor."

"Consider it granted," Charles said.

"But I haven't asked yet."

"I shall say yes whatever you end up asking."

"How very gallant," she said, feeling a bit of heat rising on her own cheeks. "Still, in order to fulfill the request, I shall have to disclose it."

"Very well then. How may I serve you?" He made another playful bow, this one slightly deeper than the last.

"Beryl and I have received a request to attend on a client in London."

"I will miss you both," Charles said. From the tone of his voice, Edwina was certain he meant it.

"How very flattering. However, I doubt you will be as troubled as will poor Crumpet. I cannot take him with me, and I believe he will be inclined to fret if not sufficiently distracted. Simpkins has promised to walk him, but I am quite sure that he will simply turn him out in the gardens to wander about."

"It would be my pleasure to take him out for a ramble. You'd like that, wouldn't you, boy?" Charles asked.

"He would be overjoyed. He has a very soft spot for you, as you can plainly see." Edwina glanced down at Crumpet, who lay on the ground with his chin resting on the toe of Charles's leather brogue.

Charles bent down and scratched at a particularly favored spot between Crumpet's ears. She couldn't be sure, but Edwina thought Charles murmured, "If only your mistress felt the same."

Chapter 3

The soothing rhythm of the road had begun to work its magic, and Beryl's mood brightened as soon as they had traveled only a mile or two out of Walmsley Parva. Edwina had slowed their departure more than Beryl would have preferred by a tearful leave-taking of Crumpet and a last-minute flurry concerning the quantity of luggage. She was happy for the excuse of making up for lost time as they darted along the narrow country lanes. The sun shone agreeably overhead, and for the majority of the journey she put Ralph and their thwarted visit from her mind.

She might have forgotten it altogether if not for Edwina doing an uncharacteristically good job of holding her tongue on the subject of Beryl's driving. Not once had she uttered the words *reckless* or *harrowing*. Although Beryl had often wished that Edwina would keep her thoughts on the subject of her driving skills to herself, she found it unnerving once it had finally happened.

Was Edwina holding her tongue as a form of apology for accepting the visit to Miss DuPont's? Or, more alarmingly, had

Beryl lost her adventurous spirit to the point she no longer dazzled behind the wheel? Surely not!

Edwina had spent the trip with her eyes firmly fixed on some sort of woolen item steadily taking shape on her knitting needles. That had to be a far more reasonable explanation of her uncharacteristic quietude than the absurd notion that Beryl had lost her edge. Still, by the time they had reached the city she was rather relieved when she heard a sharp intake of breath from Edwina.

She expertly maneuvered around pedestrians and horse-drawn carts and carriages as she nosed her beloved motorcar toward their destination. The traffic thinned bit by bit and the buildings began to appear farther and farther apart with each passing block. In even less time than she had estimated, the towering wrought-iron gate supporting a discreet placard proclaiming that they had arrived at MISS DUPONT'S FINISHING SCHOOL FOR YOUNG LADIES appeared before them. As they rounded a wide bend in the drive, the building reared up in front of them. Beryl eased off the accelerator as she felt Edwina's hand clamp down on her arm.

"If we are lucky, we will get to the bottom of Miss DuPont's concerns in less than a day and be back home to the Beeches by teatime tomorrow," Edwina said as she tucked her knitting safely away into a small bag.

Beryl felt a slight lift to her sagging spirits. She had always thought herself mightily favored by fortune. Was there any reason to expect her luck to have run out? She squared her shoulders and shot the motorcar into motion once more. As they drew closer, memories of the place came flooding back, prompted in large part by Edwina's excited exclamations.

"It looks just as I remembered it. After all this time you'd think that it would appear altered, but it doesn't, at least not at first glance," Edwina said.

The second the vehicle halted in the gravel-covered semicircle in front of the three-story building with its long, glinting windows flanked by manicured boxwood topiaries, Edwina launched herself from it with remarkably little decorum. If Miss DuPont were watching from behind one of the heavy drapes framing the windows, she would certainly be heard clucking her tongue in horror at such an unladylike display from one of her graduates.

It was the sort of behavior much more likely to be displayed by Beryl than by Edwina. Beryl had a sneaking suspicion that Edwina's exuberance would be marked down to a bad influence on account of the questionable company she kept. Beryl spared a thought to what might have happened had they arrived with Simpkins in tow rather than leaving him back home at the Beeches. She took a deep breath, tugged firmly at her red leather driving gloves, and slid out from behind the wheel.

As much as she would have preferred to avoid the whole thing, once she had committed to an expedition, she would see it through with the best attitude she could muster. For her this was a personal code of conduct and a point of pride. There were those with whom she had set off from time to time who regretted their decision and spent entire journeys tormenting those around them with their grumbling. No matter the circumstances, Beryl would never comport herself in such an unsportswomanlike way.

Feeling more cheerful than she had since Edwina had announced her intention to accept the case, she rounded the front of the motorcar, giving the dear old bus an affectionate pat on the hood as she did so.

"Your gloves will be soiled beyond saving if you insist on touching something as filthy as a motorcar's bonnet," a reedy and unfortunately familiar voice called out from the building's wide front steps. Beryl had not expected Miss Glover to still be alive, let alone still at the school. Perhaps her luck had run out after all.

"Miss Glover, what a pleasure to see you once again," Edwina said, stepping forward and giving Beryl time to compose herself.

Miss Glover had been the bane of Beryl's existence the entire time she had been at Miss DuPont's. If her memory served, Miss Glover had made her sole purpose to break the spirit of any of the young ladies who did not fall immediately in line with the program set out for them. Beryl had proved the most recalcitrant of her class and had come in for the brunt of Miss Glover's relentless criticism.

"I see you have not outgrown an unfortunate predilection for keeping questionable company, Miss Davenport," Miss Glover said. "I would have thought you would have learned by now to choose your companions more carefully. I had hopes that your lack of judgment was simply a youthful folly. It appears I was mistaken."

"You're just exactly as I remember you," Beryl said, stepping forward and delivering the most dazzling smile she could muster.

Faced with adversity it was always her strategy to ignore it and proceed as though everything was going her way. It had seen her through countless adventures and misadventures. Besides, she was not the same person she had been all those years ago, when last she had been at the school. At least not in terms of experience.

While she liked to imagine that she had kept a firm grasp on her youthful spirit, she was far more seasoned in dealing with adversity than she had been as a girl of sixteen. Over the course of her life, she had encountered more than her fair share of naysayers and had learned a thing or two about how best to deal with them.

"I would attribute that to my healthy diet and committed abstinence from all forms of vice. I can see that you have not followed my example," Miss Glover said, peering over the top of her glasses and glancing up and down at Beryl's figure.

It was true that Beryl had become slightly less fit in her time living at the Beeches. There was something about village life that was easily conducive to putting on a bit of weight. She had never had any trouble keeping her slim figure while she was trekking through jungles or riding camels across the desert. It wasn't until she dined most days on one of Simpkins's gourmet meals, rather than simply spooning beans directly from a tin down her gullet, that she had developed such troubles. How Edwina managed to stay so slim despite a lifetime in Walmsley Parva she would never understand.

"Beryl has always been one to follow her own inclinations. I'm sure you must have read all about her triumphs in the papers," Edwina said, shooting her a reassuring glance.

Miss Glover sniffed loudly. "I would sooner describe them as exploits. Given your education at Miss DuPont's, I should have thought both of you would understand nothing good can come of having your name appear in the newspapers unless it is to announce your wedding or your death. I will say that I have noticed wedding announcements on more than one occasion for you, Miss Helliwell."

"As you mentioned, I have not been one to turn my back on vice," Beryl said.

"Since you seem to be in such good health yourself, can we hope to expect the same of Miss DuPont?" Edwina asked. Beryl had to admire her friend for her skill at steering the course of conversations into safe waters. Conflict was not something Edwina generally sought out and did her best to smooth over when it swirled around, threatening to engulf herself or those around her.

"Miss DuPont is the same as she ever was. She has asked that

I keep an eye out for you and bring you to her directly. If you will both follow me, you can see for yourself how she fares," Miss Glover said.

She turned her back on them abruptly and strode into the school's grand foyer. Richly hued oil paintings hung on the paneled walls, some of which had been presents from parents of former students or even the students themselves once they completed their course. Beryl knew that a number of them were quite valuable, or at least they had been while she was in attendance.

She had made the mistake of reaching out to adjust a crooked frame one afternoon not long after she had first arrived at the school, and had been sharply admonished by one of the teaching staff never to touch them. Over the years more paintings had been added to the collection—so many, in fact, that they were displayed on the wall beside the grand staircase extending from the first to the second floor. Beryl recognized none of the pieces of art as they trailed behind Miss Glover.

The elderly woman stopped abruptly in front of a heavy wooden door at the far end of the second-floor corridor. Beryl remembered the first time she had stood in this very spot awaiting permission to enter to meet the headmistress. Miss Glover rapped on the door, turned the knob, and shoved it open.

Edwina stepped over the threshold, following closely on Miss Glover's heels. As Beryl towered above the other two women, over their heads she could see the figure of Miss DuPont seated behind her enormous mahogany desk, just as she had done on Beryl's first day at the school.

"Thank you, Eunice. Please, don't let me keep from your duties any longer. I'm sure the girls will be eager to have you all to themselves once again," Miss DuPont said with a dismissive bob of her head. Without a word Miss Glover turned on her heel and strode out of the room, pulling the door firmly closed behind her.

Chapter 4

Just as Miss Glover had said, Miss DuPont had aged exceedingly well. Her hair was a steely gray with a few white streaks rather than the deep chestnut of the past, but her posture was erect, and her face mapped with far fewer lines than Edwina would have expected from one as aged as she remembered her former teacher to be. When Miss Glover had knocked discreetly on the door before pushing it open, the voice that bid them enter was clear and firm.

Their former teacher's eyes were still bright and held an undeniable softening of relief as they stepped out from behind Miss Glover and moved to take the seats she indicated across from the same wide oak desk she had held court from behind all those years ago. Miss DuPont looked them up and down and Edwina felt a wave of déjà vu wash over her. She could well remember the very first time she had sat in the same chair opposite that scrutiny.

Her stomach had clenched from the discomfort of that interview. Her mother had enumerated her many faults and missing graces to Miss DuPont as a sort of to-do list for the school to address. Miss DuPont had given nothing away as she had looked adolescent Edwina up and down, and she gave nothing away now. That is, not until she leaned forward and gave them each a smiling nod.

"Miss Davenport and Miss Helliwell, I cannot tell you how pleased I am to see you both. It was so good of you to accept my invitation. I am sure neither of you were particularly eager to return and I am in your debt for doing so," she said.

Edwina willed Beryl to keep her thoughts on the visit to herself, and for once she managed to hold her tongue long enough for Edwina to speak first. Beryl had always felt on the back foot at the finishing school, and it seemed she had not grown out of it.

"There is no debt to be considered," Edwina said without looking at Beryl. "I am sure any of your graduates would be honored to help you however they could."

"It is very kind of you to say so. I have a fondness for all of my finished young ladies and would hope that the feeling is reciprocated."

Once again Edwina willed Beryl to refrain from commenting. Perhaps it was a tribute to Miss DuPont's tutelage, but Beryl did not even let out the merest guffaw. She simply sat in the chair next to Edwina, holding her posture completely erect and her hands folded neatly in her lap before launching into the reason for their visit.

"Your letter said you are interested in our professional services. How may we be of help?" Beryl asked.

Edwina was pleased to note that Beryl sounded just as she always did at preliminary client interviews. There was nothing in her voice that hinted in the least at her reluctance to assist. The knot between Edwina's shoulder blades unkinked ever so slightly.

"Straight down to business, I see. How very practical you are, Miss Helliwell. You always were remarkably forthright. It has served you well in your endeavors, I dare say. So, I shall be equally forthcoming. I fear someone is attempting to drive me out of business."

With that, Miss DuPont placed one hand over the other atop her desk blotter and looked from one to the other. She held her head cocked to the side in the exact pose she had adopted when questioning the pair of them years earlier about an incident involving one of the other young ladies.

"Drive you out of business?" Edwina asked. "Are you sure?"

"I flatter myself that I am not one to overreact, Miss Davenport. I would not have troubled you to come if I had any doubt," she said.

"What has happened to convince you of this?" Beryl asked.

"There are reports of missing items, unexplained noises, and even, if you can credit it, strange lights in the night. There is a persistent rumor amongst the girls that the school is haunted," she said.

"I assume you don't give credence to a supernatural explanation?" Beryl asked.

"I have never been one to indulge in such nonsense. I am certain there is a logical explanation for it all, but I have not been able to root out the perpetrator on my own."

Edwina looked over at Beryl and met her friend's gaze. "Is there any reason to think it is sabotage? Could it be that some of the young ladies are indulging in girlish hijinks? I seem to remember that such things were not unknown in our time here."

How well she remembered nighttime raids on the cook's jam cupboard and sneaking off to the local shops during the hours set aside for music practice.

"I'm afraid it has gone beyond high spirits. Personal items are constantly going missing and noises that defy explanation are waking the household night after night."

"That seems like a concerted effort to make things uncomfortable, but is there any reason to think it is aimed at the business rather than at one or more of the enrolled young ladies?" Edwina asked.

"Business for all finishing schools has seen a steep decline since the war, and there is increased competition for young ladies. I think it is possible that putting me out of business might benefit the schools that remain."

"Are you truly concerned that incidents like the ones you describe could be as damaging as all that?" Edwina asked.

"I am very much afraid that if this foolishness keeps up it will spell the end of my establishment. Why would anyone choose my school if the reputation is of a place more known for theft and disruption than for deportment and grace?"

"Is anyone on staff concerned by what is happening?" Beryl asked.

"I'm sorry to say that many members of staff have been quite unnerved by it. But the sad fact is, I am not sure if any of them are feigning discomfort because they are responsible. Which is why I asked you to come here under the guise of looking for a finishing school for a goddaughter acquired in the course of your travels, Miss Helliwell," Miss DuPont said.

"Have you discussed your concerns with any member of the household?" Edwina asked. "Surely there must be someone you could trust." The idea that Miss DuPont might feel entirely surrounded by enemies seemed terribly sad.

"Under the circumstances I have felt it best to strictly keep my own counsel. I'm not saying that there is no one I generally trust, but I deemed it best to share my concerns only with the two of you."

"Why don't we begin by you telling us who's currently in residence, as well as their connection to the school," Edwina said, pulling her ever-present notebook from the pocket of her skirt and withdrawing a tiny pencil.

Miss DuPont nodded. "Besides myself and Miss Glover,

Mary White is our only other teacher. Jennings and his wife remain as butler and cook, and most grateful I am to have them too. We have a maid named Ellen as well as a gardener," she said.

"So few?" Beryl asked, her eyes widening with surprise. "Surely there were at least three times that many when we attended."

"Our staff is tragically diminished in size. It has been impossible to get help for the most part, even when you can afford to pay them handsomely, which unfortunately I cannot. As the number of girls has dwindled, so have our coffers."

"Mary White doesn't happen to be a former student herself, does she?" Edwina asked. A vision of a small girl with scraggly pigtails, her nose invariably buried in a book, rose up in her mind's eye. After the difficulty Mary had with one of the older girls, Edwina could hardly imagine she would have wanted to make a career in a place that had provided her with so much unhappiness.

"The very same. Mary has been with me for some time now, and I don't know what I would do without her. I know that she is very eager to renew your acquaintance. When I told her you were expected she expressed delight at the prospect."

"I look forward to seeing her too," Edwina said. She had always thought very highly of Mary White and her ability to endure a difficult situation.

"Is there anyone else that makes up the household?" Beryl asked.

"Besides the students, there are two people here viewing the school with an eye to enrolling a prospective student, just as you supposedly are. A third is expected shortly."

"Could any of them have been involved?" Beryl asked.

"At this point I suppose anyone could be responsible. Although, considering who they are, it seems unlikely."

"Why is that?" Beryl asked.

"I expect you'll remember Veronica DeLisle. She is here with her husband and younger daughter, Florence."

"And why is it that you think Veronica or her family might not be involved?" Edwina asked.

How well she remembered Veronica DeLisle. When they had attended the school, Veronica had been the most unrelenting bully she had ever met. She was ruthlessly unkind, especially to the smallest and youngest of the girls in their class. That girl just happened to be Mary White.

"It just seems to me unlikely that someone who wishes to enroll her daughter for the upcoming term would be actively working to undermine the very same institution. And as for the husband, he seems perfectly happy to agree with any of Veronica's opinions."

"Have you had any rumblings amongst the staff? Anything that would indicate that someone was unhappy enough to make mischief for you?" Edwina asked.

Edwina wasn't entirely certain, but she thought Miss DuPont paused just a beat too long before shaking her head. "There are always minor complaints in any organization, but nothing that seems serious enough to explain what has been happening. No one is ever entirely satisfied with his or her lot, and I would not presume to say that anyone here is completely without complaint. But no, there's nothing I can think of off the top of my head. Believe me, I've tried."

"Do you have a suggestion as to where we should begin our investigation?" Edwina asked. "If not, would it be acceptable for us to speak with some of the girls?"

"I really have no idea where you should start. I am relying on you as to how to proceed. This is completely outside of my scope."

"Then we shall start with them. Where will they be found?" Edwina asked.

Miss DuPont consulted a large diary opened on the desk before her. "They are having a painting lesson on the east lawn with Mary White, who serves amongst other things as our art and culture mistress. But I would ask you not to do anything to upset them."

"Do the girls appear worried?" Beryl asked.

"I assume that at least some of them are, and that sort of thing is contagious. The number of students who have already left before completing the term is distressing. Worse still, is the low number of inquiries about upcoming terms. I'm sorry to say that I am very much afraid that if you don't get to the bottom of this, the school will be forced to close," Miss DuPont said.

Although Miss DuPont had looked extremely well for her age, Edwina could see there was an underlying frailty to her former headmistress's countenance. Despite her first impression that Miss DuPont looked vigorous and much as she had done more than twenty years earlier, upon closer inspection she could see marks of tension around her eyes and at the corners of her mouth. Her hands fidgeted on the blotter of her desk in a manner she never would have permitted any of her girls to have exhibited during the school's heyday. No, despite her best efforts to keep up appearances, Miss DuPont was a very worried woman indeed. Edwina got to her feet and Beryl did the same.

"In that case we had best get to work as quickly as possible," Edwina said.

"I'll have Ellen show you to your room. I thought for old time's sake I would put you together in the same one," Miss DuPont said as she reached for a needlepoint bellpull hanging on the wall behind her chair. After the briefest of pauses, the door opened and a snub-nosed young woman with bright blue eyes stepped in and dropped a slight curtsy.

"You rang, Miss DuPont," she said while keeping her eyes firmly fixed on the pair of visitors.

Edwina was quite sure that the pretty little maid recognized Beryl for the celebrity she was. Despite a slowdown in the number of articles featuring Beryl's adventures of late, she was, after all, a household name and had spent years with her image in newspapers over and over again with each new attempt at derring-do.

"Yes, Ellen. Please escort Miss Davenport and Miss Helliwell to the Lilac room. I've already asked Jennings to have their luggage sent there, so I expect you to help see to their unpacking," she said.

"Yes, miss. If you will follow me," Ellen said, indicating the door with a tip of her head.

"Please feel free to stroll about the school and the grounds in order to reacquaint yourself with all that we have to offer your goddaughter, Miss Helliwell," Miss DuPont said with a voice pitched just slightly louder than her conversational tone.

Edwina suspected it was for Ellen's benefit that she did so, reinforcing the idea that the two of them were there on behalf of a prospective student. As she followed behind the energetic young maid she wondered if she could possibly be involved. Edwina had known of many troubles with the servants throughout the years, both at her own household and the household of friends and acquaintances. One of her first orders of business would be to speak with Jennings and his wife in order to ask their opinion. If anyone would know what was going on behind the scenes at Miss DuPont's, it was the butler and his wife.

Chapter 5

At first glance, the second-floor hallway still looked just as it had when they were girls. Although, as Beryl gave it a closer inspection, it seemed that things were perhaps ever so slightly shabbier than they had been in decades past. A slight layer of dust could be spotted if one was peering into the corners or along the tops of the baseboards. The carpet runners seemed clean enough, but the hardwood floors beneath could have done with a fresh layer of polish.

Had it always been that way? Beryl wondered. Perhaps she had simply not noticed such things in her youth. She never had been much of a housekeeper, and she wondered if rather than viewing things through her own eyes she was now seeing them through Edwina's.

After all, her dear friend had been exceedingly grateful for the ministrations of their recently acquired housekeeper, Beddoes. In the months Beryl had lived at the Beeches she had never noticed that the draperies might benefit from a starching or that the silver did not gleam sufficiently, but there was no stopping Beddoes once she got her teeth into the project of entirely bottoming out her new domain.

The whole incident had been extremely disruptive and fraught with misunderstanding, and it had left Beryl with a heightened sense of what accounted for housekeeping standards, at least as far as Edwina was concerned. Her friend had been absolutely delighted with the changes in her beloved home; and while she would not have bothered to go to any such lengths of her own accord, Beryl could clearly see that Beddoes would have found Miss DuPont's school failing to meet her own exacting standards.

As they followed Ellen down the hall and turned right toward the west wing of the building, she thought of the overall decline at the school and found herself surprisingly moved by the elderly woman's plight. How difficult it would be to see one's life's work falling to rack and ruin. She wondered if it was not already too late to help save Miss DuPont's legacy. As they approached the door at the end of the hallway, Edwina spoke.

"Thank you, Ellen, for showing us the way. We shan't need any help unpacking, as I'm sure you have more than plenty to get on with in your usual course of duties. Tell me, does Jennings still ring the gong for dinner every evening?"

"Yes, miss, he does, at eight o'clock sharp. You won't tell Miss DuPont about the unpacking, will you?" Ellen asked.

"Our lips are sealed," Edwina said.

Beryl smiled at the little maid and watched as she bobbed a final curtsy and hurried off down the hallway and out of sight. She turned to Edwina. "I suggest we leave the suitcases just as they are until it's time to dress for dinner. I know we're in agreement about tying this case up as quickly as possible."

"I agree. After we meet the girls, I think it would be very helpful to chat with Jennings and his wife," Edwina said.

"If you don't mind, I shall leave interrogating the servants to you. We both know that you have a knack with them that is simply beyond me," Beryl said.

"That suits me very well. I would enjoy reacquainting myself with them. They were very good to me when I was a girl."

"Somehow, I am not surprised in the least," Beryl said.

Edwina did have a knack with servants that entirely eluded Beryl herself. Her friend seemed to have a magical ability to command respect and loyalty without appearing to make any effort whatsoever to do so. Beryl, on the other hand, try as she might, never seemed to garner either from the hired help.

Edwina had suggested that her efforts to treat the domestic staff as social equals was the problem and that despite her efforts to befriend them, she had created a cavernous rift. Edwina had pointed out that the better sort of servant was even more of a snob than his or her employer, and that by attempting to cross an invisible divide she had offended them. Beryl would never understand it.

"But were you as surprised as I at hearing that both Mary White and Veronica DeLisle are here?" Edwina asked.

"As a matter fact, I was astonished that Mary White would have returned to the school if she had a choice in the matter," Beryl said. "That said, I'm not in the least surprised to hear that Veronica has returned with a child of her own in tow. She was in her element at finishing school, and I can well imagine her daughter as a miniature version of herself, so it seems perfectly plausible for her to be here."

Beryl was not in the least bit eager to reacquaint herself with Veronica DeLisle. Nor was she looking forward to witnessing Edwina encountering her anew. In fact, it was during a confrontation with Veronica DeLisle that Beryl had first noticed Edwina. Her dearest friend had been a self-contained and quiet sort of person until she had finally had enough of Veronica's ill treatment toward little Mary White.

Edwina's usually reserved manner completely abandoned her, and she had taken Veronica to task in front of the entire rest of their cohort. She had dressed Veronica down in no uncertain terms with a vigor and forthrightness that would have commended her to a career as a military drill sergeant, should such a thing be allowed for women. Veronica had continued to make sport of Mary throughout the rest of their time at the school, but she had rarely done so in Edwina's presence after that day. Beryl did wonder if Veronica would be likely to hold a grudge and how that might play out during their work on the case.

"Most unfortunate indeed, and even more so for Mary, I should think," Edwina said. "I don't expect it places her in a very good position for Veronica to have returned as a paying customer. Especially not if business is as slow as Miss DuPont indicated."

"I suppose we shall have to go out and see for ourselves. Shall we?" Beryl asked, hooking her arm through Edwina's.

Chapter 6

The rolling lawn sloping gently toward the dense copse of trees on the eastern side of the property bustled with activity. A slim woman who appeared to be of approximately the same age as Beryl and Edwina stood at the front of a mere half dozen girls. She was demonstrating some sort of technique for the group by passing a long-handled paintbrush over the surface of a canvas mounted on an easel in front of her. Surely this could not be the entire number of students. If so, things were dire indeed. When she and Beryl had attended, their group of fifty had been the smallest in years.

But some things had not changed despite the diminished numbers. Just as in their day, each girl wore a muslin smock and wide straw hat. Not only that, but they also stood facing the same vista that had proven so popular with the arts mistress all those years ago. Even the wooden easels made famous by the French Impressionists standing before them were the same. Although she viewed their work from a distance, Beryl could tell that there was a wide degree of variation in skill on the part of the young artists.

Although, truth be told, most of the girls seemed far less interested in working on their paintings than in chatting with each other or in ogling a strapping young gardener trundling a wheelbarrow along a mixed flower border at the edge of the lawn. One of the bolder girls had attempted to capture him in paint. The girl next to her elbowed her in the ribs and stifled a giggle as the teacher shot them both a scolding look. As she turned to admonish the students, her gaze fell upon the sleuths.

She let out a small cry of surprise and abandoned her paintbrush on the tray of her easel. The girls all turned to watch her as she hurried toward Beryl and Edwina with her paint-smeared hands outstretched.

"Edwina Davenport, is that you?" she said as she strode toward them, a broad smile across her face.

"It is, Mary. How lovely it is to see you again," Edwina said. "You look very well, I must say."

Edwina tipped her head to the side as if reconciling her memory of Mary with the woman she had become. Beryl could see her point. It was so strange to think that the meek and bullied young woman they had known during their time at the school had grown into a woman in a position of authority at a school devoted to confidence and poise. Beryl had difficulty seeing the Mary White she had known so many years ago in the self-assured, middle-aged woman standing before her.

Her memories of the younger version were primarily comprised of images of Mary huddled in an oversized wingback chair in a dark corner of the school's library, or more bleakly, at the center of a gaggle of girls haranguing her with mocking comments. There had been one girl in particular who had acted as the ringleader of the attacks, and until Miss DuPont had named her, Beryl had put her almost entirely from her mind. Perhaps she had blocked it out on purpose. Beryl did not buy completely into the theories of the subconscious as espoused by Freud and his ilk, mostly because she had found his attitude toward women tedious in the extreme whenever she had encountered him socially. That said, if there were ever anyone she would wish to forget, it would Veronica DeLisle. Beryl never could abide a bully.

"I had no idea you had made a career of education until Miss DuPont told us you were here," Edwina said.

"I've come to it rather late, I'm afraid. Economic woes and all that, you see," Mary said with a shrug of her slim shoulders.

"I am well aware of such matters. Still, you seem to have done well for yourself here," Edwina said.

"It's early days, but so far I like it far more than I would have expected. I have always loved art and travel, and the position here offers both."

"How long have you been back?" Edwina asked.

"This is my second term as a teacher. I lost my mother last year and found myself at loose ends, so when I heard through the grapevine that there was an opening here, I wrote to Miss DuPont straightaway. I've been here ever since."

"I am very glad to renew our acquaintance," Edwina said, turning slightly. "You must remember Beryl, don't you, Mary?"

As Mary nodded at her, the tall young gardener, with his dark hair curling romantically just over the top of his collar, caught Beryl's eye. Perhaps, she thought, her stay at Miss DuPont's might not be quite as miserable as she had anticipated. She returned her attention to Mary and Edwina, determined to make a tour of the grounds before the trip was through.

"Of course, I remember our most famous graduate. I've been following your adventures as reported in the newspapers for years. Your most recent exploits as private enquiry agents have been amongst the most exciting, in my opinion."

"As far as I am concerned, Davenport and Helliwell has been the most exciting adventure of my career too," Beryl said.

"I doubt the last time we saw each other it would have been expected that we would all turn out to be career women rather than wives of prominent men," Mary said.

Beryl wasn't sure, but she thought she saw a flicker of pain pass over Mary's face. Was there someone in particular that pained her not to have married? Beryl rather thought that the remark was not a general observation. But the expression passed as quickly as it had arrived.

"I have always been interested in thwarting expectations," Beryl said.

"I should never have expected you to return to the school. If you don't mind me asking, why are you here?" Mary asked.

"My goddaughter is considering finishing school and has asked if I will recommend this one to her. I did not feel I could in good conscience do so without seeing it for myself after all these years," Beryl said.

"I see. Will you be with us for some time?"

"A day or two at most, I hope," Beryl said. She could not say for sure, but she thought she detected a flicker of relief pass across Mary's features. Surely, she was not one to be involved in the sort of mischief taking place at the school.

"Would it be possible to speak with one or two of the students?" Edwina asked. "Beryl would like to have a girl's opinion as she considers the options."

"Of course. Why don't you speak with Adele and Lois." Mary lowered her voice and leaned forward. "Adele is far enough advanced that a bit of distraction won't hurt her studies, and Lois would rather be doing just about anything besides painting, anyway."

"That would be most helpful," Edwina said.

"If you will excuse me, I had best get back to the class. Otherwise, one of them may decide to make a fool of herself with the gardener."

Chapter 7

"What a remarkable job you've done. Although it's been more than twenty years since I last viewed the east lawn, I would have recognized it anywhere," Edwina said, leaning toward Adele's canvas.

The girl turned toward her and smiled. "Do you really think so?" she asked.

"Absolutely. You've caught the slope of the land and the way the trees rise up and head off toward the horizon. The quality of light is just exactly how I remember it too," Edwina said. "Have you developed your talent under Miss White's tutelage, or have you always been such a gifted artist?"

"I shouldn't like to say that I am particularly talented, but I do enjoy it. Miss White has been wonderful, giving me a lot of extra attention and encouragement, so I feel as though I've made great strides while I've been here," Adele said.

"You are lucky to have such a generous teacher," Edwina said. "Since you have such a small class size it must be a wonderful time for you to be at Miss DuPont's."

Adele dabbed her brush into a bit of dusky blue and added velvety shadows beneath a line of trees on her painting.

"I suppose that is one way to look at it." Adele slipped the end of her paintbrush between her teeth and chewed on it. Edwina could not tell if it was a sign of nerves or contemplation.

"Would you say that these are not the best of times to be at Miss DuPont's school?"

"I shouldn't want to influence you unduly but, no, I should say that they are not. I appreciate the one-on-one instruction, but with fewer girls I haven't met as many new people as I would have hoped."

Edwina looked over at the handful of girls standing in front of the easels. Such a small number would completely change the experience, although Edwina thought there might be some merit in spending time with a smaller group of people. She had never been one for crowds and perhaps would have enjoyed her time much more had there been only a half dozen girls in her cohort.

"The number of students is certainly smaller than when I was here. This is the entirety of your class?" Edwina asked.

Adele nodded and dabbed her paintbrush into a crimson blob of glistening paint. "This is all that remains now. There were at least twice as many when the class started."

"What has happened to the rest of them?" Edwina asked.

"They've all given different reasons for leaving. Some have claimed there are emergencies in their families or sudden trips abroad that are too interesting to resist. Others have been more honest about their withdrawal."

"And what reason is that?" Edwina asked.

Adele's hand hovered above her canvas, and she turned to look Edwina in the face. "Perhaps I've said too much. I wouldn't wish to cause any more problems for Miss DuPont."

"We are here to evaluate whether or not this would be a good place for my companion's goddaughter to attend. The insight a student could give might spare another girl from the disappointment you have experienced."

Edwina hoped she had not overplayed her hand by appealing

to the girl's compassion. She held her breath as Adele spread a bit of dark red paint into the leafy canopy portrayed on her canvas. She stood back and squinted at her efforts before continuing to speak.

"There have been a few incidents that have rattled most of the girls."

"What sorts of incidents?" Edwina said.

"Most of us have had the experience of our possessions being inexplicably moved about or even going completely missing," she said.

"Do you think that someone here at the school is a thief?" Edwina asked.

"I'm sure that could be the explanation for the missing items, but it wouldn't necessarily explain the noises," Adele said. She lowered her voice. "I think that's what is worrying people the most."

Edwina took a step closer to Adele. "What sort of noises?"

"The sounds are sort of hard to describe. They always happen at night after lights-out. There are moaning noises and rattling, dragging, scraping, and even thumping. Some of the girls are saying they think the school is haunted," Adele said.

"That doesn't sound much like a common garden-variety burglar," Edwina said.

"It doesn't feel like that when you hear them either," Adele said.

"Does that mean that you've heard them yourself?" Edwina asked.

Adele nodded. "I wish I could say that I haven't, but I have."

"How often have you heard them?" Edwina asked. "Do they happen every night?"

"The thefts are happening most days and the noises almost as often."

"And no one has been able to explain them away?" Edwina asked.

"Miss Glover insists it's all nonsense and has suggested that the noises are caused by the heating system or air passing through gaps in the window sashes. Miss White makes light of it and says no manor house worthy of the name would be content not to have at least a few ghosts on the premises."

Edwina looked over at Mary and wondered about her lighthearted attitude toward her employer's difficulties. Should she really have been encouraging the girls to believe that the school was haunted? With so many students withdrawing from the program, surely it would be in her own best interest to discourage them from thinking any such thing. Or perhaps her lighthearted attitude was meant to signal to the girls that they also ought to be unconcerned with whatever was causing the disruption.

"What about you? Do you plan to leave the school?" Edwina asked.

"I expect that I will stick it out. I'd rather take my chances with whatever is happening here than by returning home."

"Your home is a place of uncertainty?" Edwina asked.

"Not uncertain in the least. It is a fact that my parents are so grief-stricken by the loss of my brothers that they are practically ghosts themselves," she said.

Edwina's heart gave a squeeze. As poised as Adele appeared to be, she still was very young, and it saddened her to hear a girl of her age sound so disillusioned. Although, it seemed as though all the young people of her generation were similarly marked by the events of the preceding years.

She wondered if the downturn in Miss DuPont's business had more to do with the fact that young people had very different expectations for their futures than had their parents and all previous generations. There was something so destabilizing about the ghastliness of the Great War, and it was no wonder its effects were felt in big things and in small.

Perhaps Adele's disillusionment explained the depth of emotion she conveyed in her painting. Edwina felt she had taken up enough of Adele's time. The girl eyed her pallet of wet paint and then glanced at the scene in front of her. Edwina knew from outings with her friend Charles that capturing the light was a constant difficulty and there were times of day where it seemed the most fleeting. She could always come back and ask Adele more questions later if she needed to.

"Thank you for your forthrightness. I'll let you get back to your work. I wouldn't want you to miss the light," she said.

Adele smiled at her and nodded. Without a word she turned her full attention back to her canvas and gave every indication she had completely forgotten Edwina was there. She looked over at Beryl to see how she seemed to be getting on with Lois. Her friend appeared to be trying to silently signal for her to join them, so Edwina surmised that things were going about as well as they generally did when Beryl attempted to engage with children. Without appearing to hurry, Edwina crossed the lawn and came to a stop at Beryl's side.

Chapter 8

"Lois please allow me to present my friend Miss Davenport. Would you care to tell her what you've just been telling me?" Beryl asked.

Lois nodded enthusiastically. Apparently, she was not immune to a desire to curry favor with the celebrity. Perhaps Beryl's look of discomfort had stemmed not from a problem convincing Lois to speak but rather in convincing her to stop.

"I was telling Miss Helliwell that there's no end of trouble here at Miss DuPont's."

"What sort of trouble?" Edwina asked. She wondered if Lois's story would tally with that of Adele.

"Thefts and odd noises at night. It's just like something out of the pictures. I can't decide if I think that there's a cat burglar who's responsible for all the creaking and groaning or if there's a poltergeist with a penchant for jewelry and lipsticks and the like."

"Lois tells me she's had several of her own things stolen and most of the other girls have had things either moved about or they completely disappear," Beryl said.

"How very lamentable," Edwina said. "And you have no notion of who the culprit might be?"

"None whatsoever. It's a complete mystery. I try and try to stay awake at night to see if someone's moving about in the room pilfering things, but I can't seem to keep my eyes open long enough to spot anyone. I always have been quite a heavy sleeper," Lois said.

"Do any of the other girls or the staff have any suggestions as to what might be going on?" Edwina asked.

"Miss Glover says we are making it all up just for attention. She has threatened us with being asked to memorize longer passages of poetry if we don't come to our senses. Miss White has listened with concern to what we've had to say, but she can't explain either. Miss DuPont changes the subject when anyone brings it up."

"Have you heard any of the household staff discussing it amongst themselves?" Edwina asked.

"Not between themselves, no, but Adele and I were talking to the gardener about it, and he seemed to think that the whole place was probably haunted," Lois said, bursting into a fit of giggles as she allowed her gaze to roam toward the gardener bent over the flower border at the far end of the lawn.

Edwina was not sure she would credit something a gardener might say in the presence of two impressionable and attractive young ladies. That was just the sort of staffing difficulty she wished to speak with Jennings about. Unless he had allowed things to slip considerably since she had been in attendance, she could not imagine that an imperious butler like Jennings would hold with such nonsense from the junior staff.

"When did all of this start?" Beryl asked.

"It started a few weeks into our term. There were no troubles at all for the first month or so, and then all at once things started to go wrong. In fact, I think that I was the first one to notice a stolen item."

"Do you remember what it was?" Edwina asked.

"It was a mother-of-pearl brooch that I planned to wear on an outing we were taking to the theater one evening. I was sure that I had left it in my jewel case, but when I went to retrieve it, it was gone."

"Did you ever find it?" Beryl asked.

"That was the strangest part of it. The brooch reappeared in my jewelry case two days later with no explanation."

"Do you think one of the other girls borrowed it without your permission and was too embarrassed to admit it?" Edwina asked.

"I'm sure that I would have noticed if someone else was wearing it. The group wasn't large enough for me not to have done. I'm afraid it's much more likely that someone on staff helped themselves to it and then put it back. Maybe one of the maids wanted to dress up her own ensemble for a half day off or some such a thing."

"And no one has come forward to admit it?" Beryl asked.

"No, never. And no one's been caught with their hands where they ought not to be either," Lois said. She crossed her arms over her chest as if she were suddenly slightly cold. "The incident with my brooch was the first of many. Since then, there hasn't been a week gone by without at least one girl reporting a missing item."

"Have any of the other items been returned like yours was?" Beryl asked.

"I would say that about half of them have been returned," Lois said.

"Does there seem to be any sort of pattern to what's returned and what isn't?" Beryl asked. "For example, would you say that items of value are returned, and cheaper items are kept, or vice versa?"

Lois pursed her lips as if thinking deeply about the question. "I don't think there's much of a pattern to that either. One girl loses a compact never to see it again, and another finds hers returned the day after she misses it. A pair of pearl drop earrings have never been seen again but a diamond bracelet showed up in the owner's bed without explanation."

"And no one has seen a thing?" Edwina asked.

"Nothing at all. I will say that people tend to notice something missing in the day after there are the unexplained noises. I don't know if that makes any difference. Why are you asking all these questions? Is it because you are worried about sending your goddaughter here?" Lois asked.

"We just want to be sure to understand the sort of environment she will find herself in should she decide to attend," Edwina said.

"She's a really rather nervous sort of girl and I'm not at all sure that she would flourish in an environment with so much unsettled," Beryl said.

Without warning, any response Lois might have attempted to make was drowned out by a roaring noise from overhead.

Chapter 9

Edwina looked around as she felt a stirring wind rushing across the lawn. The girls' smocks began to flap wildly about their legs, and those with the greatest presence of mind reached for straw hats before they blew to the ground. The sound became deafening, and Edwina looked up. Making straight for them with alarming speed was an airplane.

Edwina glanced over at Beryl for reassurance and saw that her friend's face was wreathed in a smile. Beryl held both of her hands extended over her head and her arms waved back and forth as if to greet the pilot. In the space of only a couple heartbeats the airplane jounced down onto the lawn and skidded to a stop, barely missing the gardener and his wheelbarrow. Overturned easels and canvases scattered across the surface of the lawn, sending the girls running to collect their windblown supplies. Beryl lowered her hands before reaching for Edwina's arm. She tugged her swiftly alongside her, striding toward the plane, her red silk duster and wide-legged pants flapping in the stiff breeze as they made their way across the lawn.

A man in his late forties with dark curly hair working to escape from beneath his aviator's helmet sprang from the cockpit and landed with grace on the turf beside the plane. He tugged the helmet from his head and Edwina's heart flip-flopped in her chest.

"You always did know how to make an entrance, Desmond," Beryl said.

"I learned from the best, Beryl," Desmond said, his face breaking into a broad smile as he stepped toward Beryl with obvious enthusiasm. "When was the last time we saw each other? It must have been before the war. At an air show, wasn't it?"

"Yes, I believe it was. You were there with an airplane you were trialing for the Air Ministry, if I remember correctly," Beryl said.

"And you crept around behind my back and took it for an unauthorized test flight, if I remember correctly," he said with a laugh.

"I just wanted to be sure that the plane had any of the bugs worked out of it before it was tried out on the boys in the Air Force," Beryl said. "It was an act of patriotism."

"The ruckus you caused turning loops in the air and buzzing over the tops of the officials' heads was not viewed in quite that light," he said.

"You got the contract, didn't you?" Beryl asked. "If memory serves, it was a very lucrative one at that."

"It was, and I took you out to dinner as a way to thank you," he said.

"While we are reminiscing, surely you remember my dear friend Edwina Davenport," Beryl said, turning toward Edwina.

Edwina felt her face flush slightly. Desmond Montrose had been the most eligible young man of her acquaintance while they were at Miss DuPont's school. He had been one of the many young suitors to appear at dances and dinners held throughout their course in order to provide the young ladies with an opportunity to practice their social skills. Desmond had been the only young man to turn Edwina's head of all those she met that season.

As far as she had been able to tell, he'd had that effect on her entire cohort. It had come as a bitter disappointment to the vast majority of them when he had fallen under the sway of Veronica DeLisle. The two had married not long after she completed Miss DuPont's course.

For just one fleeting moment Edwina felt a pang of envy. Life had proven so unfair for so many in the past few years—between the war, the flagging economy, and the ravaging effects of influenza. It seemed all the more unjust that someone as unpleasant as Veronica DeLisle had managed to make it through with her handsome husband, a daughter, and unless she missed her guess, her wealth intact. Still, she would not have been one to display such sentiments. Only someone petty would give in to that sort of temptation. Instead, she simply smiled and nodded at Desmond as he turned toward her.

"Of course, I remember Miss Davenport. Anyone as capable as you were of putting Veronica in her place is someone most definitely unforgettable," he said as he reached for her hand, and lifted it to his lips.

Edwina's neck flamed hot. She had never quite learned how to take a compliment without feeling flummoxed. That sort of attention from the likes of Desmond Montrose left her feeling even more flustered than ever.

"I'm sure I meant to give no offense to you or your wife," Edwina said, certain that her cheeks were growing warm as she met Desmond's gaze.

"You've given none whatsoever, especially considering Veronica is no longer my wife. I only wish I had been as skilled at putting her in her place for the interminable years of our marriage as you were so long ago," Desmond said.

"I had no idea that the two of you had parted ways," Beryl said.

Edwina noticed a note of interest creeping into Beryl's tone of voice. She hoped for the sake of the case that her fellow enquiry agent would not end up distracted by extracurricular activities and fail to give the investigation her best effort. They had a far greater chance of wrapping things up quickly and returning home if they both threw themselves wholeheartedly into their work.

"Even Veronica could not have managed to bump war reporting from the front pages of the newspaper with the sordid details of our divorce. Mind you, it seemed to me that she gave it her very best effort to do so."

"Then you were very fortunate indeed. As someone whose divorces have attracted an unpleasant amount of attention in the press, I can tell you that there is little worse than being harassed by photographers and insistent reporters every time one attempts to leave home."

"I remember seeing some of the coverage. I thought you bore up under it remarkably well, considering," he said.

Edwina too had seen the news reports. She had judiciously refrained from clipping those sorts of articles from the papers to add to the scrapbook she had kept for years documenting Beryl's travels and accomplishments. For all her friend's ability to turn a press feeding frenzy into an opportunity to increase her public renown, Edwina had thought it had cost Beryl a great deal to do so each time it occurred, and she did not wish to spoil a book dedicated to fond memories and triumphs with something so likely to stir up bad feelings.

"How kind of you to say so. In the end, it all worked out for the best. Who would have predicted that the skills I developed at sneaking out the back of hotels and train stations would serve me so well when Edwina and I decided to open a private enquiry agency," Beryl said, smiling at Edwina.

"I had read in the papers about that too," Desmond said. He leaned toward them and lowered his voice. "You aren't here to work on a case, are you?"

Edwina's heart stuttered in her chest. They had not been

there for two hours yet and their veil of secrecy might already be rent in two. She pulled herself up to her full height, and although it pained her to adopt such a tone with someone she had such a soft spot for as Desmond, she responded as though he were a cheeky parlor maid who needed training.

"Miss DuPont's irreproachably respectable school is hardly the sort of place one would expect to require the services of private enquiry agents. Do you not agree?" she asked him, careful to keep one eyebrow arched with feigned indignation.

"Your point is well made. I meant no offense," he said.

"I am sure that you spoke in jest, but an institution is only as good as its reputation," Edwina said. From the contrite expression on Desmond's face, she doubted he would reassert the notion that they were at the school in a professional capacity.

"I couldn't agree more. But if business does not bring you two lovely ladies back to Miss DuPont's, may I be permitted to ask what does?"

"Of course, you may. I have a goddaughter looking for a finishing school and I offered to verify that Miss DuPont's was all that we remembered it to be," Beryl said. "We are spending a few days here to do just that."

"I would have every expectation that it is. My eldest daughter attended two years ago, just as soon as it reopened after the armistice. She loved it here just as much as her mother did. I flew down in order to tour it myself with an eye to our younger girl, Florence, enrolling for the next term."

"Is your daughter looking forward to the prospect of attending?" Edwina asked, hoping she could smooth any feeling of discomfort her previous criticism might have created.

Desmond shook his head. "Even though her mother and sister have praised the experience of finishing school, particularly this one, to the skies, it has fallen on deaf ears. I'm afraid that Florence is no more likely to be interested in such things than you were, Beryl."

Edwina stole a glance at her friend. Beryl had done a creditable job when they had been students of disguising the extent of her misery at being a part of something that went so decidedly against her wishes. She had made every effort to keep her chin up throughout the experience, but it had not been easy.

Edwina had admired her from the first time she noticed Beryl at a sewing lesson. She had been seated in front of a large window, squinting with total concentration as she repeatedly failed to poke a strand of embroidery floss through the eye of a needle. Miss Glover had hovered over her shoulder, tut-tutting and using her as an example to the other students of the evils of failing to attend to rudimentary needleworking skills.

"Whyever would you consider enrolling her if she was so lacking in interest?" Beryl asked. Although Edwina hated to hear the surprised tone in Beryl's voice, she thought that it was no longer likely that her friend would be distracted from her professional duties by Desmond.

Desmond raised his hands and dropped them abruptly. "Veronica insisted upon it and I'm sure you know that when she gets an idea in her head it's very difficult to dissuade her. Besides, I have to say that I think it would do Florence a world of good if only she was willing to give the place a try. The pair of you benefitted from being here, didn't you?" he asked, looking from one to the other.

Edwina tucked her arm through Beryl's. "There is usually something good to be found in any experience if one is willing to look, isn't that right?" she asked, turning to Beryl.

"I have most often found that to be so," she said.

"I expect that Florence will come to feel the same. Now, do you happen to know if I have arrived in time for tea? Flying is remarkably thirsty work."

"I'd like to remind myself of just how thirsty," Beryl said. "Any chance you'd let me take your plane up while I'm here?"

"Is there any chance that I could stop you?" Desmond asked.

"I rather expect not," Beryl said.

"Why don't we plan to take it up sometime before I leave?" Desmond asked. He turned to Edwina. "You are most welcome to take a turn yourself, if you'd like."

Edwina glanced at the airplane and felt her stomach lurch. Beryl's driving had been quite enough motorized excitement for one week.

"Although I appreciate your kind offer, I am happiest with my feet firmly planted on the ground," she said.

Chapter 10

After promising to allow Beryl to put his new plane through its paces, Desmond excused himself and crossed the lawn. His long legs quickly covered the ground, and her interest was piqued as he stopped abruptly beside another man, who appeared to be at least fifteen years his junior. Desmond leaned forward and poked him in the chest.

Beryl hurriedly took her leave of Edwina and swiftly moved closer in order to better witness the confrontation. From the look on his face, it was clear that the younger man was barely in control of his temper. She wondered if he would manage to resist swinging the golf club clutched in his hand at Desmond. But almost as soon as the confrontation began, Desmond stepped back, then strode off toward the gardens that led around to the front building.

The man, clad in a sporting outfit of plus fours and a newly fashionable Fair Isle jumper, wrapped both hands around his golf club and began hacking savagely at a swath of long grass directly in front of him. She approached with her most dazzling smile in place, hoping to disarm him. She extended a hand to him and was relieved to see him release his grip on the golf club in order to shake it.

"Unless things have been much changed since I was a student at Miss DuPont's, there is no golf course nearby. Have you lost your way?" she asked.

"Sadly, no. I expect I am here for the same reason as you."

"You're here shopping for a finishing school for your goddaughter?" Beryl asked. It would be a remarkable coincidence indeed. Especially if his goddaughter was as much of a cover story as her own.

"A stepdaughter, actually. Not that I expect a visit to the school will have much bearing on what happens to Florence," he said. "At least not as far as her parents are concerned, poor kid."

With so few girls at school, or expected to enroll for the upcoming term, Beryl did not think it likely there would be more than one young woman named Florence in residence that week. After all, Miss DuPont had indicated that Veronica was there with her husband, and Beryl had simply assumed she meant Desmond. Beryl tucked away that bit of information to mull over with Edwina later. From the looks of things, Veronica was not having greater luck with her second marriage than her first.

"Are you speaking of Florence Montrose?" Beryl asked.

The man nodded and redoubled his assault on the unfortunate tufts of grass. "That's right. I'm her stepfather, Paul Deering. I've told Veronica that Florence would hate attending a school like this, but she just waved off my concerns. I only agreed to accompany them in order to provide Florence with a shoulder to cry on if she needs it. Her mother certainly won't offer one."

"I know just how you feel. I had not planned to be here this week either. In fact, I'm missing a golfing trip of my own right now. I hope you won't mind me saying so, but it didn't appear as though Desmond is any happier with you being here than you are," Beryl said.

"You can say that again."

"I suppose it's only natural that the former husband and the new one don't get on that well," Beryl said. "I know that my ex-husbands can't be left alone in a room together without bloodshed."

"It's not as bad as all that. Desmond has no residual animosity about the breakup of the marriage."

"He looked more than a little angry just now," Beryl said.

"That had nothing to do with Veronica. Desmond is an incredibly devoted father. He's got his nose bent out of joint about the fact that I suggested that Florence be allowed to make up her own mind about attending finishing school. Anyone who has ever met her can see it's a terrible fit for the girl."

"Desmond was angry at you for advocating for his daughter?" Beryl asked.

Paul nodded. "He's very protective of his position with Florence and accused me of meddling in things best left to him," Paul said.

"Is Florence very different from her mother?"

"I've never seen two women who are more dissimilar. Florence. She prefers the company of books to other people and couldn't care less about table settings or how to properly address a duke," Paul said. "She's a lovely girl in her way, but although I think the world of my wife, I must admit that anybody with the least of motherly feeling would never consider sending Florence to finishing school."

Beryl did not like to consider the possibility that she and Veronica might share any traits whatsoever, let alone something as central to her notion of herself as a lack of maternal instinct. She never wanted to have children of her own, in fact she had insisted that she not find herself in such an odious position. That said, she felt as though perhaps it was not the lack of maternal feeling that made Veronica wish to send her daughter to Miss DuPont's.

Although she thought she would not be inclined to do the same, she did understand the value most women found in such experiences. The opportunity to arm themselves with a skill set encouraged by society against a world so tilted toward favoring men, could be considered a loving sentiment, even if it was unpleasant to endure at the time.

Although Beryl had not on balance enjoyed her time at Miss DuPont's, she had come out of the institution with an enviable skill set of her own. She never found herself discomfited in a social situation. She understood how to dress herself to create the effect she most wanted to exude, and she graduated with the understanding that she could endure difficult situations with grace and confidence.

Most importantly, she had become friends with Edwina. It might just be that Veronica was making a difficult choice in the short term for a long-term benefit. As she looked up at Paul Deering, she thought it unlikely he would understand such sentiments. After all, he was a man.

"Speaking of my wife, it's high time I tracked her down. Do let me know if you're looking for a round of golf. I happen to know of a course nearby." With that, he raised his club slightly and strode off in the direction of the school building.

Beryl watched him until he passed out of sight around a bit of shrubbery. While she had a great deal of experience with ex-husbands, she had none whatsoever when those relationships included the messiness of children. Not only had she expressly avoided bearing any children of her own, but she also made it her policy not to entangle herself with those who already had children.

The stepparent role was not for the faint of heart and she vastly preferred to conserve her energy for exotic adventures instead of the tedium of hiring governesses and selecting finishing schools. How strange it was to think that her choice of current career had brought her to exactly the sort of situation she never wished to find herself in.

The irony of it made her laugh out loud. She glanced at her wristwatch and decided to head back to her room to prepare for dinner. With any luck she would find Edwina there, and was eager to share what she had discovered.

Chapter 11

A pea-gravel path wound its way past overflowing mixed borders of late-blooming perennials and woody shrubs. Butterflies and droning bees busied themselves taking advantage of the autumn sunshine. The grounds sloped away from the grand manor house containing the school and toward a sunken rose garden.

Edwina leaned forward and buried her nose in the depths of a clove-scented shrub rose. Her stroll round the grounds could not make up for missing the second flush of bloom on her own beloved roses, but it offered a bit of solace. The gardens at the school had been one of the few places she had felt at home during her time there as a young woman.

The small pool at the center of the garden looked much as it had more than two decades earlier. Anchored in the middle of it stood a marble statue of a nymph pouring water from an upturned pitcher. The splashing sound masked any other noise, and Edwina was caught off guard when a wheelbarrow trundled into view.

The same dark-haired young man the students had found so distracting bobbed his head in deference as he parked the wheelbarrow nearby and knelt next to it. Weeds were a constant plague in gravel paths, as Edwina knew much to her sorrow.

In the years before Simpkins had once again provided the funds for additional jobbing under-gardeners at the Beeches, she had despaired of ever keeping the wretched weeds in check. From the looks of Miss DuPont's gravel paths, things were much the same for her. Sadly, the staffing shortages seen everywhere across the country had made themselves felt at the school too.

Somehow, Edwina had not considered that a place so etched in her memory could have been altered in the least. How foolish she had been, she thought as she nodded at the young man sliding a dandelion knife below a well-rooted specimen of bindweed.

She stopped short, debating whether or not she ought to advise him on his technique. To her way of thinking he was approaching the task in an entirely incorrect manner. She decided to err on the side of not giving offense.

After all, servants could be a very prickly sort and with such high demand for them, they were forever threatening to give notice over the smallest of grievances. She would not want to be responsible for costing Miss DuPont one of hers. It was far better that he inexpertly attack the weed problem than fail to attack it at all. Still, perhaps she could work her way round to it in the conversation if she approached it obliquely.

"Good afternoon. May I offer my compliments on a very fine show of blooms for this time of year? The roses are especially lovely," she said.

"Thank you," he said, not raising his head, as if to discourage conversation. He remained steadfastly bent to his task, jabbing at the offending weed as though it had done him a personal affront.

Edwina nimbly stepped round him and halted beside the stone-ringed pond. The flash of coins glinted up at her from beneath the rippling water and she was transported back to her girlhood when she would toss in a coin of her own with an accompanying wish.

She brushed a section of coping stone topping the stone wall surrounding the pond with her handkerchief and moved to sit upon it. The stone wobbled just as her skirts touched its surface. Before she could even become alarmed, the gardener sprang to his feet and reached for her arm, steadying her.

"You mustn't sit there, madame. The pond stones have become unstable and are not safe to sit upon," he said. "There is a pleasant spot to rest and view the pond just beneath that willow." He inclined his head toward a wrought iron bench in the shade of a nearby tree.

"Thank you. If you hadn't helped me, I fear I would have toppled headlong into the pond."

"It is a dangerous spot, make no mistake."

"Has Miss DuPont been informed?" Edwina asked, her heart thumping irregularly in her chest.

"I couldn't say. I report to Jennings, and he decides what is or is not important to pass along to Miss DuPont."

"But you have informed him of the danger?" Edwina asked.

"I have, and more than once. But there aren't nearly enough staff on the premises to keep up with all that needs doing, and it isn't for the likes of me to tell him what is important."

Edwina could well imagine that Jennings would not welcome any suggestions from younger staff members as to how he ought to hand out work assignments. No one rose to the sort of position he held if known for incompetence. He would be offended by any interference from a young upstart like an under-gardener many decades his junior. The lad might not know the best way to handle a dandelion weeder, but he certainly knew his way around the politics of domestic hierarchies. Beryl could learn a thing or two from him.

"Jennings will see to it at the appropriate time, I am sure. I expect there are not enough members of staff to see to everything, at least not at once."

"As you say, madame. I've heard that there were a half dozen gardeners here at one time but now there is only me to see to things. I don't mind telling you that it is too big a job for one man. If I manage to mow the lawns and weed one of the herbaceous borders each week, I consider it a roaring success," he said.

Edwina squinted at the flower bed to her left. A wave of sadness washed over her as she took in the lamentable state of the plants. If she had not been so intent on admiring the blooming roses, she would have seen the signs of neglect straightaway.

Lupines and delphiniums, long past flowering, still sported tall stalks covered in withered seedpods. Powdery mildew mottled the leaves of a clump of rudbeckia. If nothing was done to stop its spread, the whole bed would succumb before long. She knew from difficult experience how quickly such infestations got out of hand.

Her fingers itched to pull on a pair of gardening gloves in order to set the garden to rights. She suddenly wished Simpkins was at her side, loudly clucking his tongue at the disreputable state of things. How things had changed over the past few months.

If anyone had told her a year prior that she would miss the former jobbing gardener turned condiment magnate and housemate, she would surely have scoffed. But, just as so many other things in the world had changed since the war, so had her attitude toward the scruffy and stubborn old man.

Still, even if he had been there, she and Beryl had not been invited by Miss DuPont for a spot of weeding. She had far more pressing things to attend to before the week was out. She looked over at a stand of tall phlox that sadly needed a seeing-to with a pair of secateurs and sighed. Perhaps if they got to the bottom of Miss DuPont's mysterious troubles, she might find a bit of time to give the overworked gardener a hand before they returned to the Beeches. But first, it was time to head back into the school for tea.

Chapter 12

As she looped her arm through Edwina's, Beryl couldn't help but be grateful that she had put in considerable effort throughout the course of the summer in improving her fitness. She never felt quite as much like herself as she did when wearing her favorite red silk pajama pants suit with its flowing trousers and fluttering dramatic duster jacket. It was not the sort of thing one would have been encouraged to wear when she was a girl at Miss DuPont's school, which was likely the chief reason she was so fond of it. It would have been a great shame not to get to wear something quite so daring and unexpected simply because it no longer fit in a way that was flattering.

Edwina seemed more at ease than Beryl would have expected. She had not bothered to change out of the sensible and conservative blue dress she had worn for the journey, and her steps did not falter as they approached the drawing room where they had spent so many teatimes together in the past. How like Edwina it was to face this sort of situation with aplomb.

While Beryl herself was much more suited to feats of derring-do or to taking bold action in the face of social convention, Edwina was the one who knew how to step up to the line of duty. She would have made a tremendously fine soldier had such an opportunity have been afforded to women.

Beryl suspected that if Edwina's mother had not been so insistent that her daughter wait on her hand and foot, Edwina would have found a way to volunteer closer to the front during the Great War than she had. She looked over affectionately at her friend and gave her arm a bit of a squeeze as they entered the drawing room.

"I do hope there will be something stronger than tea on offer," Beryl said as she looked around.

An ancient-looking man with surprisingly erect posture stood to one side of the room, giving orders to young Ellen, the maid. Beryl assumed he must be the butler, and with a small frisson of surprise realized that was the same man who had so often glowered at her during her tenure at the school.

How elderly he had seemed when she was a mere girl, and now he appeared positively cadaverous. She thought it unlikely he would feel inclined to provide her with any unauthorized menu items, but seemed to recall that such members of staff always warmed to Edwina.

Perhaps her friend would take pity on her and make a request for at least the makings for a stiff gin fizz. Although Beryl was incredibly adept at managing many of life's difficulties, the one thing she never could seem to conquer was the deft handling of domestic staff. It had been the first of many abject failures in her time at the finishing school. She still could not see how treating another human being with such clear disdain could be considered the right way to go about things.

What caused her even more astonishment was the fact that the servants were the most eager to disrespect her if she was not inclined to put them in their place. The more she tried to be friendly or collegial, the less they appeared to like her. She racked her brain for the name of the butler and decided she must have blotted it from her memory as a way to protect herself. It wasn't until he slowly and stiffly approached with what appeared to be a softening of his face and came to a creaking halt in front of Edwina that she was reminded of it.

"Jennings, how very gratifying it is to see you still here at the school," Edwina said, her voice tinged with what Beryl was shocked to recognize as real warmth. Even more astonishingly, the elderly man went so far as to permit himself an uncharacteristic slight smile.

"There was a rumor amongst the staff that you would be joining us for a few days, Miss Davenport, and I hope you will not find me too forward in expressing my pleasure in finding such assertions to be correct," he said, sketching a very slight, arthritic bow.

"It is always a pleasure to be remembered with fondness, Jennings," Edwina said. "But tell me, is Mrs. Jennings still on staff as well?"

"I am so pleased to tell you that she is." He tipped his head conspiratorially. "We thought we might lose her during the influenza, but she rallied valiantly and is back in the kitchen terrorizing the younger staff."

"I am delighted to hear it. I shall have to beg her permission to visit her in her domain," Edwina said.

"I'm sure she would be very pleased if you were to do so. She asked me to mention that she has set aside a jar of her best gooseberry preserves should you care to sample them during your stay," he said.

Beryl hid her astonishment with difficulty. The only thing she had ever managed to pry out of the crusty old butler was a withering look. The thought that he had defrosted to the point of exchanging pleasantries with Edwina made her wonder about how different their time at the school may have been. Perhaps Edwina's mutual admiration for the butler and his wife explained something that Beryl had never quite reconciled with Edwina's risk-averse mentality.

When they were students, Edwina had often suggested making midnight raids on Mrs. Jennings's jam pantry. Perhaps the cook had a habit of setting aside tasty morsels for Edwina, who truth be told, could have used a bit more meat on her bones in the past just as much as she could in the present. It had been uncharacteristically adventurous of Edwina to sneak down into the kitchens in the dead of night. She had also seemed to have a rather remarkable understanding of just the place where the jam jars could be found.

"And what of the other members of staff from the time I was enrolled here? Are any of them still at the school?" Edwina asked.

"I'm sorry to say that there are far fewer of us in general than there were during what I think of as the golden years. I'm sure you are well aware of the difficulty in procuring quality individuals for positions of service," he said, shaking his head solemnly.

"Indeed I am. It was only through the very best of fortune that we were recently able to acquire the services of our excellent housekeeper, Beddoes," Edwina said. "I can only imagine the difficulty of trying to find sufficient staff for an establishment as grand as the school."

"It has been a constant struggle, but what cannot be cured must be endured. I hope that we manage to give satisfaction despite the current circumstances." He broke off and turned to face Ellen, who drew near, pushing a wooden cart heavily laden with a variety of pastries and rattling teacups.

He gave a slight bob of his head once more and stepped toward the young serving girl, a storm brewing across his face. Beryl was relieved not to have been included in the conversation or for Jennings to have expressed any recognition of her.

That said, it was rather disconcerting to not be instantly recognized by a member of the public. Perhaps, she consoled herself, he was too proper a servant to have indulged in such gawking behavior. After all, he must have been exposed to other celebrities throughout the years and would have known not to make anything of it. Surely, it couldn't possibly be because she had fallen so far out of the public eye as to be just another middle-aged woman considering the school for a prospective student.

"I had no idea you were so well acquainted with the butler," Beryl said as a way to distract herself from unpleasant ruminations. "Or with the cook."

"I have always found it best to be on good terms with members of staff, wherever I find myself. They are amongst the very most useful people you could possibly get to know," Edwina said.

"I couldn't agree more, but they never seem to warm to me the way they do with you," Beryl said. "I simply do not understand it."

Edwina squeezed her arm reassuringly and then drew herself up to her full, still not particularly impressive, height. "There's Veronica," she said, pitching her voice low.

There she was indeed. Veronica DeLisle stood in a shaft of light that cut through a French window at the end of the drawing room. Her hair was the exact same shade of blonde as Beryl's own and it glimmered in the light. Her attention focused on her former classmates, and she crossed the room with both of her hands outstretched before her, more theatrically than Beryl would have expected.

"I can hardly believe my eyes," Veronica said, coming to a stop before them. "Surely it can't be Polly and Wog. Whatever brings the pair of you here?"

Veronica had given most of her classmates unflattering or frankly demeaning nicknames. Beryl had not thought of the ones bestowed on Edwina and herself since she had put the school behind her. It spoke volumes that Veronica not only remembered but that she pulled them from the storage cupboard of her mind and slung them at women she hadn't seen in more than two decades. Beryl was about to answer when Edwina beat her to it.

"I'm afraid you must be mistaking us for someone else. Allow me to introduce my dear friend Beryl Helliwell and myself, Edwina Davenport. And you are?" she asked without a bit of disingenuousness to be heard in her voice.

Beryl was simply astonished. She thought of Edwina as someone who adhered to a strict moral code that almost always included far more dollops of truthfulness than Beryl felt was strictly necessary. To realize that her friend was not only exceptionally good at ferreting out lies from others but dissembling herself when she felt the need to do so was eye-opening.

It was particularly gratifying to see a flicker of surprise pass across Veronica's face. Beryl was certain she was someone who thought herself to be unforgettable. But then a familiarly nasty smile chased away the look of surprise.

"Oh, you poor thing," Veronica said, reaching out a slim, manicured hand and patting Edwina on the shoulder with it. "Not everyone is blessed with keeping ahold of their faculties throughout their life. I would say that not many are so unfortunate as to be quite so senile at such an early stage, however. Perhaps if I tell you my name it will jostle your brain cells about a bit. I'm Veronica DeLisle."

Edwina turned and looked up at Beryl before looking back at Veronica. "The name rings a faint bell. I know, you're the one who trod on the dancing master's feet and broke his toe," Edwina said. Then she smiled broadly at Veronica. "How do you do?"

Veronica drew in a sharp breath, then managed to don a tepid smile of her own. "What brings you back to the school? I had heard through the grapevine that neither of you have any children. You're not considering enrolling for a refresher course, are you?" She let out a tittering laugh that drew the attention of all the other eyes in the room.

Beryl had had just about enough of Veronica DeLisle. It was one thing to imply that either of them was past their mental prime. It was quite another to try and pick at a particularly soft spot in Edwina's heart. Beryl knew that, had things in life turned out differently, one of Edwina's dearest wishes was to have children of her own. But somehow, such a thing had never come to pass.

Although Beryl was certain that Edwina's longtime friend, Charles Jarvis, would like nothing more than to convince Edwina of the delights of marital bliss, it was unlikely, although not impossible, that such a union would result in progeny. Beryl couldn't see why an absence of children was a thing to regret, having never wished to become a mother, but she did not think any less of Edwina for sorrowing over it.

"We happen to be here on behalf of Beryl's goddaughter," Edwina said.

"Really? Is she someone I might know?" Veronica asked.

"I think it unlikely. Samira is the daughter of a sultan I met several years ago while on an expedition. There was a bit of a mishap with my hot-air balloon, and he was good enough to provide me with accommodation until repairs could be made. We've stayed in touch ever since. So naturally when he wished to have his daughter educated at a finishing school in Europe, he came to me for suggestions. Miss DuPont's school was of course the only one I would consider recommending."

Veronica arched a well-plucked eyebrow. "I'm quite shocked to think that anyone would consider you to be a voice of authority when it came to modeling ladylike behavior for anyone's daughter," she said. Then she let out a bell-like laugh and turned as if to include the rest of the assembly in her joke at Beryl's expense.

"Your surprise would be warranted if the sultan had any interest in churning out daughters who could be easily interchanged one for another. Instead, he's a forward-thinking sort of man who wished for his spirited daughter to cultivate an independent outlook. So, he thought to ask for my opinion."

"I see. In addition to fraternizing with foreigners, I had heard something about the two of you making a bit of a spectacle of yourselves as professional meddlers of some sort," Veronica said.

Before Beryl could remind Veronica that as an American, she was as much a foreigner as any sultan, Edwina piped up once more.

"There are those who look at our work that way, but we have found that most often they are members of the criminal class," Edwina said.

"I'm afraid I have very little experience with criminals, something I cannot regret."

"Edwina has a great deal of such experience, not only as a result of our thriving private enquiry business but in her capacity as the local magistrate for our district," Beryl said. From the thickening tension in the air, she thought it time to steer the conversation to some other topic. "But enough about us. What brings you to the school?"

"Oh, this and that," Veronica said. "My elder daughter attended the school last year and now my youngest is considering attending as well. But in addition to that, I'm happy to say that I've made myself available to Miss DuPont as a source of support during her declining years. I don't think it would be too much to admit that the poor dear would be simply lost without me."

"I wasn't aware that you were a member of staff," Beryl said. She watched as the smile faded once more from Veronica's face.

"Certainly not. I leave such things for those women who are more suited to that sort of tedium than I, like another of our former classmates, Mary White. I'm sure she's very grateful to have found such a soft landing after the recent collapse of her family fortunes. I'm happy to say I've had no such difficulties myself. Which reminds me, I simply must speak to her." She jabbed them with another of her icy smiles and turned on her heel.

Beryl watched as she made a beeline for Mary, who had just entered the room from a door at the far end. From the look on Mary's face, she was no happier to see Veronica than Beryl had been.

"She may be older, but she hasn't changed one bit, has she?" Beryl asked.

"I'm very much afraid that she has not," Edwina said.

Chapter 13

Mrs. Jennings looked older and a bit frailer than the last time Edwina had seen her, but she had maintained her plump figure probably through the auspices of her own good cooking. Even her floral pinny reminded Edwina of the ones she wore so many years ago. Perspiration drenched her brow, and her white hair framed her face in a frizzy halo. Her face split into a wide, welcoming smile and she bustled toward the well-scrubbed wooden worktable in the center of the room. She pulled out the chair and indicated Edwina ought to sit.

"Let me get a good look at you, Miss Davenport. It did my heart a world of good when Jennings told me that you were expected. I see he was right to say that you could do with a few solid meals while you're here," she said.

"It's lovely to see you too, Mrs. Jennings. And you know I have never been one to turn down your cooking," Edwina said, taking the same spot at the worktable she had preferred on those treasured visits to the kitchen when she was a girl.

Mrs. Jennings bustled over to the cupboard and pulled out a cake tin, which she placed in front of Edwina. She lifted the lid with a flourish. "Victoria sponge with my own lemon curd. Now you just let me brew up a pot of tea and then you can tell me all that you've been up to since last we met. Not that I haven't been keeping tabs on you, mind. Jennings and I have a scrapbook where we keep notices from all of our old girls, and I'm happy to say that you and Miss Helliwell have been filling up most recent pages at a rapid clip."

Edwina's cheeks blushed faintly. While she was incredibly proud of their successes, it was particularly nice to be remembered by someone she thought of so fondly as Mrs. Jennings. Edwina's relationship with her own mother had often been fraught with difficulties. Her mother had been a hypochondriac who seemed to require any available attention to be placed on her other than on her dependents. Edwina had loved her mother, but they had not rubbed along together without friction.

When she had arrived at Miss DuPont's and had been feeling homesick for the Beeches, she had made her way down to the kitchens one night and made the excuse that she had lost her way. Edwina never knew if Mrs. Jennings believed her or not, but she had made her a plate of sandwiches and a cup of hot chocolate before giving her directions to find her way back to the dormitory wing. Before long Edwina was finding excuses to return to the kitchen whenever she needed a break from the incessant chatter of her classmates.

In fact, it was because of Mrs. Jennings that Edwina was such a competent cook herself. Edwina had expressed interest in Mrs. Jennings's baking and jam making, and the older woman had enthusiastically and patiently passed along what she could during their impromptu visits.

"That's very kind of you to say," Edwina said.

"What's kind about it? It's nothing but the honest truth. To think that one day quiet Miss Davenport would be presiding over her local court, a gavel in her hand. Jennings and I just about burst with pride," she said. She sat down at the table opposite Edwina and lifted a cake knife, deftly slicing off a generous wedge and placing it before Edwina.

"You seem to know all about my news. What has been going on with you?" Edwina asked as she took a bite of the cake and chewed slowly, savoring the texture and the burst of flavor. She never could get her lemon curd to turn out quite as well as Mrs. Jennings's always did.

"We've been well enough, all things considered," Mrs. Jennings said.

She toyed with the cake knife and Edwina glanced up sharply to observe her face. There was no doubt about it, Mrs. Jennings's eyes were filled with unshed tears. Edwina dropped her fork and reached across the table to give the older woman's gnarled hand a squeeze.

"Mrs. Jennings, whatever is the matter?" Edwina asked.

"Everything seems so topsy-turvy. Sometimes it just gets the better of me when I think about how happy we were in the old days," Mrs. Jennings said. "Perhaps it is seeing you here that makes me feel overwhelmed with nostalgia."

"Are there problems here at the school?" Edwina asked. She felt disloyal posing the question as though she did not know the answer, but she was mindful of her duty and pushed down her feelings of discomfort.

"I should say there are. She doesn't say much about it, but it's easy to see that Miss DuPont is ever so worried."

"What does she have on her mind?" Edwina asked.

"Enrollment, of course. I have never made so few meals the entire time I've been here. This incoming class was the smallest in years, fewer than twenty girls there were to start, and now we are down to a mere half dozen."

"How can such a thing be explained? Miss DuPont has always had such a sterling reputation."

"It's the ghosts that's done it. The poor lady has spent a

whole lifetime building up her business and then some unquiet spirits have gone ahead and ruined everything for her," Mrs. Jennings said.

"Restless spirits? Are you saying you believe that the school is haunted?" Edwina asked.

Mrs. Jennings nodded, setting her multiple chins wagging gently. A drop of perspiration rolled down from her forehead and landed with a plop on her floral pinny. "Too right I do. I've heard them myself, woken from a sound sleep with all the creaking and groaning. Ghastly, it was."

"But this has not always been the case, has it? I do not remember that there were rumors of hauntings when I was here."

"Well, that's just as it should be because there weren't any. And quite a surprise that was too, with a building as old as this one. But circumstances change, don't they?" Mrs. Jennings said. Her eyes filled with more tears and this time they loosed themselves to run down her plump cheeks.

"Is it really as bad as all that?" Edwina asked, squeezing her hand again.

"I'm afraid it's my fault, you see," Mrs. Jennings said.

"How could it possibly be your fault if the school is haunted?" Edwina asked, trying to keep the incredulity from her voice.

Edwina was not one to believe in spirits herself, but she hardly liked to discount the spiritual practices of others. After all, she was absolutely certain that talking to her plants made them grow all the faster and a great deal more robustly besides. Many people would not credit that either.

"It all started a few weeks back and nothing's been right since," Mrs. Jennings said. "Which is exactly the same time that I invited a spirit medium to hold a séance here in the kitchen."

Edwina was surprised to hear it. Mrs. Jennings had always seemed like such a sensible woman. The notion of her turning over her sanctuary for a séance circle struck her as preposterous.

"You must have had a good reason to do something like that," Edwina said.

"Indeed, I did. I was trying to contact my grandson," Mrs. Jennings said. "Jennings has been quite torn up about his loss, you see, and I wanted to see if I could have a message for him from our William." She pulled a handkerchief from the pocket of her pinny and blew her nose loudly.

"Was William in France?" Edwina asked.

"That he was. Only eighteen years old. He hadn't been gone two months before we received word that he was missing. Of course, we never were able to bury his body. Jennings and I were both distraught by it. I thought that if a medium was able to make contact with him maybe we'd have a little peace."

"I understand why you would want to contact your grandson, but I still don't see why that should make you feel responsible for the disturbances at the school," Edwina said.

"I think that I may have helped to open up some sort of portal that won't close," Mrs. Jennings said. "Myrtle, my medium friend, said that that can happen sometimes. I've had her back again to try and close it, but she hasn't had any success."

Edwina looked down at her cake as if it might provide her with words of comfort. But nothing whatsoever occurred to her. It was in no way surprising that Mrs. Jennings would seek solace through spirit mediums. In fact, it was an incredibly common thing for people to do.

Still, Edwina had no belief in portals being forced open or cracks between dimensions allowing a flood of poltergeists to inhabit a building. Not that she was at all sure Mrs. Jennings would believe her. No, Edwina was certain there was a far more reasonable explanation for the goings-on at Miss DuPont's school. If she had felt committed to assisting because of lingering loyalty to Miss DuPont, she was all the more eager to do so on behalf of Mrs. Jennings.

"How did you come to meet Myrtle the medium?" Edwina asked. While some so-called mediums were simply interested in providing comfort to others, no matter how misguided, they were vastly outnumbered by those who wished to do so for monetary compensation. Perhaps the mystery of the disturbances at the school was already solved. Maybe the medium was enhancing the séance experience in order to keep Mrs. Jennings paying for her services.

"I've known Myrtle longer than I've known you. We grew up together on the same street."

Edwina's heart sank in her chest ever so slightly. Still, perhaps she was on to something. "Do you in any way compensate Myrtle for her sessions?"

"If you're asking if I pay her, certainly not. Myrtle would never take a penny. She does stay for a bite to eat if we meet around a mealtime, but nothing more."

"What does Jennings think about your theory?" Edwina asked.

Mrs. Jennings leaned forward slightly. "Since Myrtle never made contact with our William, I couldn't bring myself to tell him. He's never had much patience with that sort of thing and I'm quite sure he wouldn't approve."

So, Jennings had no knowledge of any of it. No wonder he was concerned about his wife behaving oddly.

"How often have you met with Myrtle for a séance?" Edwina asked.

"Half dozen times or so. Why do you ask?" Mrs. Jennings asked.

"I just wondered if there is any connection between the number of times and the occurrences reported by the girls or the other staff members about the noises and thefts," Edwina said.

"That I am not sure about. The thefts have been happening at such odd intervals and I don't rightly know what a ghost would want with pairs of stockings and pressed-powder compacts, do you?" Mrs. Jennings asked. "I'm sure William would not be inclined to pilfer anything at all, let alone things like that."

"Do any of the other staff members know about your séances?" Edwina asked.

"Once Ellen came in and found us, so she knows about them. But she's a good girl and agreed not to bother Jennings about it or to tell anyone else."

"How early on in your sessions did Ellen find out about Myrtle?" Edwina asked.

Mrs. Jennings tapped her chin with a plump forefinger. "I suppose it was the second time she was here. That's right, it was because she came in and found me teary-eyed. I was so disappointed that we hadn't been able to reach William after attempting twice. Ellen must've heard me crying and had come in to see what was the matter. Like I say, she's a very good girl."

Edwina thought that was certainly one explanation for Ellen's willingness to keep her own counsel. But there was another as well. There was no one in a better position in the household to steal things than the servants. Maids were able to go in and out of most every room in the house without calling attention to themselves. Moreover, the types of items Mrs. Jennings described as being stolen were certainly the sort of trinkets Edwina would expect a girl like Ellen to be interested in acquiring. She didn't like to think ill of anyone with no proof, but knew she would be naïve not to consider it.

"You're very fortunate to have her. It's almost impossible to acquire staff at all, let alone those who are worth having," Edwina said.

"That's partly what I meant when I said that I was nostalgic for the old days. When you were here, we had a full contingent of highly trained servants. Now, when Jennings is older and finding it more difficult to get around, he's ending up shouldering far more duties than is right for a man his age and in his position."

"How are you managing to run such a large place with so few staff members?" Edwina asked.

"We're not. Much of the house is closed up now. Even before the trouble started a few weeks ago, enrollment had been down for years. Things were becoming a bit worrisome before war broke out, but since then it's been nothing but a dramatic slide downhill."

"Miss DuPont said something similar when we spoke with her earlier. But she hadn't been quite so forthcoming."

"Well, she needs to save face now, doesn't she? It's not her fault though. It's the way of the world. The school closed down during the war, and afterwards it seemed as though the rules had changed somehow."

"Girls don't seem to be interested in the same sorts of things now as they were in the past, do they?" Edwina asked.

Mrs. Jennings shook her head. "No, they do not. They go out dancing and drinking, covering their faces with muck. The dresses they wear and the music they listen to is downright scandalous. The niceties of finishing school just don't appeal. Thank God for those few stalwarts like Miss DeLisle who uphold traditions and send their own daughters. Otherwise, we'd all be out on our ear."

"I'm so sorry to hear of all of your troubles. It seems that the lack of staff extends out-of-doors as well. From what I've seen on the grounds, you could really do with another gardener or two if you could possibly find one," Edwina said.

"Jennings has said as much. I'm sorry you were so easily able to notice any neglect on the grounds. I know you were always partial to them in years past," Mrs. Jennings said. "Some of the flower borders were plowed under to be put to use growing potatoes and vegetable marrows during the war. But at least the kitchen garden has been well maintained. We had a bumper crop of currants this year." Mrs. Jennings gave Edwina a smile and scraped back her chair. "Let me go fetch a jar and you can taste some for yourself."

As Edwina watched the old lady make her way into the storage cupboard at the back of the scullery, she wondered about the many things Mrs. Jennings had said. Could Ellen be involved? What about the fact that so much of the school building was closed up? As much as she was looking forward to tasting Mrs. Jennings's jam, she was going to need to cut their visit short. She had so much she wished to talk over with Beryl.

Chapter 14

Beryl slowed her steps and ducked into an alcove. Her years of crisscrossing the globe on one sort of expedition or another had honed her skills at tracking elusive prey. When she wished to be, Beryl was exceptionally light-footed and difficult to detect. She had caught sight of Veronica's daughter, Florence, she was sure of it.

The family resemblance left no room for doubt. In fact, when Beryl had spotted the girl a few yards ahead along the corridor, she had felt as though she had slipped through some sort of time-traveling portal and a young Veronica had appeared before her.

The girl looked around as if she wished to remain as undiscovered as Beryl herself did. It seemed to her that the girl was not where she was expected to be. She should have been attending one of the activities devised to convince prospective students that Miss DuPont's was an agreeable place to hone their skills.

But what she decidedly ought not to have been doing was prowling about on her own. Maintaining a discreet distance,

Beryl crept after her, wondering if the solution to the pilfering mystery could possibly be so easily discovered. If so, this case would be one for the books.

Despite her striking resemblance to Veronica, the girl had at least one thing more in common with Edwina than she did with her own mother. She had silently slipped through the door of the school's vast library and to Beryl's surprise made a beeline for a particular shelf of books near the back of the large room.

Although the electric light had not been switched on, and the sun was beginning to sink in the west, the long windows provided sufficient light for Beryl to make out Florence's figure leaning against a shelf, her face tipped toward the text of the open book she held in her hands. Beryl abandoned her attempt to disguise her presence as she strode toward the younger woman. Florence looked up and slapped the volume shut, keeping her place with a finger wedged between the pages of the book.

The way she had angled the spine and cover made it impossible to read the title, and Beryl wondered if Miss DuPont had added something vaguely salacious to what had always been a mind-numbingly tame collection of books. Why else would someone wish to keep the nature of their reading material a secret?

Not that she spent a great deal of time reading herself. She simply couldn't find it in her to sit for such long stretches of time. No, a newspaper was far more her speed, and even that was something she made her way through with the utmost haste, simply skimming the vast majority of articles in favor of getting on with things in her own life.

"Good evening," Beryl said, closing the gap between them. The girl's eyebrows shot skyward as light from the window cascaded over Beryl's face.

"You're Beryl Helliwell," she said, allowing the book to sag forward away from her chest. "You were in my mother's class."

"You are correct on both counts. But you seem to have the advantage, although I would hazard a guess that your mother is Veronica DeLisle. You look just like her when she was a girl, you know," Beryl said.

"That's what everyone who knew her when she was young tells me. I assure you, that's where what we have in common ends," she said. "I'm Florence Montrose and very pleased to meet you. Have you really flown all over the world solo?"

"I certainly have. Are you interested in flying yourself?" Beryl asked.

The young woman nodded, her shiny, pale hair swishing back and forth as she did so. "I am interested in airplanes but am more intrigued by the possibility that women can take on any jobs they fancy rather than the ones they are told are appropriate for them."

It was with a jolt Beryl realized that Veronica had produced offspring whose company she might enjoy. Florence Montrose was nothing like her mother, despite her looks. Even though Paul Deering, the girl's stepfather, had mentioned that finishing school was not a good fit for Florence, Beryl was still surprised to hear her espouse views so contrary to her mother's. But the more she thought about it, the more she realized how unreasonable such an assumption to be.

After all, she had never seen eye to eye on any topic with her own mother. They had never been aligned in matters of taste, entertainment, or even the possibility that it would rain later in the day. And as she thought of it more, Edwina's mother was brought to mind. She and her daughter had not shared many points of view, at least as far as Beryl had been able to ascertain. Perhaps she had made the error of assuming that appearance on the outside would reflect attitudes from inside. She felt slightly chagrined at her assumption and she chided herself for such shortsightedness.

Beryl was acutely aware of how the newspapers had enhanced

her reputation and popularity. She had carefully cultivated a glamorous appearance in order to make the controversial modern-woman message more palatable to those who resisted it. She knew better than most how little crossover there might be between one's exterior and interior.

It did not do her any credit as a detective to enter into an investigation or to question possible suspects with such preconceived notions. She resolved to be more open-minded toward the rest of the people she might meet during her stay at Miss DuPont's.

"You sound like quite a modern woman yourself," Beryl said. "Still, I am surprised to find you here on your own instead of at one of the sanctioned activities for the young ladies."

"I am supposed to be sitting in on a grace and deportment lesson. But I realized that if I had to listen to another minute on how to walk across the ballroom floor with my head held just so and my shoulders pulled back and parallel to the floor, I might begin to throw things," Florence said.

She tucked a strand of her fair hair behind her ear and Beryl thought the girl would benefit from having it bobbed. It had done a world of good for Edwina, after all. Beryl had been tempted to throw things about during her own classes at Miss DuPont's and she felt her heart warm to the girl even more.

"So, what is it that you are reading, some sort of escape plan?"

"I suppose that is one way of looking at it." She glanced down at the cover of the book before thrusting it impulsively toward Beryl. "I would like to learn to fly, but my real interest is in the airplanes themselves. What I would like to do is to become an engineer," Florence said. "Engineering doesn't tend to line up with the plans that my mother has for me however."

Beryl felt a shudder run through her involuntarily. Her parents had valued just the same sort of path for their own daughter, which was how Beryl had come to attend the school despite her own unwillingness to do so. In fact, Beryl had to wonder if that was one of the reasons she and Veronica had not gotten along during their time at school together. Veronica had been exactly the type of daughter Beryl's own mother had most wanted, instead of the one she had disappointingly received.

Miss DuPont's school had been touted as an antidote to her antisocial interests. Despite that, her rehabilitation had not taken place, much to the dismay of her parents. But her mother had taken it the worst. Beryl thought she completely understood what would drive young Florence to hide out in the library rather than risk making a scene by tossing about the crockery.

"Does your father agree with her?" Beryl asked.

Florence lifted her slim shoulders then dropped them with an air of defeat. "When my sister was here, he hinted that it would be fine with him if I chose not to attend."

"But now?" Beryl asked.

"Now he keeps pointing out all the reasons schools like this can be of benefit to women."

That seemed to align with what Paul Deering had mentioned when she first met him. "What does your father think of your interest in engineering?" Beryl asked.

"Daddy is all for it, even though he says he thinks I am choosing an unnecessarily difficult road. But how could he possibly object, considering it likely I came by my interest quite naturally? After all, he is an engineer himself."

But of course he was. Montrose Aeronautics was a British firm specializing in airplanes for both military and civilian purposes. There were rumors that his company had positioned itself to be a major contractor should further hostilities break out with the Germans. As much as Beryl kept such thoughts to herself, especially within Edwina's earshot, she strongly suspected the country would have need of as many airplanes as could be procured before too many more years had passed.

"So it is only because of your parents that you are considering the school?"

Florence let out a deep sigh. "You make it sound like I had any part in the notion. Mother would not listen to me when I said I had no interest in attending. I tried to convince her to be content with my older sister following in her footsteps, but it was not enough."

"So, you have not yet agreed to attend?"

"No, and I don't want to, but I may have no choice. My mother is insistent, and I don't want to burden my father, particularly at present. He is just finishing up a new airplane design and I wouldn't want to trouble him with something far less important."

"From what I remember of your father, I would think he'd want you to be happy and would be willing to speak up for you."

"I would rather end up at finishing school than to give my parents another excuse to argue. It is painful to witness the two of them together and my mother always ends up the winner, no matter what. I probably shouldn't admit this, but it was a tremendous relief when they divorced."

As she spoke, an image from the past reared up in Beryl's mind's eye. She could picture the baffled look on Desmond Montrose's face as Veronica DeLisle had hooked her arm through his and guided him away from a conversation he had been having with Mary White and out onto the dance floor. It had been a brazen and calculated move at the time, and he had not been savvy enough to resist it. Perhaps he was no more accomplished at thwarting Veronica, despite the passage of years.

She was surprised to hear that Veronica and Desmond had quarreled spectacularly. Since she had been far from England at the time, she had been able to avoid any notices in the newspapers chronicling the dissolution of their marriage. The divorce had provoked even less fanfare in the press than their wedding had, when she came to think of it. She wondered if there was any chance that he and Mary White had fanned the flames of what had been young love.

"If that is the case, it sounds as though the breakup of their marriage was the best thing. I would love to have the chance to reminisce with your father. Do you know where I might find him?" Beryl asked.

"He has been keeping to his room mostly, but I happen to know that Miss DuPont took pity on him and gave him a key to a classroom in the disused west wing so he could get some work in while he hid himself from Mother. You won't tell her, will you?"

"I shan't say a word to anyone except Edwina," Beryl said. "And I won't tell where you are, either."

She winked at Florence and made her way as quietly as possible to the library door. She turned back to look at the girl before she stepped out into the hallway, but did not catch her eye. Florence's full attention was already back on her book.

Chapter 15

Dark had finally settled over the school, and with it the opportunity to move on to the next phase of the investigation. Edwina had changed into her walking shoes and Beryl, unnervingly, had unearthed her pistol from the bottom of her valise and placed it in the pocket of her long duster. Edwina felt certain she would never become accustomed to the notion she shared a home with someone so comfortable with firearms.

"Are we ready?" Beryl asked.

Edwina nodded, holding her torch aloft, but her stomach felt tight. Not only was she uncomfortable with the idea of sneaking about, spying, simply because it felt underhanded and somehow grubby, but it also reminded her far too much of her time as a student at Miss DuPont's. Beryl had had a craving for adventure even then and the idea that any parts of the building would be left undiscovered had seemed to her unthinkable. Somehow, she had managed to convince Edwina to accompany her on her many tours through the far reaches of the school.

Together they had explored the attics, the cellars, and uninhabited outbuildings without detection. That said, they had

had a number of narrow escapes that occasionally still haunted Edwina in her dreams. She had no desire to add more fuel to her library of nightmares, but she could think of no valid reason to shirk her duties as an investigator. She couldn't very well claim that they would be likely to incur the wrath of Miss DuPont if they were there at her behest.

"Where do you propose that we start?" Edwina asked.

"Based on your conversation with Mrs. Jennings, I think the empty servants' quarters of the school would be an ideal place for us to begin."

Beryl pressed her ear against the door to their room, and after listening for a moment, carefully turned the knob before slipping out into the hallway. Edwina followed closely on her heels, as light-footed as ever. As they made their way along the darkened corridor, she realized she acutely missed her dog. While he could not have been counted on to remain silent if they had encountered someone intent on harm, she would have felt much braver knowing that he padded along beside her, his ears and nose alert for any danger. Her heart squeezed as she thought about him curled up in his basket that night back at the Beeches, wondering what could possibly have become of her.

She so rarely spent an overnight away from him that she could well imagine his distress. Once again, she felt an overwhelming surge of gratitude for Simpkins and his willingness to coddle the little creature during her absence. With a fresh surge of determination to complete the case as quickly as possible, she quickened her step.

Beryl led the way to a set of stairs that mounted to a disused wing of the servants' quarters. She paused on each step, waiting for it to settle silently beneath her weight before proceeding to the next one. By the time they reached the top of the stairwell, Edwina's heart hammered in her chest. Beryl turned the knob at the top of the stairs and carefully creaked it open.

Edwina pointed the beam of her torch into the room that appeared in front of them, bathing the space in meager light. A line of bedsteads with thin bare mattresses stretched out along each wall. Assorted chairs and wardrobes took up the rest of the space, but it was clear to see that it had been disused for some time.

Even in the low light a heavy coating of dust could easily be seen clinging to all of the surfaces. Beryl brushed away a cobweb with the back of her hand as they stepped further into the room and began to inspect it more closely.

Prominently displayed on the far wall was a series of bells attached to wires that sank down along the wall and into a series of holes drilled into the floor beneath. Edwina stepped toward them and pointed her flashlight beam directly on their reflective surfaces. They seemed less dusty than any of the surrounding flooring and furniture.

She ran a finger lightly over several of the bells and noted a far lighter coating of dust than was evident elsewhere in the room. She made a mental note of the position of the bells and wondered if they connected to areas of the house that were still occupied. Primarily she wondered if they connected to the bellpull she had seen in Miss DuPont's office when they first arrived.

Something entirely different had caught Beryl's attention along a bank of small windows set high up on the walls. She motioned with her hand for Edwina to join her and pointed out the window. Edwina was forced to reach up on tiptoe in order to peer out, but as she did so she noticed two pinpoints of light bobbing along the far end of the lawn near the line of trees that signaled the entrance to the woods.

Beryl pitched her voice low. "Can you think of any good reason why someone would be prowling around the grounds at this time of night?"

Edwina could think of many reasons why occupants of the school might be out after the time they were expected to be abed, but none of them could be considered good. She was reminded once more of the sorts of nocturnal wanderings she and Beryl had gotten up to during their girlhood. There was every reason to expect that the current crop of students was no more rule-abiding than they themselves had been.

"If you are asking me if I think that ghosts are about, I would say no. That said, I can't think of any legitimate business that would take anyone outside at this late hour."

"Then we shall have to go after them," Beryl said.

"Are you certain? After all, it might prove rather awkward if we sneak up on a romantic tryst," Edwina said, feeling the back of her neck flush with heat.

Whatever had come over her? She blamed it on the reappearance of Desmond Montrose. That and perhaps the inclusion of a love interest for her cowboy protagonist in the novel she was writing. Or perhaps it was being back at Miss DuPont's that reminded her of all the hopes and aspirations she had had for herself when she was so very young. At that time, she would never have predicted that she would have become one of so many women who would not marry. She had reconciled herself to her solitary circumstance many years prior, but something about being on-site at the place she had been before she had come to that disappointing conclusion had brought it all rushing back and had turned her mind to things romantic.

Beryl raised an eyebrow at her and then set off for the stairway. "I have caught most of my ex-husbands in compromising romantic positions. I doubt very much that I will be the least bit bothered by whatever it is that we come across on the grounds of Miss DuPont's. But we had better hurry."

Edwina threw caution to the wind and quickened her steps to match up with Beryl's long stride. It seemed impossible to move both quickly and quietly, but Beryl made an incredibly good stab at it. Edwina, usually so light on her feet, felt like a rhinoceros in comparison with her almost silent friend. Beryl's expeditions into the bush in search of game on safari surely must explain her ability to move like a ghost down the darkened stairwell and on along the disused corridor. Edwina abandoned her concerns about disturbing the household and simply focused on keeping up. But despite their rush, by the time they reached the first floor and rushed out onto the lawn, there was no sign of another soul about.

"Where do you think they could have gone?" Beryl asked, turning one way and then the other.

"Whoever it was could be anywhere by now. I don't think we are likely to find them, given how much of a head start they had on us," Edwina said. As much as she loved the school grounds, she had no desire whatsoever to pursue an unidentified party into the woods, even whilst clad in her stoutest walking shoes. She could only hope that Beryl would agree.

"I suppose it could have been someone no more bent on real mischief than we were. You remember that time we decided to play a game of badminton under the full moon?" Beryl asked.

"How could I forget? We must have been hiding up in that tree for half an hour before Miss Glover gave up her search for whoever had been making such a racket and headed back to school," Edwina said, smiling in the dark despite herself.

"Not that it did us any good in the end, considering she just checked the dormitory to see whose beds were empty," Beryl said.

"Are we turning into our own versions of Miss Glover?" Edwina asked. "After all, now we are the ones running around checking to see who's up to mischief."

Beryl turned to her and pointed her torch toward Edwina's face.

"I sincerely hope you will never make such an odious suggestion again. The very idea that either of us has anything in common with Miss Glover is quite possibly the most frightening thing I have ever faced, and that includes an emergency ejection from an airplane."

An involuntary shudder ran up Edwina's spine. She glanced over at the section of the lawn where Desmond's plane had touched down and thought about her friend being forced to exit a similar machine in midair. It didn't bear thinking about. She looped her arm through Beryl's own and turned back toward the school.

As they picked their way back across the dew-covered grass, Edwina looked back over her shoulder. She strained her eyes, hoping she might catch a glimpse of the bobbing lights once more. While Beryl was right that they had little in common with Miss Glover as far as their motivations for discovering who was wandering about in the night, she couldn't shake the feeling that it would have been better had they tracked down those persons. Still, she felt she owed Beryl something of an apology and so she put her worry aside and turned to look up at her friend.

"Since we're already sneaking around, why don't we creep into the scullery, and I'll make us each a cup of cocoa. I might even be able to remember where Mrs. Jennings keeps the biscuit tin."

Chapter 16

Beryl awoke at an hour she felt was rather too early the next morning. And even though Edwina had indeed been able to not only locate the biscuit tin but a jar of jam and a wedge of cake, Beryl found that she was ravenous. In fact, she would call her appetite almost girlish. Perhaps it was simply the psychological effects of finding herself back in school once more.

Or perhaps it was a natural response to too little sleep. She had always prided herself on being able to function on very little sleep should the need arise, but worryingly she had noticed over the past year or two that although she could drag herself out of bed in the morning after such shortages, she would find herself dozing off in a chair by late afternoon.

Edwina seemed to have no such difficulty. By the time Beryl had awakened, Edwina was fully dressed and appeared to be restlessly waiting for Beryl to be ready to start the day. She hurried through her own ablutions and in short order the pair of them appeared in the breakfast room.

Although Beryl considered herself to be an outlandishly fortunate person, she had to wonder if there was something about

Miss DuPont's school that turned such things on their heads. Miss Glover was the very last person she wished to meet, and that included Veronica. It only seemed the civilized thing that one might be permitted to down at least one cup of coffee before being required to face a dragon.

Miss Glover looked up as they entered the room and shook her head disapprovingly.

"The pair of you look like something the cat dragged in. Should I assume you were out for a midnight game of badminton like the one I caught you at as girls?"

"What a charming notion. Perhaps we should plan for that for this evening, Edwina," Beryl said, flashing Miss Glover her most dazzling smile.

Although Beryl never preferred to face down early morning dragons, if she found herself in a position of doing so, she intended to be triumphant.

"I see you are as keen an observer as you ever were," Edwina said. "Beryl and I found that we were disturbed in the night by some odd noises and even some lights flashing out on the lawn. You weren't bothered by any such things too, were you?"

Miss Glover arched an eyebrow and then looked down at her plate. With excruciating slowness, she began spreading a generous amount of butter across a triangle of toast. She added a dollop of jam before lifting her gaze to Edwina once more.

"There have been so many disturbing sounds at the school lately that I'm rather afraid I would find it more difficult to sleep without them than with them. And I might add that it is not uncommon for there to be lights out on the grounds."

Beryl stepped around the table and made her way to a long mahogany buffet placed against the far wall of the breakfast room. Mrs. Jennings had done herself proud as usual. If Miss DuPont's school was having financial difficulties, it was not evident from the breakfast offerings.

More than a dozen covered dishes and open bowls spread

across the surface of the buffet. She lifted a silver lid and peered underneath. There were so many peculiar things offered by the British when it came to breakfast items. Although Beryl did not consider herself to be a finicky eater, she was not inclined to anything involving fish so early in the day.

With relief she identified the contents of the dish as sausages. Plucking two from the dish with a pair of silver tongs, she placed them on a translucent plate of bone china. Edwina joined her at the buffet and the two of them filled their plates with a variety of comestibles. By the time they returned to the table Miss Glover was nearly finished with her piece of toast and had moved on to peeling a boiled egg.

"You mentioned that there has been a great deal of noise lately. With so few girls currently enrolled I would have thought that the amount of noise would have reduced," Beryl said. "When we met the girls yesterday, they did not appear to be a particularly unruly group."

"I suppose they're no more unruly than you were at the same age. Adele and Lois are as thick as thieves, and I've caught them getting up to the some of the same sorts of mischief I would have expected from the pair of you when you were students."

"I suppose that with two of them it would explain the pair of lights that we saw bobbing across the lawn," Edwina said, taking a seat opposite Miss Glover and addressing her remarks to Beryl.

It occurred to Beryl that Miss Glover had much in common with the postmistress back in Walmsley Parva, Prudence Rathbone. Both seemed entirely discontented with their own lots and incredibly inclined to stick their noses into the business of others, with enthusiasm. She thought it likely that Edwina had come to the same conclusion and thought it best to use a similar approach with Miss Glover to the one they often employed when wishing to question Prudence about some juicy bit of gossip. Prudence would never relinquish what she knew if one made it obvious that her input would please them. But if she were excluded from the conversation or her claims were put in doubt, she eagerly worked to convince them that she had something worth saying.

"I'm sure you must be right. The lights were nothing more than a pair of girls out on a bit of a lark when they ought to have been abed. I'm sure that none of the adults here would have so little sense as to be scurrying about after dark when they have work to do the next day," Beryl said.

Miss Glover let out an indelicate snort and reached for another piece of toast from the rack in front of her. Edwina appeared to turn the majority of her attention to removing the shell from her own egg. Her small, nimble fingers tapped it expertly with the back of a spoon and then neatly peeled off a long curl of eggshell.

"I would have to agree. I've been favorably impressed by the faculty and staff we've encountered thus far. I can't imagine any of them jeopardizing their ability to perform their duties properly by neglecting their sleep. They all seem far too sensible for such childish pranks," Edwina said as she reached for the saltshaker.

Miss Glover snorted even louder. Beryl thought the elderly lady's face had turned an unhealthy shade of puce. She wondered if perhaps they had gone too far until Miss Glover dropped a half-eaten piece of toast onto her plate and dabbed at the corners of her mouth with her serviette.

"That just goes to show what you know. I seem to remember you suffering from the same fault of thinking you knew more than you did, so many years ago. I keep a very close eye on the staff, and I'll have you know that if someone was roaming the grounds, I'd be sure that it was Mary White."

That did it, Beryl thought. Edwina was an expert at managing to convince others to show their hand. Although her friend was not a particularly adept bridge player, Beryl thought it possible that Edwina would be excellent at poker. She wondered if there was any chance she might convince her friend to give it a try. Edwina tended to be unwilling to even consider participating in those things she thought bore a whiff of immorality.

But perhaps if Beryl posed it as a bit of research for her Western novel, Edwina would be willing to give it a try. She cut off a bit of sausage with the side of her fork and popped it into her mouth. Edwina seemed to be doing a marvelous job of taking the lead and she thought it best not to interrupt.

"I'm sure that couldn't be the case. I can't imagine she would be less responsible as an adult woman who's a member of the staff than she was as a girl. Surely it must be someone else," she said.

"I see you haven't outgrown your contrariness, Miss Davenport," Miss Glover said.

A vein in Miss Glover's neck fluttered wildly and Beryl thought once again about the possibility they might require medical assistance. She wondered how long it would take for a doctor to reach them and scolded herself for entertaining the notion that it might take far too long to provide the aid Miss Glover might need.

"I'm sure I meant no offense, Miss Glover. I'm sorry if you felt I was being contrary. Just can't imagine Mary White scuttling furtively around the grounds in the dead of night. But perhaps you know best," Edwina said.

"You have assessed the situation entirely incorrectly. One of the reasons Miss DuPont is seeing such a downturn in enrollment is that the staff is woefully inadequate. Nothing is as it used to be, but Mary White is in no way qualified to be a teacher here at the school, let alone any other role she might be offered," Miss Glover said.

The throbbing of her vein became even more pronounced, and Beryl risked darting a warning glance at Edwina. Edwina, however, continued to pay careful attention to the contents of her plate.

"Beryl, I seem to remember that Miss DuPont had nothing but praise for Mary yesterday when we visited with her in her office. Is that your recollection too?" Edwina asked.

"That was my impression. It sounded to me that she was more than pleased with Mary's performance," Beryl said.

"Although I would say that she only made reference to her as a teacher. She said nothing whatsoever about another sort of role. Was there something else that you had in mind?" Edwina said, looking up from her breakfast and widening her eyes innocently as she trained them on Miss Glover.

"It's not for me to go sharing school business with outsiders. Goodness knows that only leads to trouble." Miss Glover glanced at her wristwatch and then pushed her chair away from the table before standing. "I must get on with my duties." Without another word she exited the breakfast room, half of her breakfast still on her plate.

Edwina turned in her seat to face Beryl. "It would appear that there is no love lost for Mary White," she said.

"Apparently not. Why do you think that is?"

"It could be anything, I expect. Miss Glover never seemed to need a good reason to dislike any of us when we were students, and I can't see why she would have become more agreeable as she has grown older. In my experience most people don't do so," Edwina said.

"She definitely has always been disagreeable, but she certainly sounded like she had it in for Mary even more than the students. That said, I think the most interesting thing was her mentioning other roles. What do you suppose that was in reference to?"

Edwina shrugged. "From the looks of things, Mary is already shouldering more roles than teachers did when we were here. Perhaps that's what Miss Glover is referring to."

"I can't see why Miss Glover would be against the notion of

Mary performing more jobs at the school. After all, someone needs to do it."

"It was interesting that she didn't want to come out and tell us exactly what was on her mind, wasn't it?"

"Perhaps there's nothing to anything she says, and she just wanted to make trouble for Mary. Do you think there's anything to her claim that Mary is likely the one who was roaming around the grounds last night?" Beryl asked.

"I think she was just trying to cast blame on her for reasons we have yet to understand. I think it is far more likely that it was just girlish hijinks that we saw. But she was right about one thing."

Beryl looked at Edwina with surprise. It seemed unlikely that Edwina would credit Miss Glover with being in the right about just about anything.

"And what was that?"

"We both look as though we could've done with some more sleep."

Chapter 17

While Edwina was off on her mission to find out what sort of roles Mary White might be interested in obtaining, Beryl remained in the breakfast room, lingering over a second cup of coffee. Although, truth to tell, she might require a third cup considering how weak the brew had turned out to be. No matter how long she remained on British soil she could not reconcile herself to what was passed off as coffee.

She vastly preferred to partake of her morning beverage in the Middle East or South America. She spared a thought for Desmond's airplane and wondered if it was fueled up sufficiently for a quick jaunt to Italy. A diminutive cup of espresso would hit the spot after a night of such inadequate sleep.

She leaned against the back of her chair and looked about the room. If memory served, little had been changed since her days as a student. The walls were papered in a dull yellow covered in highly stylized pink and rose flowers, the names of which might even defy Edwina to decipher. Along each side of the windows heavy velvet drapes hung and minimized the amount of light.

The weighty, dark wooden furniture was the same too and had held up remarkably well, considering that so many young women had breakfasted on it over the decades. Beryl would not have been in the least surprised to be informed that the silver toast racks and accompanying covered dishes were the very ones that had stood on the same long buffet when she was a girl.

Beryl heard footsteps hurrying along the hall and looked out to see Adele and Lois passing by the breakfast room door. She called out to them, and they turned and stuck their heads through the opening.

"Did you need something, Miss Helliwell?" Adele asked.

"As a matter fact I do. Why don't you join me for a moment?" she asked, waving them into the room.

The girls gave each other a worried look before walking toward her.

"I don't want to keep you from your lessons or anything else you have planned for the morning, but I have a question for you," she said. "I wanted to ask you if you noticed anything unusual last night?"

The girls looked at each other once again and Lois gave Adele an encouraging nod.

"There seemed to be quite a lot of creaking and thumping all around the building last night. There were some strange noises overhead as well," Adele said, turning to Lois, who nodded.

"I didn't fall asleep easily because of it," Lois said, lowering her voice. "I thought it might have been rats."

Beryl thought it more likely that the sounds they heard above them had come from her own and Edwina's feet. If her memory served, the servants' wing they had been exploring was placed directly above the girls' dormitory. But she didn't need to admit to her part in any of the disruptions they had heard.

"And there was another theft," Lois said. Two bright spots

of color had appeared on the girl's cheeks. If Beryl didn't know better, she would wonder if Lois was involved. The girl seemed to be showing a great deal of enthusiasm for what had transpired. Beryl would not have thought that the average girl would be thrilled that there were thefts taking place where she resided.

"What was stolen?" Beryl asked.

"A pressed powder compact," Lois said. "One of the other girls, Bernice, was mentioning it over breakfast this morning."

"Have all the thefts been from the girls' dormitory?" Beryl asked. "Or have they occurred elsewhere in the school as well?"

Adele shrugged. "I have no idea about thefts anywhere else. It's not as though the faculty or staff would tell us about anything like that occurring in the rest of the building. We only know for sure about thefts occurring in the girls' dormitory."

Beryl knew that the thefts had been widespread, but she did find it interesting that Miss DuPont had managed to contain news of how widespread they were from the girls. In her experience bad news like that traveled quickly within a group. Either Miss DuPont was exceptionally skilled at keeping things under wraps or Adele had just told her a lie. Perhaps Adele and Lois knew much more than they were letting on.

She suddenly wished that Edwina was there with her. Edwina was not generally one to tell untruths herself, but she was exceptionally good at recognizing them from others, especially young ladies. She claimed it was from her years of supervising girls in the Women's Land Army during the war, but Beryl thought it was perhaps more than that. After all, she always seemed to know when Simpkins had been dissembling about how much work he had put in at the Beeches.

"Are you sure that Bernice's compact was stolen? Could she have simply mislaid it?" Beryl asked.

"I suppose so. She's not the tidiest of us all and I suppose she might have simply mislaid it," Lois said. "Her things do tend to be scattered all over the place. Miss Glover has scolded her for it more than once."

Beryl could well imagine that Miss Glover would be sure to remark on slovenliness from the students. She had always been quick to do so when she and Edwina were in attendance. As she thought about it a memory came flooding back. Edwina had been instrumental in, for the most part, halting Veronica's taunts, jeers, and scathing criticisms of Mary White, but she had not managed to entirely quell her harassment.

One of the ways that Veronica kept it up was by leaving bits of trash or stray personal items on Mary's bed in the dormitory. Miss Glover had invariably taken her to task for the mess. On the rare occasion that Mary spoke up for herself and mentioned that she was not responsible, Miss Glover had scolded her hotly for lying. It had been an effective way to continue to make poor Mary miserable throughout her time at the school.

"When Bernice reported it to Miss Glover, she even scolded her about it going missing. She said that it was no surprise that her things had a habit of disappearing, considering how little care she took of them. It was as if she thought it was Bernice's own fault that someone had taken it."

"If we discount the idea that Bernice is making off with her own possessions, are you sure that there hasn't been the slightest indication of who might be responsible for the thefts?" Beryl asked.

The girls looked at each other once more, then shook their heads.

"There hasn't been any evidence of who the thief might be," Adele said.

"That's one of the reasons why people are saying that they think the school might be haunted. It is as if the items have simply disappeared without a trace. Unquiet spirits could be the ones at fault," Lois said, her eyes shining with excitement.

Beryl took a sip of her rapidly cooling coffee. She did not usually feel her age, but there was something about the keen pleasure that Lois so obviously took in imagining an otherworldly explanation that suddenly made Beryl feel just the teensiest bit jaded and ever so slightly older than usual. After all, how long had it been since she would have entertained such a possible scenario? Had she ever been so credulous? She thought it was unlikely. She made a face as she took another sip of her coffee and steered the subject back to less metaphysical possibilities.

"So, no one admitted to hearing or seeing anything else unusual besides the noises overhead?" Beryl asked.

The girls looked at each other once more. Beryl wondered if she and Edwina had looked anything like Lois and Adele when they had first known each other. Adele was dark and slim and below average height with a serious air about her. Something about her did put Beryl in mind of her friend in the years of her youth. Lois, she somewhat shamefacedly hoped, did not seem a great deal like her own recollections of herself other than her fairer hair and height. She was altogether more frivolous than Beryl thought herself to be. She might be impulsive and inclined to take risks, but she never thought of herself as someone others would describe as the least bit silly. And Lois could be called that without the observer being considered too harsh.

"No, but we wish we had. We were rather put out to have missed out on the excitement," Adele said. "It's not every day one of your teachers takes a tumble."

"Someone suffered a fall?" Beryl asked.

"That's right. Miss White fell all the way down the north stairwell from the second to the first floor. A doctor was called and everything. She's ended up with a badly sprained wrist and our art lessons are canceled for today," Lois said with a giant smile spreading across her face. "Maybe we will be lucky enough that they will be for the rest of the term."

"You needn't seem so happy about it, Lois," Adele said. "Art lessons are the only thing I really enjoy here at the school, and now we won't be having them for who knows how long."

"I'm sure that you will, since you are such a good artist, but I'd rather do just about anything than dab blobs of paint onto a canvas. I'm simply hopeless at it," Lois said.

On that point, Beryl would have to agree with her. Art had been one of the many classes at the school at which Beryl had not excelled. Surprisingly, it was one of the few that Edwina had not proven much of a success at either. She distinctly remembered standing with her friend at the back of the painting studio wondering aloud at the value of capturing a bowl of fruit for posterity and Edwina sharing her bafflement.

"You say a doctor was called. Do you know who did so?" Beryl asked.

"I heard it was Florence's father. The maid said that he was the one who found her at the bottom of the stairs," Adele said. "Why do you ask?"

"I just wondered if she was so badly injured that she could not even make it to the telephone herself," Beryl said.

In fact, she thought it strange that in a house where so many strange noises filled the air at night, no one had been roused by Mary's fall or the arrival of the doctor. But perhaps those sounds were simply conflated with all the other noises.

The girls exchanged another look and cast worried glances over their shoulders at the sound of footsteps in the hallway behind them.

"Is there anything else? We don't wish to hurry you, but we are supposed to be attending a flower arranging lesson with Miss DuPont," Lois asked.

Beryl shook her head, thanked the girls, and sent them on their way. She pushed away her coffee cup and drummed her long fingers on the tabletop. Could the lights she and Edwina had seen in the night been caused by the arrival of the doctor? Was it simply a coincidence that Mary had taken a dramatic fall down the stairs on the same night that an unexplained presence lurked on the grounds? Somehow, it seemed unlikely that two such incidents were entirely unrelated.

Chapter 18

While Miss Glover might have been content to drop hints about the source of the disruptions, so little information would not get them very far in their investigation, Edwina thought. She determined that the best thing to do would be to go straight to Miss DuPont and ask which roles Mary fulfilled at the school and whether or not she was satisfied with Mary's performance. After inquiring of Ellen, the maid, as to Miss DuPont's whereabouts, she tracked her down to an airy room with a decidedly utilitarian appearance at the back of the school.

The walls were covered in white plaster, and stone flags covered the floor. Workbenches made with slatted wooden tops ringed the outside walls of the spacious room. Miss DuPont glanced at her as she came through the door, and nodded in acknowledgment.

"Are you as fond of flowers as you were when you were a girl?" Miss DuPont asked.

Edwina crossed the stone floor quickly, her footsteps ringing through the air, and closed the gap between them.

"I find I grow fonder of all manner of plants with each passing year," Edwina said. She gestured toward a large wooden gardening trug filled with late roses and sprays of goldenrod. "May I help in some way?"

"That would be lovely, my dear. I need to get these into some water while I wait for the girls to arrive for their flower arranging class." She nodded toward a shelf where galvanized buckets of assorted sizes sat cheek by jowl.

Edwina stepped toward the shelf and carried two of the pails to the deep stone sink she remembered fondly from her own hours spent in that very same room. The faucet was as arthritic as she remembered, and she contemplated how to approach Miss DuPont with an impertinent question as she watched the water fill first one pail and then the other.

As she carried buckets to the bench next to Miss DuPont, she decided the best way would be to simply ask the question directly. After all, she was not there as a student but rather as a professional hired to get to the bottom of Miss DuPont's problem. Although she and Beryl had been acting as private enquiry agents for the better part of a year, she had still not reconciled herself to how frequently the job required her to break the rules of etiquette. She thought it unlikely she ever would become entirely comfortable with prying into the affairs of others, but she reminded herself that Miss DuPont was depending on her. She reached into the trug and began placing sprays of roses carefully into the pail in front of her.

"You have something on your mind, Miss Davenport. You'd best come out with it," Miss DuPont said not unkindly.

"Do you have any reason to believe that Mary White is not adequately fulfilling her duties as a member of the faculty?" Edwina asked.

Even as the words left her lips, she felt a heavy sense of guilt settling over her chest. Somehow it felt disloyal to Mary even to ask the question. But it had been so many years since they had known each other that Edwina had to entertain the possibility that although she might not give credence to anything Miss Glover might have to say, she really did not know Mary as an adult.

"Mary is an exceptionally able instructor, and I am grateful to have her. It has not been easy to attract or maintain faculty, even before the war. Honestly, I don't know what I would do without her. Why do you ask?" Miss DuPont asked, a deep furrow appearing between her gray eyebrows.

"It was just something that Miss Glover said to Beryl and me in the breakfast room a few moments ago," Edwina said. "She implied that she felt that none of the employees here at the school met her expectations, but Mary particularly did not come up to scratch."

Miss DuPont nodded her head slowly. "I was afraid something like this might happen. Miss Glover is inclined to be critical of others and it can be one of her strengths. She demands a great deal from our girls, and I think that they end up with a better education as a result of it. That said, she can be equally critical of her colleagues, and that is less helpful."

"Has Mary done something that would cause Miss Glover to single her out? She was emphatic in her criticism although maddeningly unwilling to provide detail."

"I rather doubt it has anything to do with what Mary has done and more to do with me," Miss DuPont said.

"What could you have done to cause Miss Glover to criticize Mary?" Edwina asked.

Miss DuPont reached for a handful of goldenrod stems and placed them in the second bucket. "Miss Glover's concern comes not from the fact that Mary is inept at her job but rather that she is excelling at it. I recently asked Mary if she would be willing to consider taking on the duties of my deputy head."

Edwina felt her eyebrows raise in surprise. Miss DuPont had never, to her knowledge, had a second-in-command. She had always run the school as a one-woman show. Edwina looked at her former headmistress with concern. While Miss DuPont still seemed capable and vigorous, she was more than twenty years older than she had been when Edwina was a student. Perhaps she was feeling the effects of time more than it was easy to see on her relatively unlined face.

"What made you decide to create that role?" Edwina asked.

"None of us are as young as we used to be, Miss Davenport. And I must confess that while I am grateful that I recovered from the influenza, like so many others I have never been quite the same since. And once the troubles at the school started to crop up, it became all the clearer to me that I would value having someone to help shoulder the day-to-day responsibilities and to discuss how best to take the school into the future, providing there will be one."

Edwina suddenly felt her heart give a squeeze. Her own mother had succumbed to influenza after spending most of Edwina's life lurching from one imaginary bout of illness to another. It had come as quite a shock when someone who had been such a confirmed hypochondriac had actually fallen grievously ill.

"I had no idea that you had been unwell. I'm sorry to hear that your strength has not entirely returned," she said. "I expect you gave Miss Glover quite a fright."

Miss DuPont nodded. "She was terribly upset by the whole thing. I know not everyone finds her easy company, but we have rubbed along right well all these years. I expect that is why she has taken the news about my offer to Mary so poorly."

"You think that she is upset that you offered the position to Mary rather than to her?"

"I do. After all, she would be well within her rights to consider she would be the most qualified for the job."

"But you didn't offer it to her. Whyever not?" Edwina was surprised. Although she did not like to think about Miss Glover wielding even more power at the school than she already did, there was no arguing the fact that she had vastly more experience than Mary White.

"In order for the school to continue long into the future, as I dearly hope that it will, a younger person will need to be ready to take over. Mary has abundant energy and the right sort of rapport with the girls as well. The school would be in good hands. As much as I appreciate all that she has done, the same cannot be said for Miss Glover. She has no more vigor than I do, nor does she possess that certain spark that fosters loyalty from the students."

Edwina could not disagree. It was impossible to imagine Miss Glover receiving Christmas cards from students long after they had left the school, or that they would extol the virtues of attendance to their friends once they in turn sought a finishing school for their own generation of daughters. Still, it must be galling for Miss Glover to find herself passed over.

"Has Mary accepted your offer?" Edwina asked.

"As a matter of fact, I'm still awaiting her answer. She told me she needed some time to think about it, and now I'm afraid her response will be even more delayed," Miss Glover said.

"Even more delayed? Has something happened to make her less likely to accept?" Edwina asked.

Miss DuPont leaned heavily against the bench and for just a moment Edwina felt concerned for her health.

"Mary had rather a bad fall down the stairs during the night and will need to focus on recovering before she can worry about the future," Miss DuPont said.

"Was she badly injured?" Edwina asked.

"She was very fortunate. She came out of the whole incident with only a sprained wrist. I'm sorry to say she won't be leading any of the art classes until it is healed completely," Miss DuPont said.

Miss DuPont appeared agitated. Her knobby fingers fussed with the rose stems, moving them this way and that, rearranging them for no real purpose. What was it that Miss DuPont was not saying? A grim thought occurred to Edwina as she watched the older woman fidget.

"You say she fell down the stairs. From the look of worry on your face I have to wonder if you think that her fall was not an accident," Edwina said.

Miss DuPont drew in a deep, ragged breath. She exhaled slowly, then nodded. "With all of the disruptions that have been going on at the school, I would be a fool not to consider someone had done it maliciously."

"Do you think that Miss Glover may be behind it?" Edwina asked.

"Surely it couldn't be her, could it?" Miss DuPont asked, her eyes wide in her face.

"You know her better than I do. Do you think it might be possible that she would have been so overcome with anger about the offer you made to Mary that she could have pushed her down the stairs?" Edwina asked.

Miss DuPont paused just a hair too long before responding. "No. No, of course not. I'm sure she had nothing whatsoever to do with it."

The sound of more feet clattering across the flagstones stopped Edwina from pressing Miss DuPont further. She watched as the headmistress forced a smile to her face as she greeted the students and instructed them to choose a spot somewhere around the room and to ready themselves for a flower arranging lesson.

Edwina slipped out the door feeling gravely concerned. Thefts and nocturnal mischief were one thing. Pushing someone down the stairs was another matter entirely. But something else was bothering her. What time had Mary's accident occurred? Could she have been the one she and Beryl spotted out on the lawn?

Chapter 19

Mary White's room sat at the far end of the faculty wing of the school. It was right next to a steep flight of stairs; a fact Edwina took particular note of as she considered Mary's fall. An enormous window looking out over the broad lawn bathed the stairwell in light and an agreeable warmth as Edwina made her way to the second floor. She rapped firmly on Mary's door and entered upon hearing a voice from within beckon her to do so.

As she stepped inside, Edwina was charmed by the simple but welcoming room. It was more than just a bedroom. In fact, the door opened into a sitting room of sorts. A second door further into the room stood open and Edwina could see the footboard of a bed through the opening.

Mary sat propped up on a small settee, her legs stretched out in front of her, and her arm wrapped in a sling. She smiled at Edwina and gestured for her to take a seat in a wingback chair beside her. The room was almost as sunlit as the stairwell, and the yellow floral wallpaper lent a cheery note. Bucolic pastoral scenes rendered in watercolor hung on the walls and a bookcase with well-thumbed volumes sat near to hand.

A small fireplace with a carved marble mantel appeared as though it would provide a welcome source of comfort in the cooler months. A large vase filled with flowers sat in the firebox and cheered the empty space. As Edwina glanced toward the far side of the room, she noted a table with a gas ring and a tray filled with tea-making paraphernalia.

A bellpull, like the one found in Miss DuPont's office, hung down near the settee, but from the presence of the tea-making supplies Edwina wondered if Mary ever bothered to ring it. With the shortage of staff, she thought it likely members of the faculty were encouraged to fend for themselves whenever possible.

"I thought I would come to ask how you were doing after your escapade in the night," Edwina said, nodding toward Mary's arm.

Mary smiled at her. "That's very thoughtful of you. I still can't quite believe I've gotten myself into this mess."

"Miss DuPont said you fell down the stairs. How does a thing like that happen?" Edwina asked.

"Do you remember when we were girls and I had quite a difficult time of things due to my sleepwalking?" Mary asked.

Edwina did remember how much Mary had suffered as a result of her nighttime excursions. She had unfortunately been found wandering out in the grounds in her nightdress by one of the gardeners. Veronica DeLisle and a few of her friends had implied that Mary was behaving inappropriately with the young man, and even more scurrilously indicated that she had a taste for the lower classes. They had teased her mercilessly throughout the rest of the term and made a point of calling her Mrs. Gardner instead of Mary whenever possible. It was just one of the many petty cruelties in which Veronica and her friends indulged.

"I'm sorry to say that I do remember you being plagued by

nocturnal ramblings. Is that what happened in the night?" Edwina asked.

Mary nodded. "Apparently so. Of course, I don't remember leaving my rooms or even falling down the stairs. All I remember is waking up in pain and Desmond standing over me with a worried look on his face."

"Desmond found you?" Edwina asked.

What, she wondered, was Desmond doing up in the night wandering about the school? As far as she knew, he had no reputation for sleepwalking, and besides, what was the likelihood that two adults would be suffering from the same unusual activity at the very same spot and time?

As far as Edwina knew, it was rare enough for sleepwalking to persist into adulthood, in any case. It was just Mary's luck that she had never managed to outgrow it. Edwina's mother had always maintained that the sleepwalking was an indication that one's mind was troubled. She thought it likely that Mary had a great deal on her mind. With enrollment down at the school and the position of deputy head on offer, she had a lot to consider. Surely Veronica DeLisle making a reappearance had done nothing to ease her thoughts.

"I was fortunate that he did. I seem to remember having a dream that my arm hurt terribly, but it wasn't until Desmond started to shake me that I truly woke up," Mary said.

"Even the fall didn't cause you to awaken?" Edwina asked. The length of the stairs was such that it could hardly be credited that Mary would not have awakened on her way down them. The notion of being so vulnerable made Edwina's heart begin to race.

"I'm afraid not. Although to be fair I'm not sure how far I actually fell. For all I know I had made it more than halfway down the stairs before I lost my footing. All I know is that when I did awaken, I couldn't move my wrist. As a matter of fact, it was bad enough that Desmond insisted on telephoning for a doctor since he thought it might be broken."

"How did Desmond manage to locate a doctor in the middle of the night without rousing the entire household?" Edwina asked.

She herself had slept quite soundly once she and Beryl had finally turned in for the night, and hadn't heard a thing after her head touched her pillow. Although to be fair, when she was awakened in the night it was usually by the sound of Simpkins stumbling in after a night of merriment down at the Dove and Duck, or even more likely, Crumpet springing from his basket and barking at something only perceptible to his canine ears. Without either of them at the school she had slept more deeply than she would have expected.

"Apparently, he's an acquaintance of Desmond's and was willing to hurry right over. I was so embarrassed by the whole thing, I asked that Desmond try to keep the incident as quiet as possible. My habit of sleepwalking has long been an embarrassment and I didn't want to draw attention to it if it was possible to avoid it. I'm sure you understand," Mary said.

Edwina could well imagine that Mary would not want to go through a repeat of her adolescent experience. It would be all the more vexing as an adult who needed to be viewed as an authority figure by her students. In fact, Edwina would not be one bit surprised if Mary would have preferred to give out a completely false reason for her accident. As much as Edwina for the most part did not hold with lying, she wouldn't blame Mary if she wished to keep the details of her injury to herself.

"Indeed, I do. You are most fortunate that Desmond was able to help you out. Miss DuPont said that fortunately your injury ended up being simply a sprain," she said.

Mary looked down at her sling and sighed. "I am very grateful that the damage wasn't worse, but I must confess, I feel just terrible about the whole thing. The doctor gave me a once-over and diagnosed it as a sprain, but he said that it would require complete rest for some time. Apparently, a sprain can take as long, if not longer, than a break to heal. Since my right wrist is the one affected, I'm very concerned about my students and for letting Miss DuPont down."

"I'm sure Miss DuPont understands and would want you to spend your energy on recovering rather than worrying. Did the doctor say how long he thought it might be?"

"He said these things are unpredictable but that it would be at least a couple of weeks before I could rely upon it for regular activities. With all of the problems at the school, I can't believe something like this has happened," Mary said.

Edwina wondered if Mary was referring to the pilfering and odd noises or the low enrollment numbers. Either way, she could see why Mary would be concerned.

"What is it that concerns you the most?" Edwina asked.

"Surely you must have noticed how few students are enrolled this term." She waited for Edwina to nod before she continued. "Art is one of the major draws for attendance at any finishing school, and without a teacher to continue with their instruction, I'm afraid that even someone as dedicated to completing her program as Adele might be inclined to leave."

"It had not escaped my notice that the school is having a difficult time. Adele really does seem very talented. Do you really think she would leave just because you are out of commission?" Edwina asked.

"I think she would be very tempted to do so. She is a devoted artist and is already chomping at the bit to leave. She has a European tour scheduled for as soon as she completes the program here, and she plans to visit all the major art galleries and to paint in France and Italy. She may just take my inability to provide instruction as permission to get started on her plans even earlier," Mary said.

"As disappointing as that might be, she is only one student," Edwina said.

Although even as she's said it, she understood how hollow the words of reassurance sounded. With so few girls still enrolled, even one leaving would be discouraging.

"Adele is the sort of girl who the others look up to. Especially girls like Lois. I'm afraid that if Adele leaves the others may follow. I cannot believe that I have put Miss DuPont in such a difficult position, especially considering how much she seems to rely on me."

Edwina wondered if she should mention knowing that Mary had been offered the post of deputy head. Was that what she was referring to? Was it a role that she wished to take on? Edwina could see how it could be viewed as a promotion. On the other hand, how difficult was the role? And how much work did it represent?

It seemed to Edwina that while it was a compliment to be offered the position, it also represented a tremendous amount of work, most likely strenuous and tedious. Edwina was not sure that any of the finishing schools, even ones with a reputation as good as Miss DuPont's, could make a comeback from their decline. She thought of the girls she knew back in Walmsley Parva and found she could not imagine any of them enthusiastically embracing the notion of attending finishing school. These were modern girls with modern ideas, none of which aligned with the proper use of cutlery or how to make polite conversation at a dinner party.

"Miss DuPont told me that she had offered you the position of deputy head. It sounds as though she would like to rely on you even more heavily in the future," Edwina said. "Have you decided whether or not to accept her offer?"

Mary sighed. "I wish I knew what to do. On the one hand, I love working here and would be very gratified to see the school thriving once more. On the other, I'm afraid that should I accept the position it may make for a great deal of awkwardness."

"I assume you're referring to Miss Glover," Edwina said.

"Exactly. Miss Glover has already had a change in attitude toward me since Miss DuPont offered me the promotion. She seems to think that I was in some way angling for it, and it is very clear that she resents me. It's making for quite an unpleasant atmosphere, so that even the girls have noticed."

"She never was a very happy woman. I cannot imagine that this has improved things. If it weren't for her, would you be inclined to accept?" Edwina asked.

"I believe so. After all, it's not as though I have other job prospects lined up that seem more appealing. And I really do need a job," Mary said.

So many of her contemporaries found themselves in such situations. Edwina herself had been in financial difficulties when Beryl had appeared at the Beeches several months earlier. It could hardly be considered surprising that Mary might find herself similarly indisposed. But was she in enough financial trouble that she was the one pilfering things?

"Do you think Miss Glover is in equal need of a paid position?" Edwina asked.

Her stomach squeezed at the unpleasantness of discussing money. Beryl never seemed to mind such things, but Edwina supposed that was only to be expected of Americans. They seem to have absolutely no shame discussing intimate details of their financial situations. While she had grown used to Beryl breezily nattering on about pounds and pence, she herself had not found it any easier to broach the subject as time had gone by. From the look on Mary's face, she felt equally ill at ease with the topic.

"I'm sure I couldn't say. I do know that Miss Glover found it insulting that she was not the one offered the position of deputy head. Whether she would have wanted it because of the increase in her wages or the increase in status, I'm sure I couldn't say. All that I know is that she was clearly distraught not to have been offered the position."

Edwina wondered if she ought to bring up another thing on her mind. There was already so much tension between Mary and Miss Glover that she hesitated to add any fuel to the fire. Still, she could not in good conscience avoid doing so. A sprained wrist was one thing, but Mary could have been far more seriously injured.

"You don't think there's any possibility that your fall down the stairs was not an accident resulting from you losing your footing while sleepwalking, do you?" Edwina asked.

Mary glanced over, a look of bafflement on her face. "What in the world are you suggesting?" she asked.

"I'm not suggesting anything particularly. I'm simply asking if you can imagine that your fall might not have been entirely accidental," Edwina said.

"How could it not have been accidental?" Mary asked.

"Do you think there's any possibility that someone might have seen you out sleepwalking and given you a push down the stairs that you are unable to remember?" Edwina asked.

Mary's eyes widened and she drew her breath in sharply. She shook her head vigorously. "Surely you're not suggesting that Miss Glover was so angry about Miss DuPont's offer that she tried to injure me, are you?"

"I'm not suggesting it. I'm simply asking if you think it's possible. After all, you know Miss Glover far better than I do. Do you think she's angry enough to do such a thing?"

"I am absolutely certain Miss Glover had nothing to do with my fall. It was entirely my fault, pure and simple." Mary clamped her lips into a firm line.

It seemed there was nothing more to say. Edwina rose from her chair and wished Mary a speedy recovery. As she took her leave, she glanced back at Mary and couldn't shake the feeling that the other woman looked worried. She may have claimed that there was no way Miss Glover could have been involved, but Edwina was certain that something was bothering Mary. Was it just the concern about a potential loss of students, or had Edwina given her something to consider that she didn't wish to believe?

Chapter 20

"Do you mind if we step out for a breath of air?" Edwina asked as she chanced upon Beryl after leaving Mary's room.

She hoped that Beryl had understood her wish to speak where there was less of a chance that they would be overheard.

"I was just about to suggest the same thing," Beryl said, giving her a wink.

They descended the stairs with as much haste as befitted graduates of the school, and slipped out a side door. As they crossed the lawn, she felt a sharp longing to return to the Beeches. It seemed strange to think that she had once been a young girl so looking forward to the adventure of leaving home.

She didn't think it was simply her age that had changed things. She believed it was that the war years had made stability and predictability such rare and fleeting treasures. Her home had seen its fair share of upheaval too, with the losses felt by her fellow villagers and those in her own family, but somehow the world did not intrude upon her quite so much when she was there.

She led Beryl toward a gravel path that carved a circuitous route through the extensive grounds. As they walked along it, more evidence of Miss DuPont's economic woes was visible to the discerning. Every garden bed they passed showed signs of neglect. Long tendrils of wisteria reached skyward from an arched trellis and snaked under the roofing slates of one of the many outbuildings. Left untrimmed it might create a leak.

As they moved farther and farther from the school building, she wondered what had become of the grotto that had been a point of pride in better days. It wouldn't hurt to take a peek. She had been enchanted by it when she had come across it during her first week at the school.

She had been wandering the grounds in order to escape the overwhelming shyness she had felt in the company of so many strangers, and had happened upon it by sheer luck. She had wandered off the main path that wended its way through the grounds and found herself facing a dense wall of rhododendrons.

As she had drawn closer, she was certain she heard the faintest trickle of water. Lured on by her curiosity to know the source of the sound, she skirted the glossy mounds of shrubbery and stopped dead in her tracks. She had heard of grottos, of course, they had been all the rage during the Victorian era, but she had never actually seen one. It had been worth the wait.

Great blocks of jagged stone had reared up out of the ground in a convincing replication of a Roman ruin. A series of small pools, one spilling into the next, were stocked with small, darting fish. Springy mounds of moss had carpeted the ground and clumps of lush ferns had arched majestically between gaps in the rocks.

"Do you remember my favorite reading spot?" Edwina asked.

"I seem to recall it as more of your favorite bolt-hole. You could always be counted on to head there if the noise of the other girls got to be too much," Beryl said. "I wonder if it is still standing after all this time."

"There is one way to find out," Edwina said. "I don't think anyone is likely to disturb us there should we wish not to be overheard."

Edwina quickened her pace, eager to know if the grotto would create the same magical effect as it had in her youth. She swept her gaze ahead to a bend in the path, seeking the telltale rhododendrons. Her heart raced as she recognized them and stepped off the path just as she had done so many years before. She told herself not to expect it to still exist, let alone for it to hold the same power to charm her as it had done in the past. The condition of the rest of the grounds made such a thing seem unlikely.

But as they rounded the enormous clump of evergreens the trickle of water could still be heard. She pressed on, her feet growing damp despite the lateness of the day. The grass there was more overgrown than in the rest of the garden, and the shade cast by the overhanging trees left it damp beneath her feet. She stopped abruptly, her breath catching in her throat. As unlikely as it seemed, the effect of the grotto seemed only enhanced by the same neglect that was so evident throughout the rest of the grounds.

She stepped closer and noted that the sense of stumbling upon a Roman ruin was all the greater for the lack of artful trimming to keep vines, saplings, and rambunctious ferns in check. The fish had prospered as a result of being left on their own too, it would seem. The pools of water teemed with them.

"It is even more enchanting than I remembered it to be," Edwina said, calling over her shoulder.

"It looks like a ruin I visited once in India," Beryl said. "Although admittedly there are far fewer monkeys."

"I wonder if the cave is still as quiet and cool," Edwina said.

"I don't see why it shouldn't be if the rest of it is still intact. Let's go see."

Edwina nodded and picked her way along the mossy rocks in search of the alcove with its stone seats placed especially for viewing the man-made ruin. The grotto proper was constructed of enormous upright stones positioned to form a sort of cool, dim cave. Inside it lay the largest of the ponds. In the warmer months the grotto had felt several degrees cooler than the temperatures outside of it, and Edwina had loved to lie on her back on one of the stone benches during the heat of the day. As she hurried to see it once more, her feet slipped out from under her.

She grabbed at a nearby branch and managed to grasp it just before she tumbled into the nearest of the pools. Her heart pounded and she paused her ascent for a moment, pressing her free hand to her chest.

"Are you all right?" Beryl asked, a worried look flashing across her face. "Would you rather turn back? I shouldn't like you to have an accident like Mary's."

It lay only a few feet farther ahead. She was determined to experience the cave once more for herself.

"I should have changed my shoes for something more sensible. I shall proceed more slowly, and I am sure it will be fine."

She made her way slowly, scrambling over the moss-covered rocks, using nearby branches as handrails and grips to steady her progress. Beryl stayed close on her heels and in short order they reached the entrance to the cave. Edwina pushed aside a strand of ivy and stepped inside. As she waited for her eyes to adjust to the gloom, she remembered the sensation of deliciously cool air on her skin.

Despite the low light she could just barely make out the stone bench she had favored as a girl. Beryl lingered near the doorway as if to ensure one of them would be able-bodied in case of an accident. Throwing off any misgivings, she picked her way across the stone floor covered in an overgrowth of knobby tree roots and leafy vines and found the bench.

Settling onto it, she was once again struck by the way the lack of attention had enhanced the effect of the grotto. Unlike so many other parts of the property, the grotto's appearance had improved with age. The quiet trickle of the water lulled her, and she almost felt as if the years had slid away somehow and the days stretched in front of her, glittering with possibility.

"It looks like the place has been left to fend for itself, doesn't it?" Beryl said.

"It certainly hasn't received any attention from a gardener," Edwina said, fingering a vine that clambered up the standing stone closest to her.

It did not look as though it had been entirely abandoned, however. There were scuffed spots in the earth as if feet had passed that way now and again, and the bench was free of the spent leaves that littered much of the cave floor, as if someone had swept them away.

Slowly but surely the cave came into focus as her eyes became accustomed to the low light. She leaned back against the wall of the grotto and allowed her gaze to roam freely. She could make out the shape of the edge of the pool before her, but there was something strange about the outline. Had someone taken it upon themselves to add some sort of a ramp to the pond? As she leaned forward to take a closer look, she let out a small gasp and sprang to her feet.

"What is it?" Beryl said, leaving her place at the entrance to the cave and hurrying to join Edwina's side.

Edwina stepped to the edge of the pool and knelt. With Beryl's help she turned over the prone figure and wiped the water from a pale face. The side of Veronica's head was crushed in near the temple and her fair hair was darkened with blood. Even in the low light she could see that there was no hope left for Veronica.

"One of us needs to alert the authorities," Beryl said. "You know the path better than I do. I'll stay here with the body while you get someone here as quickly as you can. But please, mind how you go."

Edwina nodded and straightened. She hurried out as quickly as she dared and as soon as she reached the firm footing of the path just beyond the grotto's entrance, she broke into a run.

Chapter 21

Beryl could see how the grotto could well serve its intended purpose. As much as she prided herself on her willingness to accept unpleasant conditions in her environment as a result of her years roaming the planet in search of adventure, even she found the grotto's cooling properties a bit much to endure. There was something peculiarly clammy about the moist rocks and the misty spray splashing up from the series of pools.

She wondered just how long it could possibly take for Edwina to return with the authorities when she spotted her friend rounding a clump of shrubbery, with a middle-aged man with silver hair close on her heels. From the look on Edwina's face, Beryl had to conclude that they should not expect the same sort of collegial relationship with this police officer as they enjoyed with Constable Gibbs back in the village.

Not that their relationship with the constable had always been a pleasant one. It had taken several cases before things had sorted themselves out into an easy and supportive comraderie. Beryl was quite certain that Edwina had no intention of remaining away from home long enough to develop any such relationship with local authorities. When Edwina held out her hand to indicate the direction in which he should proceed to view the body, he pushed past her and made straight for Beryl.

"I'm Inspector Lloyd. I understand there's been an accident," he said. His voice was slightly gravelly, and Beryl found herself inspecting the inspector. Although she generally preferred to spend leisure time with men significantly younger than herself, from time to time she could be convinced to consider an older man. With his craggy features and appealing voice, he might prove one of the rare exceptions.

"Right this way, Inspector," Beryl said, turning back to the interior of the grotto and leading him toward the innermost pool. She stopped, remaining carefully out of his way as he bent to scrutinize Veronica's motionless form.

"Have you moved the body?" he asked. Edwina had stopped at Beryl's side.

"We found her facedown in the pool and lifted her out to be sure she wasn't still alive but unconscious. It seemed the only prudent thing to do. We had no intention of disrupting a crime scene," Edwina said.

Beryl could tell from the tone of her voice that she was not as intrigued by Inspector Lloyd as Beryl felt inclined to be. She had to wonder what had transpired in their walk from the school to the grotto. Beryl suspected there was every chance the inspector had behaved dismissively. It was not an uncommon occurrence when dealing with men in general. It was even less so when they discovered that Beryl and Edwina worked as private enquiry agents.

She wondered what exactly Edwina might have shared and whether or not it would affect their access to the case. It would never have occurred to Edwina to use her feminine charms to gain favor with the police. She likely did not even mention her position as a magistrate in order to exert some authority. After all, as an Englishwoman, Edwina was notoriously reticent when it came to self-promotion.

Beryl would never understand it. After all, one could never

count on others to toot one's own horn. Perhaps she should have been the one to ring for the police herself. But there was no use wasting thoughts on what might have been.

"I suggest you refrain from speculating. There is no indication whatsoever that a crime has been committed here," he said, leaning a little closer to Veronica's face. He pointed at her pale forehead where a dark bruise marred her flawless skin. "It seems clear that she slipped on one of these mossy stones, hit her head and drowned while still unconscious."

"You cannot know that for certain without a proper examination by a medical professional," Edwina said.

A strident note had crept into Edwina's voice that Beryl knew to be a sure sign that her friend was likely to say something unfortunate.

"What I think Edwina means is that her death just seems so unexpected. Surely the authorities look into this sort of thing carefully, especially when the individual is one of prominence. I'm sure that it's the sort of situation in which you'd like to cross all the t's and dot all the i's," Beryl said.

The inspector straightened and turned to face them. "I am given to understand that the two of you are staying here at the school," he said.

"We are, for the time being," Beryl said.

"What brings you to Miss DuPont's? You are clearly too old to be prospective students," he said, giving Edwina a particularly long and lingering glance.

He reached into his breast pocket and pulled out a notebook not unlike the one Edwina always carried about on investigations. He withdrew a pencil as well and began to jot something down. Beryl wondered if they ought to come clean with the inspector about the real reason for their visit to the school, but before she could make up her mind Edwina spoke up.

"Clearly you are quite a detective. Beryl has a goddaughter who is interested in attending a finishing school. As both Beryl and I are graduates of Miss DuPont's, naturally it occurred to Beryl that the school might suit her goddaughter. We are simply here to confirm that it is the right place for that particular young woman," Edwina said.

Beryl kept her face a mask of neutrality despite the fact that her thoughts were racing. It was not like Edwina to be the one of them to tell white lies, especially not to those in positions of authority. Beryl was the one who thought nothing of skirting the truth if it led to the desired outcome. But every now and again Edwina let loose with a lie and Beryl had to admit, she was rather good at it.

If Beryl had not known the truth, she would have simply accepted what her friend had to say unquestioningly. It appeared that the inspector was also inclined to do so. He wrote something down in his notebook and tucked it back into his pocket. He looked over Beryl's shoulder toward the entrance to the grotto.

"I think that will be all for now, ladies," he said. "I'll ask you to just step away from the area in order for the police to get on with our jobs."

He lifted a hand and motioned, as if to beckon someone forward. Beryl turned and saw a half dozen constables hurrying toward them, slipping on mossy rocks and crushing ferns beneath their boots. The smell of their broken stems and bruised leaves rose up in the air. Edwina let out a small gasp of dismay. Beryl tucked her arm through Edwina's and pulled her gently away. There was no profit in sticking around and causing trouble for the inspector or for themselves.

Chapter 22

"Do they need to crash about so? Like bulls in a china shop?" Edwina asked. Beryl guided her friend toward a bench nestled against a leafy shrub and pressed her down into it. They were far enough away from the swarming officers to avoid criticism and near enough to keep an eye on the investigation. Beryl sat down beside her and gave her friend her attention.

"It's not like you to lie to the police. Well, except for Constable Gibbs on occasion. What happened on the way back from the school?" Beryl asked.

"Inspector Lloyd told me it was not a lady's place to be mixed up in something as unpleasant as an unexpected death, and he suggested that someone like the gardener be the one to escort him to the scene," Edwina said. "I suggested it was more important that he get there quickly than it was for him to be led there by who he considered to be of the appropriate gender."

"You must admit he's rather handsome," Beryl said.

"Handsome is as handsome does. Simpkins is more appealing than Inspector Lloyd," Edwina said.

Beryl fought down an urge to giggle. As much as she esteemed Simpkins, she could not bring herself to agree with Edwina's assessment. Perhaps her friend was more rattled by discovering Veronica's body than she had realized.

"I suppose we should hope that he doesn't decide to ask the name of my goddaughter. We will have some explaining to do if he does," Beryl said.

"Inspector Lloyd appeared remarkably incurious to me. I doubt very much that we will have to come up with any sort of explanation whatsoever," Edwina said. "He did not seem to even consider that Veronica's death might not be an accident."

"Perhaps he simply did not wish to encourage any idle talk from the public. Constable Gibbs has often mentioned her desire to keep rumors of wrongdoing from the public as long as possible. It frequently impedes an investigation," Beryl said.

Edwina shifted on the bench and looked directly at her. "You seem surprisingly eager to make excuses for what to me appears to be ineptitude."

"I'm simply offering an alternate possibility for his dismissiveness," Beryl said.

Desmond Montrose appeared around the side of the hedge and headed straight for the grotto. He gave no indication that he had noticed the two women sitting nearby as he made straight for Inspector Lloyd. The inspector stepped off to the side using his body as a visual shield.

Desmond made no attempt to look past him in order to view his dead ex-wife. He did, however, lean toward the inspector. Beryl could see his lips moving rapidly, but between the distance and the splashing sounds from the fountains could not make out any of their conversation.

The inspector appeared to be listening carefully and then nodded. He looked over at Beryl and Edwina and said something else. Desmond looked over his shoulder and appeared to notice them for the first time. Beryl lifted a hand in greeting, but he simply turned back to the inspector.

After another moment the inspector nodded and turned away. Shortly thereafter a pair of constables exited the grotto with Veronica's lifeless form on a stretcher between them. Desmond bowed his head as they filed past him, but he made no move to follow. The inspector clapped him on the shoulder before following his junior officers back toward the school building. Desmond hesitated for just a moment and then approached them.

The two women got to their feet. "Please allow me to offer my condolences," Edwina said. Beryl was glad to hear that her tone had returned to its usual polite timbre. Edwina always did have a very soft spot for Desmond, no matter how she had tried to hide it. If there was anyone to shake her out of a testy mood, it was him.

"That's very kind of you," Desmond said. "An accident like this comes as a complete shock. I don't know what on earth I will tell Florence."

"I'm sure you will find the right words. But are you certain that this was an accident?" Edwina asked.

"What else could it be?" Desmond asked. He looked over at Beryl as if to garner her support.

"Veronica was not always the easiest person to get along with, surely you'll agree," Beryl said.

"That may be, but the inspector assured me there is nothing about the situation that indicated anything but a tragic accident. After all, the moss growing everywhere rendered the rocks around the pools exceedingly slick. He said that the bruise on her forehead made what happened very clear," he said. "This will be hard enough on Florence without anyone implying that her death was anything but an accident. I hope I can count on the both of you not to put her through that sort of misery."

Without waiting for a reply he pivoted on his heel and strode away in the direction of the school. Edwina waited until he was out of sight beyond the bushes before she spoke.

"Desmond is just as unwilling as the inspector to entertain the notion that Veronica did not simply drown," Edwina said. "Now why do you think that might be?"

"Do you really think there's any possibility that this might have been foul play?" Beryl asked. She certainly hoped not. If they could wrap up the investigation into the disturbances quickly, she had the slimmest of chances to salvage just a bit of her golfing trip. If, however, it turned out to be a murder investigation, all hope was lost.

"I think that it seems suspicious that on the same night Mary White had an accident by falling down the stairs, Veronica had an accident that led to her death. I have to ask myself if there is more trouble afoot at Miss DuPont's school than unexplained noises and a spot of pilfering," Edwina said.

"Are you saying you think that Mary was pushed?" Beryl asked. She had not considered that Mary's fall might not simply be an accident. Adele and Lois had reported it as an accident, and she had had no reason to doubt them.

"Mary claims not to remember anything about what occurred. Do you remember how she used to sleepwalk when we were all students?" Edwina asked. Beryl nodded. "Well, she still does."

"Her fall was as a result of sleepwalking?" Beryl asked.

"She says she can't imagine what else it might have been. She only remembers waking up at the bottom of the stairs when Desmond shook her awake. She is lucky that she came away from the whole incident with nothing worse than a sprained wrist."

"You make it sound as though perhaps Desmond had something to do with that," Beryl said.

"Considering the fact that he and Veronica were not on good terms, I suppose that does make things look worse for him. But no, I had someone else entirely in mind," Edwina said.

"Like whom?" Beryl said.

"Miss Glover. I hate to say it, but I can picture her being so petty as to take advantage of Mary's state and to give her a shove. Who's to say she didn't have a quarrel with Veronica as well?" Edwina asked.

Beryl tried to picture Miss Glover hovering at the top of the stairs, her hands outstretched toward Mary's unsuspecting back. She wished she could say it seemed entirely out of character, but in truth she could not.

"I suppose we could try to convince the inspector to take a closer look at the fact that there were two accidents on the same night," Beryl said. She thought it might be fun to give it a try. Edwina certainly was in no position to sweet-talk the police officer. Her attitude would be likely to make him dig his heels in even further about it being a mere accident.

"You certainly could try, but there's something else that concerns me."

"What's that?" Beryl asked.

"What did Desmond say to Inspector Lloyd? He finished up with the scene almost immediately after pulling him aside."

"I have no idea. They were too far away to make out their conversation. Are you implying that Desmond had something to do with the inspector finishing up so quickly?" Beryl asked.

"Personal relationships with the police do occur and I think we can both agree that Desmond is a powerful and well-connected man," Edwina said.

Beryl didn't particularly enjoy the idea of an old friend and someone she admired being involved in something so sordid. It wasn't that she was naïve about such things. But still, it was never pleasant when corruption wafted about someone one knew personally.

"I'd hate to think that Desmond was exerting undue influence. I thought you were rather fond of him yourself," Beryl said.

"I am fond of Desmond, but I'm not blind to what passes

right before my eyes. Neither are you, usually," Edwina said. "You're not suggesting we should ignore any suspicion simply because we've known someone for years, are you?"

"I suppose not, it just sits uncomfortably with me to suspect a friend," Beryl said.

"I realize that it's extremely uncomfortable. The cases we've solved in Walmsley Parva have put me in that position each and every time they've come up. I've known most of the people we've had to investigate far better than either of us knows Desmond Montrose," Edwina said.

Beryl had not given that any particular thought. While she did recognize that so often the relationship that Edwina had with her fellow villagers was quite different from Beryl's, she had not paid a great deal of attention to the sort of discipline Edwina must have exerted in order to pursue an investigation involving acquaintances and friends of long standing. She felt sheepish about how little credit she had given to her dear friend for a determined pursuit of the truth despite its toll on her.

"You are such a good egg, Ed. Let's look into any funny business on Desmond's part, if only to reassure ourselves of his good character," Beryl said.

Edwina sat up a little straighter and Beryl thought she could see a flush of color on the back of Edwina's neck. Her friend always blushed so easily when being complimented.

"Then we are agreed? We will look into what happened to Veronica in addition to the goings-on with the thefts and the noises?"

"Absolutely. For all we know, the cases are linked. After all, why shouldn't they be?" Beryl said.

"I think there's every possibility that the two cases go hand in hand. It's not as though Miss DuPont's school is generally known as a hotbed of criminal activity," Edwina said. "The question is, where do we begin?"

"I suppose exactly where the police most often do," Beryl said. She stood the direction of the school.

"You mean we should speak with the husband," Edwina said.

Edwina was always at heart a romantic and it never set well with her the notion that the spouse was most often the guilty party. Beryl thought it might be best that she be the one to handle that particular conversation.

"If you don't mind, I would like to be the one to speak with him. We've created something of a rapport because of a shared enjoyment of golf. That would free you up to poke around and see who else might have heard something or seen something last night. We could meet back up in our room in a few hours' time and compare notes," Beryl said. She could have sworn she saw a wave of relief pass over Edwina's small features.

"Just promise me you won't decide to give more comfort to the grieving widower than is absolutely necessary," Edwina said.

"Even I have my limits, Ed," Beryl said. Edwina lifted an eyebrow at her and smiled.

Chapter 23

Beryl waited until after the police vehicles and ambulance had left the grounds before going in search of Paul Deering. The news of his wife's death appeared to have come as a complete shock. She found him in the drawing room filling a large tumbler with whiskey from a decanter from the drinks tray. From the hazy look in his eyes, it was not the first of the day. Not that she would blame him for seeking oblivion in the face of such a shock. It was an altogether common way of dealing with unpleasant news and one she had used herself from time to time.

Although, to be fair, most of her imbibing grew out of a desire to celebrate rather than to forget. Beryl had few regrets and most of those were ones that she was willing to face head-on. After all, she had recognized very early in life that the things one tried to ignore had a habit of popping up again and again until one eventually committed to resolving them.

Paul Deering, on the other hand, did not look like he was in any condition to resolve anything whatsoever. She felt ever so slightly guilty at taking advantage of his disturbed state in order to ask him questions, but the feeling soon passed. She had assured Edwina she would ask all the right questions and she did not intend to let her friend down.

She stepped over to the drinks cart and lifted a glass. She splashed in a finger of whiskey, then topped it with soda water from a silver siphon. It was one thing for Paul to have a fuzzy head, but she had no intention of allowing her own to be similarly dulled. She hoisted the glass in his direction before taking a sip.

That was when he first seemed to recognize that he was no longer alone in the room. His eyes widened slightly at the sight of her, and he took a large gulp of his own drink before speaking.

"The police told me that you and Miss Davenport were the ones who discovered Veronica's body," he said. "I just can't seem to wrap my mind around the fact that she's gone."

Beryl took a step away from the bar and motioned that Paul should join her in the nearby seating area. She chose a chair nearest the door in case she needed to make a hurried escape. She had no idea what Paul might do when well and truly in his cups, and she had no intention of becoming trapped in a room with an enraged and drunken murder suspect.

"I'm so sorry for your loss. You must be badly shaken. A visit from the police certainly would not help matters, I'm sure," Beryl said as she crossed one long leg over the other. Despite his recent bereavement, Paul's slightly unfocused gaze paused on her legs, which, even if she said so herself, were rather good.

"They were very kind about the whole thing. To tell the truth, they couldn't have been more considerate. I suppose in an accidental death like that you have to request that the police come along and make sure everything was on the up-and-up," he said.

So, the police hadn't treated it as a homicide, at least not from anything they had said to Paul. She wondered if he had any qualms about the accident himself. If so, he hadn't let on thus far.

"Inspector Lloyd appeared to me to be quite reserved and unlikely to give offense," Beryl said. "I'm glad to hear that he did not bother you unduly." She took another sip of her drink and looked at him over the rim of her glass.

"He was really quite good about it all. He told me that he would let me know as soon as possible when they could release Veronica's body and then he went on his way," Paul said. "I expected him to ask many more questions than he did. That's the way it always seems to be done in novels."

"How very fortunate for you. I hope you will be allowed to begin making plans very soon. I think it's always best for the bereaved to be able to get on with things as quickly as possible. It doesn't do to dwell on such things any longer than absolutely necessary," she said.

That much was absolutely true. The Great War had changed so many things, including the way one dealt with bereavement. With so few of the fallen soldiers being returned to their native soil, the time between their deaths and any sense of finality about what had happened stretched on and on.

Families were never able to bury their loved ones in the way one would expect. Instead, there was a gnawing sense of unreality about their absence. Without the ceremony of a funeral in order to put paid to someone's life, many people felt mired in a murky space between before and after. Beryl had quickly realized that she needed to give up on any expectation about how such things should be handled if she were going to be able to come out the other end of things with any of her usual optimism intact. Even with her tendency to see the bright side of life, it had been a struggle much of the time.

"He said it should only be a day or two. That seems like barely enough time to make arrangements. Desmond was very civil about it all and said that he would break the news to Florence. I don't know what the poor girl is going to do," Paul said.

"You seem quite fond of Florence. Not every stepfather would have such a pleasant relationship with a girl of her age," Beryl said.

"That really was very lucky. Florence is a great kid and in some ways we had quite a lot in common. After all, when it comes right down to it, she's not all that much younger than me."

Beryl had suspected that Paul was significantly younger than Veronica, despite the other woman's best efforts to combat signs of aging. There was just something youthful about the way he held himself and the amount of energy he gave off. Still, she was surprised to think he was as young as all that. Perhaps living with Veronica had aged him somewhat. She was quite certain that if she had had the misfortune of spending much time in the dead woman's company it would have been difficult not to show signs of accelerated aging herself.

"I don't claim to know her at all well, but I can see how Florence's company might have offered a pleasant contrast to her mother's. I'm sure that Veronica had her good qualities, but she wasn't always the easiest woman to get along with," Beryl said.

"But that's exactly what I loved about her. She told you what she thought, and you knew where you stood with her. Veronica was one of the most honest people I ever knew. I admired her for it," Paul said.

Beryl never would have thought about Veronica in those glowing terms. She considered her to be blunt and opinionated and often quite cruel. The notion that those same characteristics could be given a positive spin was intriguing. She looked at Paul with renewed interest.

"You sound as though you really loved her," she said.

She noted that his eyes shimmered with moisture. She wondered if it was on account of strong emotions or strong drink. British men were not the sort to generally allow tears, at least not in her experience. Plenty of men from other cultures wept freely when speaking of love or loss, but she had rarely seen an Englishman do so. And she had seen plenty of circumstances where such a thing could easily be justified and even expected.

"I did. I still cannot believe my good fortune that she agreed to be my wife," he said.

"It sounds as though you had a happy marriage."

Paul took another long tug on his drink and placed the empty tumbler on the table beside his chair. "It really was. And things were only going to get better in the future. We were even planning a trip to the Continent as soon as Florence was settled here at Miss DuPont's."

"A romantic getaway for just the two of you?" Beryl asked.

"Exactly. I thought it would be good for the two of us to have some time alone together and we both loved Italy and France."

"Somehow that makes things all the more wretched, doesn't it," Beryl said. "You think you have so much time stretching ahead of you and then in the blink of an eye everything changes."

"I can't believe that I'll be planning a funeral instead of a romantic getaway. I suppose I best get on with it. There are a great many telephone calls I need to make." With that he staggered from his chair and tottered toward the door.

Beryl couldn't say for sure, but she thought he painted a very convincing picture of a grieving widower. Her stomach felt heavy and slightly queasy, and she placed her mostly full glass next to Paul's empty one. If Paul had nothing to do with what happened to Veronica, Desmond looked even more guilty than before.

Chapter 24

While Edwina did not want to appear to be prying, she decided it would be the right thing to do to pay her condolences to Florence. She made inquiries of Jennings, who reported that none of the household mentioned having seen her since her father broke the news to her. Edwina thought it likely that she herself would have headed straight for the library, had she received such shocking news whilst at Miss DuPont's school. Considering the fact that Beryl had discovered Florence there when they first arrived, Edwina thought it a good bet she might have taken refuge there once more.

As soon as she entered the space, memories of the library came flooding back. Whenever it had been too dark or the weather had been too inclement to spend time roaming the grounds, Edwina had sought solace in the library. With its towering bookcases filled with novels as well as nonfiction books, she had never failed to find something entertaining to read whenever she had visited in the past. Just as she suspected, toward the back of the large room she spotted a pair of feet sticking out just beyond the bottom of a tall oak bookcase. Edwina cleared her throat slightly in order to give the owner of the feet time to realize she was no longer alone, then walked in their direction.

Florence sat on the floor leaning against another of the bookcases. Towering stacks of books rose up to her left. A messy pile spilled out to her right. In her lap a volume of the encyclopedia lay open. She looked up as Edwina approached and while her face appeared drawn, her eyes gave no indication of a recent bout of crying.

With complete disregard for her usual sense of propriety, Edwina lowered herself to the floor in front of Florence in a spirit of book-loving camaraderie. Her ever-so-slightly stiff knees gave a bit of a protest as she touched them down onto the cold marble, but she tried not to allow her discomfort to show. The posture felt ridiculous, but she could not imagine how she could foster any sense of rapport with Florence by remaining on her feet and looming over her. And she certainly couldn't ask the grieving girl if she wouldn't mind awfully standing up.

"You're Beryl Helliwell's friend, aren't you?" Florence asked.

"Yes, I'm Edwina Davenport. I was a classmate of your mother's and an acquaintance of your father's when we were all young," Edwina said. "I'm so sorry for your loss."

Florence lifted her slim shoulders and then let them drop. "I know that is what everyone is supposed to say under the circumstances, but truthfully I do not expect that many people would consider my mother's death a loss."

Edwina felt of shiver of shock run through her as she kept her eyes trained on the young woman's face. While she herself had found Veronica to be an incredibly dislikable human being, it seemed surprising for her daughter to speak so honestly about her mother. Had they been even remotely close?

Considering the fact that she had found Florence hiding away in the library, barricading herself from the world with a fortress of books, it seemed like the two of them had little in common. Edwina could not recall ever having seen Veronica in that room when they had been in school together. It was difficult to picture Veronica taking pleasure in having a daughter so inclined to be bookish rather than bent on becoming a social success.

"Your mother did have a very strong personality that may not have suited everyone else. But it's your loss that I'm thinking of. I was decades older than you when my own mother died, and yet it was still extremely painful. I can only imagine that such a thing would be even more difficult to accept at your age," Edwina said.

"I know I'm supposed to be torn up about it, but somehow I can't seem to make myself feel that way. You know what's really running through my mind over and over on a loop?" Florence asked.

"I haven't the least idea," Edwina said. And she didn't. Florence seemed entirely unfazed, and Edwina wasn't sure what to make of it.

"I keep thinking about the fact that if she's dead she can no longer insist that I attend finishing school. I expect it's terrible of me, but I feel an immeasurable sense of relief," Florence said.

Edwina felt the sudden need to lean back against the bookcase behind her rather than maintain her usually entirely upright posture. While she realized that people responded to grief in a myriad of ways, she had yet to see someone reflect so honestly on how they would benefit from such a loss soon after the event had occurred. While she did understand that Florence appeared to be a poor match for the finishing school experience, even as unsuited as Beryl perhaps, she couldn't imagine that her first thought about the entire matter regarding her mother's death should be a feeling of relief.

Which begged another question entirely. It was one she truly did not wish to consider. Was it possible that Florence had had sufficient motive to be responsible for her mother's death? Before speaking with her Edwina would not have thought that a desire to avoid the finishing school experience would prompt such extreme action, but based on Florence's demeanor she had to reconsider.

"Was the notion of attending really so very upsetting?" Edwina asked.

"Absolutely. I've been telling my mother for years that I have no intention of attending finishing school and I had always assumed that my father would back me up about it, but when the time came, he simply refused to do so."

"Was it unusual for your parents to agree on such things?"

"Very. In general, they cannot agree on anything at all. I was shocked when I approached my father about becoming involved with Montrose Aeronautics instead of attending Miss DuPont's, only to have him refuse me." Florence gripped the edges of the encyclopedia so tightly that her knuckles whitened.

"Did he give you a reason for his decision not to support you?"

"He just said something about the company still being there in the future but that I would never be the proper age to attend Miss DuPont's again and that he did not want me to miss my chance."

"Your chance at what, exactly?"

"Taking a prominent place in the right sort of society. Marrying well. All that tosh."

Edwina felt a wave of indignation welling up within her. The longer she spent involving herself in roles that were not traditional for women, the less patience she felt for those who opposed such things. How was it possible that a man she had admired so much when she was young could be so unsupportive of his own daughter?

"Beryl mentioned that your father sounded very proud of

your interest in the company and in engineering. Did something happen to make him change his mind?"

"I haven't the slightest idea. I had thought for sure that he would back me up with my mother, but he absolutely refused. She was over the moon about it." Florence slapped the book shut.

Edwina's uncomfortable feeling grew stronger. Maybe Florence had been involved in Veronica's death. She certainly seemed like she did not appreciate being told she could not have her way. And she sounded particularly perturbed by her mother's delight in bringing her own plans to fruition.

Edwina remembered how unattractive a quality that had been in Veronica when they were all young. She had a knack for rubbing her triumphs in the faces of those she bested, whether whilst playing cards, having a round of croquet, or securing a partner for a dance. It might have been too much to take if she had done it to Florence on a regular basis.

The notion that her father would betray her hopes would have rankled as well. Edwina thought back to her relationship with her own mother at Florence's age and for many years thereafter. They had rarely seen eye to eye, and as much as she had not wanted to attend finishing school, it had been something of a relief to get out from under her ever-watchful eye.

She had counted on her own father to be more understanding and to allow her to follow her head much more often than her mother would ever permit. She would have felt devastated if he had agreed with her mother about anything she felt as strongly about as Florence appeared to do concerning the school. Anger, frustration, and betrayal were a dangerous mix.

It was more than just that though. Edwina had been concerned about the younger generation ever since war had been declared. The soldiers who returned were different men than they had been when they left, of course. But the rest of their generation were changed too.

There was something so unsettling about the war that it had left everyone jaded and a bit undone. The sweeping battle with influenza had only made things worse. They all seemed to be living simply in the present, as if the future was a myth that the old folks liked to tell about but that they no longer believed in.

Would it really be so out of character for a young person to feel compelled to seize the moment and try to make the best they could of it? Florence didn't sound like she bought into the reasons her father gave for her finishing-school attendance. Those were future events and Edwina was not sure the girl or most of her peers would be persuaded to value them.

Maybe that was the biggest uphill battle Miss DuPont faced for the continuing health of her enterprise. Although it would not do it any good if a prospective student turned out to be the sort of girl who didn't turn a hair at murdering her own mother.

"What about now? Has he indicated that he has changed his mind now that the circumstances have changed?"

"I tried to ask him, but he said such questions were unseemly. He never used to say things like that to me. I just don't know what is going on." For the first time, Florence appeared to be on the verge of tears.

Edwina reached over and handed her a pocket handkerchief. "I wouldn't give up hope. He is probably in shock and cannot summon the strength to make any decisions just yet."

Florence dabbed at her eyes, gathered up an armload of books and struggled to her feet. "Perhaps you're right. At least I have plenty to read while I wait for him to change his mind."

Edwina waited until Florence was out of sight to attempt to get up off the floor. If her joints had felt a bit stiff when she settled onto the cold marble, they were positively rusted as a result of the experience. She was not sure what to make of what the girl had said. Her attitude about her mother was frankly alarming.

But Edwina was not so sure that what she had revealed hadn't made Desmond look all the more suspicious. Why had he not gone to bat for her? Why had he encouraged her to attend the school? Was it in order to give him an opportunity to kill his ex-wife?

Chapter 25

Even though it had not been long since Beryl had seen her friend, she thought that Edwina looked tired. Something had transpired since they had left the grotto and the scene of Veronica's murder, that much was clear. She had encountered her friend in the hallway just as she approached their shared room, and looked forward to comparing notes on what they had each discovered during their time apart. But as they entered the room her hopes were dashed as Ellen, the friendly young maid, was within, a feather duster held above the dressing table.

Ellen turned as they entered and dropped a slight curtsy. Despite the difficulty in obtaining domestic help, Miss DuPont certainly had done well with that particular member of staff. The room looked neat and tidy, and from the look of it, Beryl expected it would even meet Edwina's exacting standards for the housekeeping.

"I'm so sorry not to have finished up your room sooner, but the household has been in a bit of an uproar," Ellen said.

"Please don't trouble yourself," Edwina said, stepping forward and nodding briskly at Ellen. "It's very commendable that the school is running as well as it is under the circumstances."

Ellen blushed prettily and curtsied slightly once more. "That's very kind of you to say, miss. We are all very upset by what has occurred."

In Beryl's experience there was nothing like a bit of an upset to set tongues wagging. Surely domestic servants, even of the caliber at Miss DuPont's school, would not be above such human behavior. Perhaps with just a bit of encouragement Ellen would succumb to temptation. Apparently, Edwina had the exact same thought, and Beryl was glad that she took the lead without any encouragement. After all, she was so much better with the servants.

"An accident such as this one would disrupt even the most well-run establishment. Everyone is quite shocked at what has occurred, I'm sure," Edwina said.

Ellen lowered the duster and passed it back and forth between her hands.

"Are the police quite sure that Miss DeLisle's death was an accident?" she asked.

Beryl felt her eyes widen slightly. Was there a reason that Ellen would have thought Veronica's death was not a mishap? She turned slightly to Edwina. "We both got that impression from Inspector Lloyd, didn't we? Although, I suppose that it is possible that there could be another explanation."

"It has been my experience that members of a house, particularly the staff, are far more likely to know more than anyone else. And certainly, they would be better informed than police officers who are new to a place," Edwina said. "I am sure that the staff at Miss DuPont's establishment is no less skilled than others. Wouldn't you agree, Ellen?"

Ellen bobbed her head as a slight smile crossed her face. She dropped her voice and leaned toward them. "That's very kind of you to say, miss. Jennings always says that we should keep our eyes and ears open, and our mouths closed. I would say there isn't much that happens that we don't know about."

"It sounds as though the police would be wise to consult any of you concerning unexplained occurrences at the school," Beryl said.

No sooner had she said it than she wished that she had let Edwina continue to take the lead. The poor girl turned bright red and dropped her duster. Her breath came in shallow gasps and Beryl wondered if she was going to faint. Edwina stepped forward and retrieved the duster from the highly polished floor. She handed it back to Ellen, whose lower lip quivered as she reached out to grasp it.

"I'm sure that Ellen is not the sort of girl to involve herself with the police," Edwina said. "Even if she does have something they might be best knowing."

"I'm not, miss," Ellen said. "What would Miss DuPont say if I were to be questioned by the police?"

"What indeed? You know, Ellen, Miss Helliwell and I might be in a position to help with this. Isn't that right, Beryl?" Edwina asked, turning to her with a look of intensity on her face. Beryl thought it best to simply follow wherever Edwina was leading.

"Certainly. Why don't you tell Ellen what you have in mind?"

"When we first arrived, you mentioned that you have followed Beryl's exploits in the newspapers, so I am sure you must be aware of her foray into the role of private enquiry agent?" Edwina asked.

Ellen nodded enthusiastically. "I have several clippings mentioning your agency."

"I thought you might. So, as I'm sure you can imagine, we have had rather a good deal of experience evaluating whether or not information is pertinent to an investigation. We also routinely speak with our local police officer back in Walmsley

Parva and would feel comfortable doing so here as well if it seemed prudent to do so. Wouldn't you agree, Beryl?"

"Absolutely. I cannot see why Ellen should need to be involved at all if she would rather not."

Beryl watched for any sign that Ellen was comforted by their words. She had no idea a maid would react so poorly to the idea of speaking with the police. After all, it wasn't as if the girl was particularly reserved. In fact, she had proved an outgoing sort thus far.

Edwina nodded and then took Ellen by the elbow and steered her to the small seating area in front of a pair of long windows overlooking the grounds. She indicated the maid should sit in one of the upholstered chairs, and she settled in the other. Beryl perched on the end of the nearest bed and crossed one long leg over the other, hoping she had struck an informal but not overly familiar pose. She had learned from difficult experience that one of the fastest ways to get onto the wrong foot with the servants was to appear too chummy.

"I wouldn't want you to think me a gossip," Ellen said, looking at them each in turn. They both nodded.

"We shall think nothing of the sort. There is a clear difference between idle gossip and doing your duty," Edwina said. "And if there is no reason for concern you need not dwell on what you tell us any further."

Ellen let out a slow breath and stared down at her hands, still clutching the feather duster. She seemed to come to a decision and began to speak.

"I had noticed that there was some tension between Miss DeLisle and several of the others here this week, but there is one incident that really stands out in my mind."

"Go on," Edwina said.

Ellen bit her lip and for a moment Beryl wondered if she would change her mind. Edwina nodded at the girl encouragingly and she continued.

"Last evening, I happened to be returning some serving dishes to the butler's pantry and I overheard a very heated argument. I wasn't eavesdropping, mind you. The voices came through the opening to pass plates through to the dining room."

"Whose voices?" Edwina asked.

"Miss DeLisle's and Miss Glover's."

"What was the nature of the argument?" Beryl asked. She felt her pulse begin to quicken. As much as she had loved setting speed records and throwing herself into one wild adventure after another, there was something even more thrilling about picking up the trail of a case. She would not have ever guessed that the merest inkling of wrongdoing would set her heart racing faster than lifting off in an airplane or hurtling along a racing track, her hands wrapped firmly round the steering wheel, but the fact remained that it did.

Maybe it was the mental challenge of it. Or maybe it was that the stakes felt higher. After all, she never much concerned herself with what might happen should her exploits end in disaster. But the notion that someone might inflict harm on another and escape the consequences felt very dangerous indeed. It was one thing to risk one's own life. It was quite another to meddle with someone else's.

"I didn't hear the entire conversation, so I am not sure of all the details. They were already in the heat of it when I arrived," Ellen said.

"That's fine, Ellen. Just tell us what you did hear," Edwina said, leaning toward the girl ever so slightly.

Beryl recognized the tone of her voice as one she regularly employed when speaking with her housekeeper, Beddoes: kindly but unlikely to brook resistance.

"Miss Glover said something to the effect that Miss DeLisle wouldn't dare. Then Miss DeLisle said there wasn't anything Miss Glover could do to stop her."

"Did you hear what Miss DeLisle proposed to do?" Edwina asked.

She slid a glance at Beryl that seemed to convey Beryl's own thoughts that Ellen might not be able to avoid speaking to the police after all.

"She said she would report her to Miss DuPont as soon as she possibly could."

"Report her about what?" Beryl asked.

Perhaps she should have left Edwina to ask, but the words left her lips before she thought. Ellen didn't seem to notice, however.

"I have no idea. They must have discussed that before I arrived with an armload of serving platters to put away."

"Are you quite sure that the voices you heard belonged to Miss DeLisle and Miss Glover?" Edwina asked.

"I know that they were. Not only did I recognize them, but they also called each other by name during the conversation. I don't want to put Miss Glover in an awkward position, but she sounded very angry. And that wasn't all," Ellen said, looking from Edwina to Beryl and back again.

"Yes?" Edwina asked.

"I hurried out of the butler's pantry and into the hallway as soon as I finished tucking the dishes away in the cupboards. As soon as I stepped into the hall, Miss Glover practically ran out of the dining room with a murderous look on her face. She actually collided with me but never stopped to apologize. I'm not even sure she noticed she had run into me."

"It sounds as though she was very worried indeed," Edwina said.

"I thought so. And no sooner had she rushed past than Miss DeLisle came out into the hallway herself. She was humming to herself, and she even smiled at me as she passed by, which is something she had never done before. I think whatever happened in the dining room, she felt that she had come out the better for it."

Ellen glanced over at the door and scooted to the edge of her chair. She fidgeted with her duster and Beryl thought it likely she was worried that she was already missed. It would not do to be seen as shirking her duties. Edwina seemed to notice too and got to her feet.

"I appreciate you informing us of this. You had best get back to work before you are missed. If anyone questions your absence you may tell them that I required assistance in winding a new skein of wool," Edwina said.

Ellen stood and took a few hurried steps toward the door before pausing and turning round. "You won't mention my name to the police, will you? I'd hate for anyone to think I made a habit of listening in when I ought not."

"You have our word that unless it proves absolutely necessary, we will look into this further without involving the police. Most often such stray bits of information do not tie into a case, so I should not worry about it overly much if I were you," Edwina said.

"That's a relief. But there is one more thing, if it isn't too much trouble," Ellen said.

"What is it?" Beryl asked.

"May I have your autograph for my scrapbook?" Ellen asked. "I've been carrying this clipping around trying to work up the courage to ask you for it." She stuck her hand into the pocket of her maid's uniform and pulled out a folded square of newspaper.

"It would be my pleasure," Beryl said, retrieving one of Edwina's fountain pens from the desk at the opposite side of the room. She penned her name across her own image emblazoned on the article mentioning Davenport and Helliwell Private Enquiry Agency with a flourish. Ellen thanked her as Beryl handed the clipping back, then held it out to Edwina.

"May I have your signature as well, miss?" she asked.

Beryl thrust the pen to Edwina, who momentarily looked uncertain. Then she gave herself a slight shake and carried it to the desk to add her name across her own image. Beryl spotted a telltale redness creeping up from below her friend's collar, but she decided it was good for Edwina to take the spotlight now and again no matter how much she found it disconcerting. Ellen thanked them, tucked her clipping back into her pocket, and hurried out to get on with her duties. Beryl waited until her retreating footfalls could no longer be heard before turning to Edwina.

"So, what do you make of her story?"

"It convinced me that we were not wrong to wonder about the circumstances of Veronica's death. I suppose we should perform the unpleasant task of questioning Miss Glover about that conversation."

"There won't be any getting out of that job, will there?" Beryl asked.

"We could confine ourselves to our original investigation." Edwina's brows drew together slightly. "But the convictions of the police have never dissuaded us before from pursuing the truth, however unpleasant."

"Miss DuPont may come to regret requesting our services before this is all over," Beryl said.

"I'm afraid you might be right. I am beginning to regret ever leaving home. I'm sure Crumpet is in quite a state in my absence. I do hope that Simpkins is looking after him properly," Edwina said.

Her brows drew even closer together and Beryl thought her lower lip trembled ever so slightly. Beryl felt a wave of dread wash over her. Edwina had been subject to bouts of homesickness when they attended Miss DuPont's as girls. She had lost weight, grown pale and had trouble sleeping for the first weeks.

Beryl had not shared her misery, not on that score at least, but she had been very unhappy for her friend. She had hoped that Edwina would not find things so difficult so many years on, but there were still good reasons that she would prefer to be home.

After all, Edwina had been eagerly anticipating a second flush of bloom from her beloved roses. And although she certainly could not be accused of being overly demonstrative, Beryl was certain she missed Simpkins almost as much as she did Crumpet. Beryl even held out hope that she might feel a pang at her friend Charles Jarvis's absence. Suddenly an idea occurred to her.

"Why don't you take some time to yourself to gather your thoughts. I have something I must do but will be sure to meet up with you in a bit."

Edwina simply nodded and made her way back to the seating area near the window. "I think I should like to sit quietly for a few moments alone, now that I come to think of it. Are you sure that you don't mind?"

"Take all the time that you need," Beryl said. If Edwina didn't follow too closely on her heels, she thought she might just be able to accomplish her task in secret.

Chapter 26

Beryl replaced the telephone receiver, feeling very pleased with herself. She strode down the hall with a renewed spring in her step. She felt sure that with any luck she and Edwina would be headed back to the Beeches before too much longer. And for the time being she had come up with what she hoped would be a good way to head off any homesickness on Edwina's part.

From somewhere toward the rear of the building she could hear the faint sound of music. She followed it and came to a stop in the doorway of the music room. A flood of memories passed over her as she remembered the failed music lessons of her youth. The music mistress, whose name Beryl had mercifully forgotten, had despaired of her. Despite her teacher's constant urging, Beryl never seemed to improve in the slightest. She simply could not be bothered to practice scales or learn to read notes when there were so many things in the world that interested her more.

That did not mean that she was not a music lover when someone else was charged with creating it. And Desmond Montrose certainly was an accomplished musician. He sat with his back to her at the gleaming grand piano, his hands moving gracefully across the keys. The tune was mournful, and Beryl waited until the piece had come to an end before she crossed the threshold and stood next to the piano.

"I didn't know that you were such an accomplished musician," Beryl said, nodding toward the instrument.

Desmond spun on the piano stool to face her. There were dark circles below his eyes, which were missing their habitual sparkle, and his shoulders sagged forward.

"I find it soothing, when things take a turn for the worse," he said.

"How are you holding up?" she asked.

"I have felt better, as I am sure you can imagine. Veronica and I made each other desperately unhappy, but I am still so sorry that she is dead."

Having gone through her own share of divorces, Beryl could easily understand the sorts of emotions and unpleasant scenes that preceded them. That said, she did not wish any of her ex-husbands ill and thought it likely she would feel real remorse at the passing of the majority of them. She had not even shared children with any of them, and yet had generally attempted to remain cordial if not genuinely friendly.

"I'm sure that her death came as quite a shock. It isn't the same at all as the deaths throughout the war years or even the influenza epidemic, is it?" Beryl said.

"Not in the least. Even those who didn't like Veronica would have to admit that she was enormously vivacious. It seems impossible to imagine that she is dead."

Desmond shook his head slowly, then faced the piano and swept his long fingers across the keys. Had he turned away from her because he found it soothing to play music, or was he trying to hide his expression from her? There had been something so surprising about his interaction with Inspector Lloyd that she couldn't shake the feeling that something about her old acquaintance was not all that it appeared. The question was, what about him was the source of her uneasiness? Before she could reach any sort of conclusion, he turned back round once more.

"The only thing to be grateful for in this whole mess is that the police inspector seems to be such a sensible sort of chap. He wasn't the least inclined to sensationalize her death in any way. I would be appalled for there to be any scandal attached to her accident."

Desmond looked Beryl in the eyes and while she did not feel threatened, she did have the sense that she was being encouraged to simply accept the accident without question. She wondered if he had kept as close tabs on her career as she had on his. If so, he could not be unaware of the private enquiry agency.

Even if he had not been following her life or Edwina's particularly closely, stories of some of their cases had been written up in national newspapers. When it came right down to it, it would be more surprising if he did not know about their roles as investigators. But did that knowledge worry him? If he thought she would refrain from questioning him because of their longstanding acquaintance, he would be disappointed.

"I must admit, I noticed that the inspector called off the investigation at the scene almost as soon as you arrived. Both Edwina and I found that more than a little surprising," she said.

"Are you suggesting that I took it upon myself to influence the investigation in some way?" Desmond crossed his long arms over his chest. Perhaps she had touched a nerve. Back in Walmsley Parva, Constable Doris Gibbs crossed her arms in front of her chest just as soon as she and Edwina began asking questions that the police officer would have preferred that they not.

"I was merely making an observation. Even in a small village like the one Edwina and I reside in, the police make rigorous inquiries into unexpected deaths. I would have thought the standard of investigation would be at least as high in a metropolis like London."

Desmond lowered his arms and reached for the piano keys once more. He plunked out a few notes before replying.

"Of course, if there is more to Veronica's death than a simple accident, I would wish to know it and I would urge the police to make the most thorough investigation possible."

Beryl could not have asked for a better opening. "So, you are convinced that what happened to Veronica was an accident?" She kept her eyes trained on his profile as he replied.

"What else could it have been?" he asked, his eyes widened with surprise or a credible approximation of it.

"You and I both know that Veronica was not the most agreeable person. And I have heard that she might have had a few conflicts with people here at the school."

"I don't know who you have been talking to, but I can assure you, if Inspector Lloyd is satisfied that her death was unfortunate rather than nefarious, I cannot see what benefit there would be in suggesting it was otherwise or belaboring it with an unnecessary investigation. After all, I have our daughters to consider."

"I am sure you wish to protect them from avoidable difficulties," Beryl said. "I expect that after what has happened you will not insist on Florence attending the school."

Desmond spun back toward her. "I think a bit of stability is what Florence needs right now. Without her mother to keep an eye on her, the finishing school seems like the best place for her to be."

Beryl raised an eyebrow. Florence had been emphatic about her desire not to attend. It seemed strange that Desmond would put their daughter through any more distress than absolutely necessary. Still, since she was not a parent herself, she did not feel best qualified to judge.

"The school is a bit less stable than it was at this time yesterday though, isn't it?" she asked.

"What do you mean by that?" he asked, crossing his arms again.

"I am referring to the mishap in the night that Mary had. I understand that she is out of commission as far as any art lessons go, at least for the time being."

"Oh, that. With Veronica's accident it had gone right out of my mind."

"I heard that you were the one to find her crumpled up at the bottom of the stairs."

"That's right, I did. I had gone to bed and had just drifted off when some sort of noise must have awakened me. I sat up and heard what sounded like something tumbling. I left the room to investigate and discovered Mary at the base of the staircase."

"Did you see anything that explained her fall?" Beryl asked.

"There was nothing on the stairs, if that is what you are asking. Mary was awake when I reached her, but she told me that she had had troubles with sleepwalking since she was a child and that she thought that explained what had happened."

"She was lucky that you found her and that your quick thinking got a doctor round in the middle of the night."

Desmond nodded. "I suppose it was. Mary was embarrassed and didn't want to call any more attention to herself than she already had, so I offered to telephone a doctor of my acquaintance to see to her."

"Was she badly injured? Edwina said it was a sprain, but that Mary said she was cautioned it might be some time before she could expect the full use of her wrist."

"That was my understanding. Still, considering the outcome of Veronica's accident it could have been far worse," Desmond said.

"You don't think it is odd that there were two dangerous accidents in such an unlikely place on the same night?" Beryl asked.

She found the notion preposterous. Nothing remotely interesting ever happened in the entire history of Miss DuPont's school. The idea that two such things would simultaneously occur simply beggared belief.

"I don't wish to speak ill of the recently departed, especially not of my children's mother, but the fact was that Veronica had been drinking more than she ought to have done all evening long. She was well into her cups during the pre-dinner drinks and continued throughout the meal that followed. I should imagine that she kept it up after we left the dining room."

No one had mentioned that Veronica was quite so fond of drink. Beryl had always thought her too careful of her reputation to allow that sort of thing to be attached to her name.

"Are you sure about that? I hadn't noticed her over-imbibing at all."

"You had no reason to do so, but since I share my children with her, I tended to pay special attention to those behaviors that might affect my daughters." A scowl had clouded Desmond's handsome face and Beryl wondered if Veronica's drinking was the reason their marriage had failed.

"Still, it is quite a coincidence."

"Coincidence or not, the only logical explanation for her death is an accident. Since you found her body, you must have noticed how slippery those mossy rocks throughout the grotto happen to be. It's a difficult place to navigate safely under any circumstances, but for an inebriated woman it would easily have proved treacherous."

"I suppose that is one explanation," Beryl said.

"I hope you won't try to convince anyone that Veronica's death was deliberate. Florence doesn't need the loss of her mother to be any more difficult than it already is."

"I should think that Florence would rather know the truth about what happened to her mother than to be comforted by a lie."

"I think I know my daughter a bit better than you do. That is the last thing Florence needs."

Beryl had to admit that he had a point. She had very little experience with children. Still, Florence had seemed to be a practical sort of young lady and even if she wasn't, it was Beryl's experience that the truth of things tended to come out in the end, no matter how hard one tried to ignore or avoid them. Besides, Beryl did not hold with murderers getting away with their crimes, no matter how much she had disliked the victim. But there had been something in Desmond's tone that gave her pause.

Why was Desmond so insistent that Veronica's death was an accident? If he wasn't responsible for her death was he worried that Florence had something to do with it? How far would any father go to protect his child? As she looked over at Desmond once more, he no longer looked quite like the fresh-faced youth that had been such a catch when he had appeared at the dances Miss DuPont had arranged for her students' enjoyment. He looked rather more like he just might be a man with a guilty secret.

Chapter 27

A stroll in the garden would do her good, even if she wasn't accompanied by Crumpet. Edwina retrieved a wide-brimmed straw hat from the wardrobe and pulled it down firmly on her head. She was surprised at herself. Perhaps it was the lack of sleep the night before and the shock of discovering a former classmate dead that was causing her bout of homesickness. She hadn't felt that way in years. In fact, it had not been since the last time she had been at Miss DuPont's.

Truth be told, she hadn't spent much time away from the Beeches since she had left finishing school, besides the odd night away to the seaside or to visit the city for an overnight shopping trip. Although, when she came to think of it, she had felt something akin to homesickness in the months just before Beryl had arrived to stay. Her home had not felt the same when she was alone in it, and it had been a curious thing to long for a place where she already was. But when Beryl and then Simpkins had moved into the Beeches, her home felt like one once more. And there was only one way to get back to it.

She nodded to herself in the glass on the wardrobe door. She and Beryl would solve the case and then they would head directly back to Walmsley Parva. She wouldn't even remark on Beryl's driving. Well, perhaps only if it was absolutely necessary.

As she reached the top of the staircase, she spared a thought for poor Mary taking a tumble the night before. She gripped the handrail and descended with more care than usual. Just as she reached the bottom step, Jennings appeared and gave her a slight nod. He looked a decade older than he had the evening before. Her heart squeezed with fondness for him, and she felt a twinge at how the outcome of any investigation might affect both Jennings and his wife.

"Jennings, you are just the person I wished to see."

"How may I help you, Miss Davenport?"

"I wondered how you and the rest of the staff are holding up in light of the tragedy?"

"That is very kind of you. We are doing our best."

"Of course, you are. No one would expect anything less of you. That said, it is never easy to keep the junior members of staff in line under any circumstance, and a disruption involving the police would be enough to try even consummate professionals like you and Mrs. Jennings."

She hoped that her words did not sound insincere. They were completely heartfelt even if they would help to grease the wheels of conversation and invite unorthodox confidences. She held her breath as she awaited his reply.

"If you do not mind my saying so, you were always such a thoughtful person, even as a girl. It is bolstering to know that the staff is appreciated, especially during difficult times." Jennings placed a white-gloved hand on his chest and Edwina wondered if he had any trouble with his heart. He had put on at least a stone since she was a girl, likely as a result of his wife's excellent cooking. Undue stress would not do him any good if he did suffer from any heart complaints.

"Young Ellen is quite a treasure. Beryl and I have been most impressed with her. She tidied our room this morning as though there had not been a tragedy," Edwina said. There was no reason to inform him of their reason for appreciating the maid. Jennings would not be best pleased to know that one of his staff had been so inclined to indulging in a cosy gossip with guests.

"That is gratifying to hear. She hasn't been here very long, but she has learned the ins and outs of the school and the way Miss DuPont prefers things very quickly. Which, I am sorry to say, is far superior to some others I could name." Jennings winced as if physically pained at the thought of incompetent staff.

"I cannot help but think you are brought to mind of your gardener," she said.

"I am sorry to hear that Evans's lackluster efforts are so easily spotted. The grounds are not what they were during your time here."

Edwina's heart squeezed again. She recalled her own troublesome gardener, who had transformed into a member of what she thought of as her family. It was almost difficult to remember how irksome she had found him only a few months before. From the look on Jennings's face, he did not feel as fondly of Evans.

"As bothersome as such things are, I am sure you are grateful to have anyone at all. The dearth of domestic servants in Walmsley Parva is not to be believed. I cannot imagine that things are much better here," she said.

"Indeed, they are not. It seems that young people feel that going into service is beneath them. Still, if Miss White hadn't recommended him, I would have sent him on his way before now."

"Mary recommended the gardener?"

"That she did." Jennings leaned slightly toward her and lowered his voice. "I don't mind telling you it has made things rather awkward. I cannot feel right about dismissing him, considering she encouraged me to hire him."

"I suppose that is why so many people prefer to find servants through agencies. It makes for far less trouble should the employee prove unsuitable." Once again, she thought of Simpkins and the way he had insisted on hiring an under-gardener on a trial basis to be sure he was worth having about. Fortunately, Declan O'Shea had proved a quick study with a strong back. Evans could learn a thing or two from him, to be sure.

"Right you are, miss. If we could have found someone we would have preferred to do so. But as there were no gardeners to be had, we were fortunate to have Miss White's suggestion."

"Speaking of Miss White and luck, she has had rather a bad bit of it, hasn't she?"

"You speak of her fall?" Jennings asked.

Edwina nodded. "She mentioned that her wrist has made it impossible for her to fulfill her teaching duties. I hope that the news of Veronica's death doesn't leave her feeling even worse."

Jennings cleared his throat and Edwina felt as though he meant it as a correction to her assumption. He was far too proud of his position to contradict her outright, but he was as happy to share his vast knowledge of the household intrigues as anyone else if allowed to save face whilst doing so.

"But now that I come to think of it, I seem to recall that Mary and Veronica were not the best of friends when we were at school. In fact, Veronica made quite a sport of Mary until someone put a stop to it," Edwina said.

"Rumor had it that the person who straightened her out was you, miss," Jennings said, allowing himself the ghost of a smile.

"I may have helped just a bit," Edwina said. "After all, I never could abide a bully."

"It's too bad you did not arrive sooner then," Jennings said.

So, she was not the only one to have noticed the tension between Veronica and Mary. But had it turned into the sort of bullying that Veronica had forced Mary to endure as a girl? Surely a grown woman would not have behaved so badly, would she?

"Had things turned unpleasant between the two of them once more?"

"Unpleasant would be putting things mildly." He lowered his voice even more. "I don't make a habit to listen to private conversations, but I cannot help but be aware of arguments that take place right in front of me. Especially when the instigator does her best to make me a part of it."

Edwina felt a wave of shock roll over her. She had not needed to attend finishing school to realize that a houseguest did not entreat the butler to participate in a squabble. How the poor man must have squirmed at the very notion of it. If she did not think it would give offense, she would have patted him on the shoulder. As it was, she simply tut-tutted as a sign of outrage.

"I am sure that you were no way encouraging of such unheard-of behavior. Veronica must have been overcome by some sort of intense emotion to subject you to such an impertinence."

Just the memory of the incident had caused a line of perspiration to appear on Jennings's forehead. She could not ever recall any such display of human frailty before, and it spoke to the gravity of the experience that he pulled a freshly pressed handkerchief from his pocket and wiped his brow. She thought once more of his heart and wondered at the morality of questioning him further. But before she could steer the conversation to more pleasant waters, he spoke again.

"Last night as I approached her to deliver a message from Miss DuPont, she seemed as though she had lost control of herself completely. While I stood right there in front of her, she accused Miss White of comporting herself with moral laxity. Then she asked me if I thought someone like Miss White should be allowed to instruct young ladies, at least not if her area of greatest expertise was in carrying on with any of the men with whom she came into contact. I didn't know quite where to look."

Indeed, it seemed he still did not. He looked past her shoulder as if he could not meet her eyes even in the retelling. His face was turning an unhealthy shade of gray, and she thought it best not to engage him much longer. Edwina would not have known quite what to do herself if she had been a party to such goings-on.

"Do you have any idea why Veronica would have made such a provocative statement?"

"I am rather afraid her comments were prompted by the fact that Miss White had been getting on rather well with Mr. Montrose." One of his eyebrows lifted ever so slightly. For a butler as self-contained as Jennings, it spoke volumes.

"I am sure you handled the situation with aplomb."

"I am sorry to say that I simply held out the salver containing the post and then bowed and left as soon as she took it. I do not wish to speak ill of any of Miss DuPont's guests and certainly not any of her finished girls, but I cannot say I am not relieved by the notion she will not put me in such an awkward position again."

"No one could blame you for that. And from what I hear, you are not alone in your sentiments. Veronica seems to have put the backs up of quite a number of people before she died."

"Then I suppose there are those who would count her accident a blessing in disguise," Jennings said. "Now, if you will excuse me, I promised Miss DuPont that I would be sure to have someone take a luncheon tray up to Miss White, who is keeping to her room today."

"I seem to remember a system of dumbwaiters that were used for trays when I was a student. Are they no longer in service?"

"We rely on them rarely now that times have changed so much, and our numbers are greatly reduced. Even if we did, Miss White would not be capable of lifting a tray once it reached her room, I'm afraid."

Edwina was not one to allow an opportunity to pass her by unnoticed. "I was planning to stop in to check on Mary just now anyway. Why don't you have the tray sent up via the dumbwaiter and I will assist her with its retrieval?" Edwina asked.

She could see that Jennings was wavering between his desire to uphold the formal line dividing guest and servant and his need for a bit of help. She nodded at him encouragingly and his practical side won out.

"That would be most appreciated," Jennings said, giving her a slight bow.

Chapter 28

Beryl was pleased to note that Edwina looked more determined than woeful when she encountered her on the way up the grand staircase to the second floor. There was a slight forward thrust to her carriage, as if she were being drawn forward by an invisible force, and a determined set to her pointy chin. Something had happened since they last had spoken, and she was delighted to see it.

"Where are you off to in such a lather?" Beryl asked, taking the steps two at a time in order to catch up with her. Edwina was shorter by a head than she but surprisingly fast, especially when excited.

"Mary's room." Edwina paused her ascent and leaned toward Beryl's ear. "Jennings tells me that Veronica accused her of poor morals and suggested she was not fit to teach young women. I thought I had better ask her about it."

"I'll join you, shall I?" Beryl asked, not waiting for an answer.

Edwina sprinted up the remaining stairs with as much dignity as such an endeavor could allow, with Beryl close behind.

Their knock was responded to immediately, and as they entered, Mary stood before an opening in the wall of her sitting area. Edwina moved swiftly past her as Beryl pressed the door firmly into place. There was no need for anyone to overhear their conversation.

"Please allow me to carry that for you. I am sure your wrist is not up for it," Edwina said as she hoisted a tray from the dumbwaiter and placed it on the low table in front of a small, comfortable-looking chair. "Please don't delay your meal on our account. You need to keep up your strength in order to mend quickly."

"Your timing is excellent. I wasn't sure quite how I would manage the tray," Mary said, easing herself into the chair and lifting a silver lid from a delicate china plate.

Edwina sat in the chair nearby and Beryl perched on the window seat, which provided a sweeping view of the grounds to the rear of the school. The window was open, and the only sounds to be heard were birdsong and the squeak of wheels. The young gardener whom she had seen puttering about off and on since they arrived, emerged from behind a clump of shrubbery trundling a wheelbarrow.

He stopped and tipped a load of compost onto a deep border of mounded flowers, the names of which she felt she ought to know but didn't. Perhaps she would make his acquaintance by asking him to identify them if she had time later in the day. She had always found there was nothing like an unexpected death to make one wish to take every advantage of living.

"This is very kind of you. I feel such a fool," Mary said as Edwina poured out a cup of tea from a diminutive pot and held it toward Mary's good arm.

Beryl noted that whoever had rigged up Mary's sling had done a thorough job of it. Her arm was pinned closely to her chest and the wrapping went almost to her fingertips. Clearly the doctor had understood how tempting it was to try to use one's hand even when it was not conducive to the healing process.

On expeditions, she and her companions had endured any number of sprains, and so she knew a thing or two about how discouraging they could be. Having seen Mary with her own two eyes, she was all the more pleased with herself for the telephone call she had placed. She glanced at her wristwatch, a gift from an admirer during the war, and smiled.

"Credit for my timing goes to Jennings. He happened to remark that you were to be sent a tray and he worried about your ability to manage it without a servant. It seems the household is not best equipped to add to the workload today under the circumstances."

"Which circumstances are those?" Mary asked before taking a sip of her steaming tea.

"Have you not heard the news?" Edwina asked. Beryl thought there was a note of surprise in her friend's voice. It seemed strange that no one would have thought to inform Mary of what had taken place that morning.

"I've been quite on my own all day. I expect that after Miss DuPont had heard about my accident, she asked the rest of the household to allow me to have a lie-in. I was awake for a good bit of the night, after all. And I am hardly of any use to the students in this state." She glanced down at her sling and let out a sigh. "So, what is it that has happened? Not more noisy mischief and petty thefts, I hope?"

Edwina glanced over at Beryl as if to ask if she should break the news to Mary. Beryl nodded. They might as well see how she reacted to the news. In their admittedly limited experience as investigators, the moment a suspect first heard about a death offered a unique glimpse into their private thoughts.

"It's rather more serious than that, I'm afraid." Edwina said.

Mary returned her teacup to the tray and looked from Edwina to Beryl then back again. "I should think that nonsense that is driving away the students is quite serious enough."

"Not as serious as a death," Edwina said.

"Whose death?" Mary asked. Beryl thought her voice sounded shaky. "Not Jennings or Miss DuPont."

"No. It was Veronica."

"Veronica? How can that possibly be? She is so young," Mary said, raising her left hand to the base of her throat.

Before the war began Beryl would have likely made the same remark, or at least agreed if another had done so. But she had learned since then that age had little to do with the end of life, given the right circumstances. In the brief years of the war and the influenza outbreaks that followed on its heels like buzzards, she had seen more deaths of the young than she had of the elderly in all the rest of her years combined.

"It appears she had an accident," Edwina said.

"What sort of an accident?"

"Beryl and I found her body in the main pool at the grotto. The police are currently considering the possibility that she slipped, hit her head, and drowned."

Edwina's upright posture, to those who knew her less well than did Beryl, would likely appear just as impeccable as always. But to her more accustomed eye, it was clear that Edwina was poised like a tuning fork. She always tipped her head ever so slightly to one side when she was listening for the sounds of untruth. Beryl was not sure how she did it, but more often than not she ferreted out lies like a trained pig located truffles. She wondered what her friend would make of Mary's reaction.

"But that is horrendous. How is Florence taking the news?" Mary asked. To Beryl's ears her question sounded genuine and as if it was prompted by real concern for Veronica's daughter.

"She is taking it better than I might have expected," Edwina said. "In fact, I am a bit worried that she is taking it rather too well. Although we do all respond to grief in our own ways."

"She is an unusual child. I shall go to see her as soon as I am dressed."

"Do you know her well? After all, she has only recently arrived to tour the school," Beryl said.

"One need hardly know her well to realize that she is not the average young lady who attends a finishing school, or anything else for that matter. She reminds me very much of you, Beryl, at that same age. It is possible Veronica's death will not be all that much of a loss, considering how little they had in common."

"I hope I am not speaking out of turn, but I had heard that maybe her death is no terrible thing for you either," Edwina said. "I understand that the two of you were heard having an argument last night."

"You must have been speaking with Jennings," Mary said with a nod. "The poor man had no idea where to look when Veronica attempted to pull him into the thick of it."

"I'm sure he was mortified, particularly considering the subject matter. I doubt he speaks freely on the matters of romance with Mrs. Jennings, let alone other women."

"I don't think Veronica could have picked a worse subject to mention in front of him." Mary lifted her teacup once more, and Beryl wondered if she was using it to shield any emotions flitting across her face.

"She must have been furious if she lost her sense of propriety to that degree. Although I seem to remember that she never did like to share her possessions with others, even if she seemed to no longer be interested in using them herself," Beryl said.

Mary tipped her head to the side as if she was confused. "What exactly did Jennings tell you about the incident?"

"He said Veronica accused you of having loose morals. He did not hear everything but inferred that she believed you to be conducting a romantic liaison with Desmond," Edwina said.

Mary lowered her teacup again. It rattled in the saucer as she placed it down. "Jennings is a marvel, but he has got the wrong end of the stick there, I'm afraid. Although I suppose he might have found Veronica's actual accusation even more disconcerting."

"So, you are not involved romantically with Desmond?" Beryl asked.

"I most assuredly am not. We are on friendly terms but that is all. Why Jennings should think differently I cannot imagine." Mary reached for a small sandwich on the plate in front of her.

"Then who was Veronica mentioning?" Edwina asked.

"The gardener, if you can believe it. She had seen me speaking with him from time to time and blew things out of proportion."

"I did not realize you were a keen horticulturalist," Edwina said. Beryl watched how her friend leaned forward ever so slightly. She never could hide her interest in chatting about plants with fellow enthusiasts.

"I am not. I was merely asking Evans about areas in the garden that would provide the most interest for my students to paint. Since he is an expert in such matters, I thought it logical to ask for his advice."

"So, it was all just a misunderstanding?" Edwina asked.

"Yes. But why are you so interested? It isn't like you to gossip, Edwina," Mary said.

"The years have brought changes in all of us. For instance, we were both very surprised to see you here at all, considering your time at the school was far from pleasant. And now we hear that you have done so well that you have been offered the position of deputy head."

Mary toyed with her sandwich and took another bite, chewing slowly before answering. Again, Beryl wondered if she was stalling for time.

"Miss DuPont has kindly made that offer, but I have not yet decided whether to take it."

"If I may be so bold as to ask, why would you consider declining?" Edwina asked.

"I am not sure that it would be a sound decision. The school is in financial trouble, and I think bringing it back from the brink may require something beyond my current skills. Besides, as a teacher I have plenty of time for my other interests, and I do not know that that would be the case if I accepted the position."

"What other interests?" Beryl asked.

"Why, my own painting and also traveling. I love to escort the girls on trips abroad, and I even act as a chaperone from time to time for a girl who needs to be brought here from overseas," Mary said. "Miss DuPont had indicated that the demands of the deputy head position would make it less likely that I could take on those travel assignments."

Beryl could easily understand why that would make the job less appealing. Her own love of travel outstripped most of her other interests and she could not imagine accepting a post that would make that more difficult.

"What do you think Miss DuPont will do if you turn her down?" Beryl asked.

"I haven't the faintest idea. I had thought that if she wanted to appoint a deputy head, she would hand over the position to Miss Glover. The fact that she offered it to me suggests she didn't want to do so. If I refuse, I am not sure she would move on to Miss Glover or would look to hire someone from outside the school." Mary tried to hide a yawn with her left hand, but it was futile. Edwina rose and Beryl followed her lead.

"We mustn't keep you any longer. I am sure you could use a rest, considering how little sleep you must have had last night. Do let us know if we can be of any help with anything you might need. We'll let ourselves out."

Beryl waited until they were well along the hallway before speaking.

"So, what do you make of all that?" she asked.

"I think Veronica was behaving even more combatively than

Jennings suggested. To suggest that one of the teaching staff would carry on with a gardener could have destroyed Mary's career, especially if the accusation had fallen into the right ears."

"So, you think she had a reason to kill her?"

"I think it is not a very strong reason, but I would like to check with the gardener, Evans, about Mary's reason for speaking with him. I don't feel entirely convinced that she was telling me the truth about something."

"I know just where to find him. He was tending a border in the rear of the school all the while that we were in Mary's room."

"We should go there directly," Edwina said.

"Why don't you question him on your own? You know that gardening is not my strong suit, and besides, someone still has to speak with Miss Glover."

Edwina paused and turned toward her. "You are going to question her by yourself? Are you sure?"

Beryl waved her hand in what she hoped conveyed a breezy lack of concern. "I've faced down wild boar in the Caucasus. I think I can do the same with Miss Glover."

Chapter 29

Edwina had a great deal to think about as she wended her way through the drawing room and out a wide French door to a flagstone veranda. The sun shone brightly overhead, and it seemed impossible that a few hours earlier the grounds had been crawling with constables.

As she went in search of the gardener, she considered Mary's situation. Would she really turn down the position in order to travel? It was difficult for Edwina to reconcile her memories of Mary as a timid girl with someone who was so bold.

She herself had changed, of course, over the years, and there was no reason to assume she was the only person capable of such a feat. Still, it did seem that someone who took a job because she desperately needed the money would turn down a chance to move into a more lucrative one.

Edwina spotted the gardener, Evans, only a little removed from the area where Beryl had reported seeing him. His broad back was bent over a lush bed of Michaelmas daisies, their purple flowers nodding in the slight breeze. He straightened as she approached and upon noticing her, doffed his cap and held it pressed to his chest. A bit of earth smudged his cheek and she thought he looked as tired as the rest of the staff.

"May I help you?" he asked.

"I certainly hope so. I was just speaking with Miss White, and she told me that you were the one I should consult."

"Are you wanting to know about which plants are blooming on the grounds too?" he asked.

So, Mary had been telling the truth about the reason for her conversations with the gardener. Leave it to Veronica to make a cesspool out of a mud puddle. She never really thought it likely that a woman like Mary would show a romantic interest in one of the servants, no matter how well-formed a specimen he might be.

The more she thought of it, the more foolish she felt to even have considered the possibility. Still, since she had his attention, she might as well make use of the opportunity. After all, they still had not gotten to the bottom of the noises and petty thefts.

"As a matter of fact, there was something else on my mind. Miss White said that as a person who is intimately familiar with the grounds, you would be able to say if there have been any unusual goings-on out of doors recently." She smiled at him encouragingly.

He scratched his chin with a slightly grubby forefinger. "Unusual how?"

"Unexplained lights or noises. Trampled spots where no one ought to walk. Discarded items?" Edwina smiled again. The thought that Simpkins would know just what she meant, without having to ask her to elaborate, burst into her mind. Her feeling of homesickness swelled once more.

"I can't say as I have seen anything like what you mentioned. I did come across two people having an argument yesterday. The man was so angry he grabbed her by the arm, and I thought

I might have to ask him to leave her be. It wasn't a position I wanted to find myself in, I can tell you that."

He most certainly would not have wished to intervene in a private disagreement between those who would surely consider themselves his betters. He would likely lose his position over such a breech. "Do you know who the pair were?" Edwina asked, a thrum of excitement building in her chest.

"It was Veronica DeLisle and her husband," he said.

That begged the question of which one. Although perhaps a groundskeeper might not be aware of the complexities of relationships between guests to such an extent.

"What did the husband look like?" Edwina asked.

"Young. Blond. Favors those golfing trousers and sleeveless jumpers. And he's the only one I've seen about the place with a golf club."

"Was it Paul Deering?" Edwina asked.

"I think I've heard him called that. She was shouting something and started to walk off. I think I heard her call him Paul as he caught up with her."

"Did you see where she was headed?"

Evans pointed toward the far end of the grounds where a familiar clump of rhododendrons stood, casting a wide pool of shade onto the surrounding grass. Just beyond them was the entrance to the grotto. Her heart hammered a little faster as she considered her next question.

"Do you remember what time this was?" she asked.

Evans scratched his chin again. "Late. It was dark enough that I could only make them out on account of the moonlight."

"What were you doing out here so late? I thought gardeners tended to rise with the larks."

In Edwina's experience the morning was the best time of the day in the garden. But perhaps Evans was an exception.

"I couldn't sleep so I decided to head out to smoke a pipe on a bench and to think about the next day's work," he said.

His tone was one of defensiveness and she wondered if he had something to hide. Had he been waiting to meet someone? If so, who could it have been? Was he one of the people responsible for the lights she and Beryl had seen bobbing along the grounds as they inspected the disused servants' wing? Maybe they saw the glow of his pipe and thought it was a torch. Or could he be involved with the disturbances at the school, and the story of a pipe was simply an excuse to explain why he was out at night?

She had not thought to consider a groundskeeper when she thought about the people who might be in a position to make mischief. Servants of all sorts were often invisible to others in the household and could be seen without their presence making an impression.

"Do you think that the couple saw you? A glowing pipe is easily spotted in the dark, isn't it?"

"If they noticed me, they gave no sign of it. Not that I called attention to myself. I might have lost my position just for having witnessed their argument."

"Why do you say that? Gardeners are not easy to find, so your job should be reasonably secure."

"She was not a reasonable woman, at least not where gardeners are concerned. I only got this post because she asked Miss DuPont to let the previous one go. I didn't want the same to happen to me," he said.

"Are you sure about that?" Edwina asked. It seemed highly irregular that Veronica would have had so much influence over Miss DuPont and the running of her school.

"All I know is what I was told. Ellen the maid was kind enough to point her out to me on my first day here and to tell me to mind myself if I didn't want to end up like the last gardener. She's a nice girl, is Ellen."

"And well informed, apparently."

Evans nodded. "If there isn't anything else, miss, I should return to my duties. Veronica may be dead, but I still wish to keep my post."

She shook her head, and he clapped his cap back on his head and turned once more to bend over the flower bed. She watched him for a moment and thought of how easy it would have been for a man of his size and youthful strength to knock Veronica down and to be sure that she drowned in the process. Maybe he was the one to argue with Veronica the previous night. Perhaps he was the one who followed her to the grotto instead of her husband. She turned back to the building with even more questions than she had had when she left it.

Chapter 30

Miss Glover sat in the morning room, a bit of embroidery lying untouched in her lap. Her attention seemed focused on some distant spot she could perceive through the open window, and she paid no mind when Beryl entered the room. Beryl stood and watched her former teacher for a moment.

Miss Glover had seemed like such a tyrant when Beryl was a student. She had been absolutely ruthless in her expectations of how her students would perform. She never tired of reminding them that they would serve as ambassadors for Miss DuPont to the wider world and that they would be judged on the skills they had learned or failed to learn while at her establishment. Beryl had never managed to master any of the subjects Miss Glover taught, but with Edwina's help she had finally squeaked through the course.

Despite her lack of fondness for her former instructor, Beryl did feel a passing wave of sympathy for the woman in front of her. The years had made Miss Glover somehow seem diminished in size and certainly in ferocity, at least as far as Beryl was concerned. Although to be honest, that likely had more to do with Beryl's own metamorphosis over the years than any fading on the part of Miss Glover.

She entered the room and stopped to take a seat directly opposite the older woman. Finally, Miss Glover pulled her gaze away from the window and focused on the newcomer.

"Miss Glover, are you all right?" Beryl asked. "Should I ring for some tea?" Although she was not entirely sure that, should she tug on the nearby bellpull, a servant would respond to the call. With everything in such disarray, she was loath to create additional work for anyone.

"I am perfectly well. Why should I not be?" Miss Glover asked.

"Everyone at the school has been deeply shocked by what happened to Veronica. Although I think of you as an extremely capable person, I should have not expected you to be entirely unaffected by her passing," Beryl said.

Miss Glover fiddled with the piece of needlework in her lap. She clutched at the fabric with one hand and jabbed the embroidery needle into it with the other. She let out a sharp cry of pain and Beryl could see a droplet of blood spreading on the snowy fabric. Miss Glover was clearly more upset than she wanted to let on. In all the many hours she had spent watching her teacher give needlework demonstrations, she had never seen her prick herself.

"Well, of course I'm not insensitive to any death, least of all that of one of our finished girls. But I pride myself in being someone who knows how to soldier on no matter the circumstances. It's a quality I believe the two of us share," Miss Glover said.

If Beryl was surprised at Miss Glover's clumsiness, she was absolutely shocked at the older woman implying that the two of them had something desirable in common. In fact, unless her ears deceived her, there had been a note of respect in Miss Glover's voice.

"I would agree with you about that. I find that one does not get far in life if one is not persistent," Beryl said.

"Indeed, one does not. Although sometimes I wonder what good all the persisting does in the end," Miss Glover said, looking down at her embroidery as if the answer might be found in the pattern of complicated stitches.

She looked so morose that Beryl felt a pang at the notion of questioning her. But there was no help for it. There was no way she could fail to follow up about the argument Ellen had heard between Miss Glover and Veronica. At least not if she wanted to preserve her sense of self-regard as an investigator.

"It's not surprising that you might have feelings of regret if the last words you've exchanged with someone before they died were combative," Beryl said.

Miss Glover's hands holding the embroidery began to shake ever so slightly. "What leads you to believe that my last conversation with Veronica was argumentative?" she asked.

"I suppose it was not necessarily your last conversation with her, but you were overheard having a loud quarrel with Veronica on the day that she died," Beryl said.

"And who, may I ask, told you that?" Miss Glover asked.

"It doesn't really matter who told me. It only matters that it occurred. Have you been questioned by the police regarding your conversation?" Beryl asked.

Miss Glover's face blanched. Her hands trembled all the more violently. "Why would the police have any reason to question me about anything?" she asked.

"When there is an unexplained death, everyone in the vicinity is questioned. If someone was witnessed quarreling with the victim the very same day that person died, the police are likely to wish to question that person more than once," Beryl said.

She watched Miss Glover's face for signs that the other woman would faint or manifest some other form of physical distress. But after drawing and releasing a deep breath, the woman seemed to gather her wits. Beryl had to give credit where credit was due. Miss Glover was demonstrating the very best qualities of Miss DuPont's finished girls. She managed to keep her head and exude a sense of poise under duress.

"It was my understanding that Veronica's death was an accident and that the police were treating it as such," Miss Glover said.

"That's one explanation, and one that would be very convenient for a number of people here at the school. An accident or not, the fact remains that you were heard arguing with her, and I am sure the police would be very interested in knowing about it if they determine her death was suspicious after all," Beryl said. "But knowing Veronica, I'm sure you had good reason to be so provoked."

"Being interviewed by the police would bode very ill for the school," Miss Glover said. "You don't actually think they will question me, do you?"

"I really have no idea. Perhaps if you told me the nature of your argument, I could better advise you as to the seriousness of your situation," Beryl said.

"It certainly was nothing to kill someone over. We simply had differing views on the subject of her daughter Florence," Miss Glover said.

Now that was interesting. It did not line up with what Ellen had reported, at least not on the surface. But Beryl had learned early on in their career as private enquiry agents that snatches of overheard conversation could be interpreted in a myriad of ways, most of which had nothing to do with the actual discourse.

"What sort of a different view?" Beryl asked.

"Veronica approached me and asked if I felt that Florence was enjoying her visit to the school. I told her truthfully that the girl seemed absolutely miserable and that I felt it would be a mistake to enroll her," Miss Glover said.

"I doubt that Veronica took that news with good grace," Beryl said.

"I should say she did not. She spoke to me like a fishwife. I never would have guessed that she had attended any finishing school, let alone Miss DuPont's, if I did not know for a fact that she had. Truly, I was ashamed of her," Miss Glover said. "If she behaved like that with any frequency, I dare say that Florence is better off without her example."

"Why did you feel compelled to tell Veronica what you thought?" Beryl asked.

"I tried to avoid it at first, but she was most insistent. I suppose it just seemed the best way to conclude the conversation. And I suppose your being here didn't help me to hold my tongue," Miss Glover said.

"I can't imagine what I might have had to do with it," Beryl said.

"Your presence here has reminded me of how difficult it is for some girls to adjust to the finishing school environment. Florence has reminded me a great deal of you when you were her age. I never felt that finishing school was the right place for you, and it seems to me that Florence was cut from very similar cloth," Miss Glover said. "Veronica did not seem to find the comparison the least bit flattering to her daughter."

Beryl did her utmost to suppress a smile. Laughing at a dead woman's expense was certainly not worthy of one of Miss DuPont's finished girls, or her own moral code, for that matter.

"I'm sure she was horrified. I cannot imagine she took your observation lying down."

"She most certainly did not. By the time we parted ways she had assured me that she would be apprising Miss DuPont of my assessment of her daughter. She indicated that if her daughter were not good enough for Miss DuPont's school, Veronica would be sure to make members of her social set aware that their daughters would not be welcome either."

That sounded exactly like something Veronica would do. It was just the sort of spiteful wielding of power she would have enjoyed. But the question was, who would be the most hurt by her fit of pique? Was Miss Glover the one with the most to lose? Would speaking to Miss DuPont cost her her position? Or was Miss DuPont the one who would be most likely to wish to silence Veronica?

After all, a woman of her status would have a wide and well-heeled social set. She could certainly have caused a great deal of harm to Miss DuPont's reputation and thus to her bottom line if she had wished to do so. As far as she could see, both women had a great deal to lose if Veronica did not manage to make light of what she perceived to be an insult.

Matters could not have been helped by Beryl's own presence at the school, especially considering she was purported to be there on behalf of a prospective student of her own. Veronica would likely have been very vexed if her daughter was deemed inappropriate to attend whilst a goddaughter of Beryl's was found to be a good fit.

"What did you say to that?" Beryl asked.

"I told her that I could not stop her from voicing her complaint but that my opinion stood firm. I did not feel that Florence would benefit from the program here or at any other finishing school, for that matter. I suggested that she hand over plans for her daughter's further education to her husband, since I felt he was more inclined to consider what the girl herself might want," Miss Glover said.

Beryl was deeply shocked. She had always thought of Miss Glover's tendencies to be rigid and unyielding as negative qualities. To be fair, Beryl had often found herself on the receiving end of such exacting standards and had always failed to measure up. She had not considered that an unwillingness to compromise her principles could be wielded on behalf of one of the students just as easily as to inflict pain on one. She looked at Miss Glover with new respect.

"Florence is very fortunate that you spoke up for her in this way. I wish someone had done the same for me when I was her age and facing the ordeal that was finishing school," Beryl said.

Miss Glover eyed her for a moment and then shook her head sadly. "One of the reasons Florence put me so much in mind of you as a girl was for just that reason," she said.

"What do you mean?" Beryl asked.

"Why, I had the very same conversation with your own mother. And like Veronica, she refused to listen. That's one of the reasons I was so hard on you," Miss Glover said.

"You recommended to my parents that I not attend Miss DuPont's school?"

Miss Glover nodded vigorously. "I most certainly did. As soon as I met you during your own prospective-student visit, I realized finishing school was not in your best interest. But your mother insisted, and so I determined that you needed to be returned to her with a set of skills that would force her to look on you with a bit more fondness."

Beryl leaned back in her chair, limp with surprise. She had been absolutely convinced Miss Glover despised her. She had pushed her and prodded her to develop some level of proficiency with the most meaningless of traditionally female tasks.

But the truth of the matter was that although Beryl did not employ any of those skills more often than she could help, she had left Miss DuPont's school with a greater understanding of the rules she would choose to break throughout the course of her life. She left no longer feeling incompetent and unsure. Rather she'd finally felt emboldened to make informed choices.

"I'm rather afraid that she never changed her impression of me despite your best efforts. For my part though, I think my time here helped me to understand her a bit better. I don't know as I have ever properly thanked you for your efforts on my part. I'm sure it could not have been easy," Beryl said.

Miss Glover allowed herself a small smile. "I'm sure that you realize that easy is never the point at Miss DuPont's school. I just hope we are going to be able to continue to turn out finished girls well into the future."

"Is the school really in so much trouble?" Beryl asked.

"I am sorry to say that even before something as damaging as a death on the grounds, our position was a precarious one. It will take a miracle to turn things around now."

With that, Miss Glover picked up her embroidery and left the room. Beryl watched her retreating back. Did her statement rule her out as a suspect in Veronica's death and perhaps even the pranks and thefts? Would she actually do anything to put the school in harm's way? Somehow Beryl couldn't quite believe that she would.

Chapter 31

Miss DuPont appeared to have aged a decade since Edwina had last seen her in the flower room. She sat hunched over her desk, her usually impeccable posture nowhere to be seen. Her voice was feeble as she bade Edwina to sit in the same chair she had taken only the day before. How long ago it seemed since she had opened the letter from Miss DuPont asking for their help.

"I wanted to stop in to check on you. Is there anything either Beryl or I can do to be of help to you?" Edwina asked.

Miss DuPont let out a long sigh. She leaned back in her chair, appearing on the verge of collapse. From Miss DuPont's demeanor Edwina could only surmise that the relationship between the headmistress and Veronica had been far closer than she had understood. Either that, or perhaps Miss DuPont knew more about Veronica's death than she had admitted to anyone.

"Unless you are able to find a way for us to salvage the school's reputation, I truly don't know how anyone could help. I was already deeply concerned about the school's longevity when I wrote to you about the mischief taking place here. But how we will overcome the blow to our reputation with a death on the premises, I cannot begin to imagine," she said.

"Do you really think it's as bad as all that?" Edwina asked. "After all, the school cannot possibly be blamed for an accident, can it?"

Miss DuPont drummed her long fingers on her desktop. "I'm rather afraid we could be. These days it seems to me that most girls are looking for reasons not to attend finishing schools rather than reasons why they ought to do so."

"Surely not every girl is so disinclined to attend and thwart tradition," Edwina said.

"Even if they do decide to swim against the tide of popular opinion, Veronica's death has handed families one more compelling reason why we should not be added to their list of potential schools. People will attach scandal to what happened, and I am sure will infer that there was negligence, if not deliberate malfeasance," she said.

"Do you think that deliberate malfeasance is a likelihood? I thought that the police were convinced that her death was an accident," Edwina said.

She kept her eyes trained on Miss DuPont's face, alert to the slightest indication of dissembling. While she was far better at ferreting out lies on the part of young girls and tradesmen, she could also claim to be fairly adept with her elders as well. Perhaps all those years of spending time with Simpkins had honed her skills to a fine point. Perhaps that was one more thing she owed to her elderly former gardener.

"To be entirely honest with you I have absolutely no idea. The police did not hang about all that long after they arrived. In fact, I was rather shocked at their cursory questioning," she said.

Edwina had also been unimpressed with Inspector Lloyd's apparent lack of thoroughness. She could not quite get over the uncomfortable feeling in her stomach that arose every time she thought about the way Desmond Montrose had pulled the instructor aside almost as soon as the police had appeared on the scene. It was hard to consider that someone who had once set her heart aflutter might have at the very least attempted to cover up his former wife's murder. There had been so many disillusionments over the last several years, and Edwina admitted to herself that discovering that Desmond was actually a scoundrel was no worse than any of the others. Still, it smarted to consider it.

"You wouldn't happen to know if Inspector Lloyd and Desmond Montrose were already acquainted before Veronica's body was discovered, would you?" she asked.

"I really know very little about Desmond other than his connection to Veronica and their daughters. That and the fact that he owns Montrose Aeronautics. I'm afraid I don't travel in the same social circles as he. Why do you ask?" Miss DuPont said.

Edwina was not sure that she wished to share that much information with Miss DuPont. Not only was it possible that Miss DuPont was a suspect in Veronica's death, but Edwina was not entirely convinced of how much more the elderly woman could take without coming to grief. Still, she was the one who asked the question and had opened the can of worms.

"I happened to see the two of them speaking right there at the grotto, and I had the sense that there was something beyond the usual police and witness interaction. Beryl and I have had quite a number of joint investigations with our local constable in Walmsley Parva, and it appeared to me that Inspector Lloyd was treating Desmond differently than our constable does with witnesses in her own cases."

"That hardly signifies though now, does it?" Miss DuPont said. "Surely, a female constable would have to be especially vigilant just to keep her job, wouldn't she?"

Edwina would have to agree. It had been an absolute marvel that Constable Gibbs had kept her job after the men had returned from the front. Between her eminent capability and her force of will, she had adamantly refused to be ejected from her position. Although Edwina and Beryl did not always agree with Constable Gibbs, she liked to think that they had developed a mutual respect. She would never have expected any member of the public to hold sway with Doris if she thought something needed investigating.

"No, I am sure that you are right about Constable Gibbs. But, setting that aside, do you think it's possible that Veronica's death was not an accident?" Edwina said, hoping she would not offend Miss DuPont with the bluntness of her question.

"I suppose that is partly why the whole situation has worried me to such an extent. An accident on the property would be a bad enough blow to our reputation and respectability. But a murder? I really don't know how we can survive it," she said.

"So, you do think it's possible that her death was no accident? Even though she was reported to have been drinking heavily throughout the night?" Edwina asked.

Miss DuPont looked at her with raised eyebrows. "I had no idea that Veronica was in the least inebriated, but I suppose that might explain some of her behavior. She was in rare form, and for Veronica that is saying something. There is good reason to think that there were people who might want her out of the way. To be honest, when it comes to suspects, one is spoilt for choice," Miss DuPont said.

Edwina was surprised to hear the older woman speaking of Veronica with such frankness. She had always appeared impartial toward all of her finished girls. What could have happened to cause her opinion of Veronica to sour? Or was it simply that like so many other women of Edwina's acquaintance, as Miss DuPont grew older she became less willing to sugarcoat her words in order to put others at ease? Edwina had been finding she herself had less and less interest in doing so, and could only imagine how much more tempting it would be to speak plainly the older she got. It was one of the things about aging she actually eagerly anticipated.

"As Beryl and I have been asking questions about the mischief here at the school, several people have mentioned arguments they overheard Veronica having with others. Did you have any particular suspect in mind?" Edwina asked.

"As a matter of fact, I'm in possession of a troubling bit of knowledge, but I am not sure that I ought to speak about it," Miss DuPont said.

"I think it would be in everyone's best interest if you were to tell me what it was. At the very least you'll feel better if you don't have to stew over it alone," she said.

Miss DuPont stared up at a spot on the ceiling for a moment before appearing to come to a decision. She met Edwina's eyes with her own bright blue ones.

"Veronica told me yesterday afternoon that she is planning to divorce her husband," she said. "It's one of the reasons she was so eager to have Florence attend the school. She wished to have her settled somewhere out of the fray when they were working out the details of the whole dreadful affair."

A divorce could be a very fine motive indeed. Paul Deering had represented their relationship as one of marital bliss. And Florence herself had seemed to get on well enough with her stepfather. Edwina wondered what sort of settlement Veronica might make on her soon-to-be ex-husband. If he was either feeling rejected or as though his position and financial wherewithal were about to be reduced, there was every possibility that he would prefer to be a widower other than a man who had been set aside. She wondered if Inspector Lloyd had any idea that the couple planned to divorce. Perhaps if he had, he might have taken more time to question members of the household.

"Are you suggesting that Paul Deering might have killed her to stop her from obtaining a divorce?" Edwina asked.

"I'm sure I cannot say what he was likely to do. What I do know is that shiftless young men like Mr. Deering don't particularly like to fend for themselves after they have become accustomed to sponging off of their wealthy wives. I cannot imagine that a young man with so few skills as he seems to possess would find it easy to compete for employment in today's job market."

"Would you happen to know if he is a beneficiary in Veronica's will?" Edwina asked.

Something in Miss DuPont's face shut down. It was clear that Edwina had asked a question that caused her the most discomfort of the entire conversation. Edwina couldn't help but wonder why such a question would bother her. While it was never particularly nice to discuss finances, she did not feel as though the question was such a very great faux pas. Miss DuPont paused for a moment before replying.

"I'm sure I couldn't give you any details. Perhaps you would be better off asking Mr. Deering directly. I'm sure you will excuse me, as I have to write a letter to the families of our girls, assuring them that the school is still a safe place for their daughters to reside."

Miss DuPont opened a drawer in her desk and pulled out a sheet of paper. She laid it on her blotter and picked up a fountain pen inlaid with mother-of-pearl. It was clear to Edwina that she had been thoroughly dismissed.

She paused as she reached the door and looked back. Miss DuPont was twisting her pen round and round in her hands as if she could not settle to the task. What was it about Veronica's will that had rattled her to such a degree? She needed to find a place to sit down to think, where she would be unlikely to be disturbed.

Chapter 32

Beryl checked her watch again. She asked Ellen the maid if she had seen Edwina recently. The girl reported that she had been seen entering the morning room only moments before. Sure enough, Beryl spotted her at a small writing desk tucked into the corner just out of sight from the doorway. Edwina's small hands could be seen jutting out past a grand column that shielded the rest of her from view.

She strode toward her and as she suspected, discovered her friend bent busily over a small notebook. Edwina kept meticulous notes throughout the course of their investigations and Beryl expected that her friend had much to chronicle since last they had compared notes. Still, there would be time for that later, after her surprise had been unveiled. Edwina looked up as she approached, and Beryl could see the strain on her face. Her surprise could not be better timed.

"You are looking a little peaky. What has happened?"

"Does it really show all that much?" Edwina asked.

"Like a bow tie on a bull," Beryl said.

"I had a disconcerting conversation with Miss DuPont. I

must confess, I am concerned that all is not as it appears with her."

"How do you mean?"

Edwina leaned back in her chair and toyed with her pen. "I stopped in to check on Miss DuPont and she told me that Veronica said she planned to divorce her husband, Paul."

Beryl let out a long, low whistle. Edwina winced and Beryl wished she had thought to spare her friend from such an unladylike display. Usually, she would have thought a bit of agitation would do her good, but under the circumstances she wished she had been more accommodating. Truly, Edwina looked distressed.

"Surely, this is not something that worries you unduly. Why such a long face?"

"It was Miss DuPont's reaction when I asked her whether she knew if Paul Deering stood to benefit under Miss DeLisle's will. She seemed flustered, and the Miss DuPont I remember was never flustered."

"Do you have any idea why she would react that way?"

"None whatsoever."

"Well then, why don't we go for a stroll around the grounds? A walk in the fresh air always brightens your mood," Beryl said.

Edwina tapped her pen on the open page of her notebook. "The sooner we get to the bottom of this, the sooner we can go home. I'm not sure that going for a walk is the best use of our time," she said. "Besides, a walk is never the same without Crumpet."

"With or without a canine companion, a walk can do wonders for one's mental faculties, I always find," Beryl said.

Edwina arched an eyebrow. "I have never noticed you extolling the pleasures of a long ramble whenever I invited you for one back at home. You always complain if I suggest that we walk somewhere instead of using the motorcar."

Beryl raised her hands in supplication. "Perhaps you have served as such a fine example that I have been inspired to reform my indolent ways. You know that you've always been an extraordinarily good influence on me. You're not about to leave me to my baser instincts now, are you?" Beryl asked.

That ought to do it. Edwina never was one to resist the opportunity to help others improve themselves. With a sigh, she pushed back the carved wooden chair in which she sat and pocketed her notebook and pen.

"I shall have to fetch my hat," Edwina said.

Beryl checked her watch surreptitiously and nodded. "I shall wait for you on the rear veranda," she said.

In no time at all Edwina had returned, hat on her head and a pair of sensible walking shoes upon her feet. Beryl tucked her arm through Edwina's and steered her around the side of the building. Beryl's hearing had always been remarkable, and as they came closer and closer to the front of the school, she felt quite certain she could make out the sound of gravel crunching beneath tires. Edwina appeared to pay no mind to the sound but rather focused her attention on bending over a nearby flower border to yank out a clump of weeds.

Beryl fought back the urge to hurry Edwina along, at least not overtly. But as soon as Edwina straightened her back, Beryl quickened her pace. As they rounded the corner of the building and the driveway came into view, Edwina let out a small cry of pleasure. A blur of fur accompanied by excited barking raced toward them, and Edwina, in a most unladylike display, dropped to her knees and scooped up the small creature in a firm embrace. She turned toward Beryl.

"You arranged this, didn't you?" she asked before burying her face in Crumpet's coarse fur.

"She certainly did," Simpkins said as he crossed the drive and stopped beside them.

He patted Edwina on the shoulder and smiled at her. When Edwina lifted her face from Crumpet's coat, Beryl felt sure she saw traces of tears on her friend's lashes. But clearly, they were tears of joy from the beaming smile spread across Edwina's face as she reached up and squeezed the elderly man's gnarled hand. How different was her response to the sight of Simpkins compared to her attitude all those months before, when Beryl had first arrived in Walmsley Parva. If she didn't know better, she might have said that Edwina was almost as glad to see him as she was Crumpet.

The cab pulled away and one more figure stood there on the drive, a pile of luggage near his feet. Charles Jarvis looked over at them and lifted a hand in greeting. Edwina, still clasping Crumpet to her chest, got to her feet, crossed what remained of the lawn in a few quick strides, and came to a stop beside him. She looked back over at Beryl and then at Charles.

"I can just about imagine Beryl convincing Simpkins to come to London, but I'm thoroughly surprised to see you here too," she said. "How on earth did she manage it?"

Charles smiled down at her. "Beryl mentioned that Miss DuPont was having a spot of bother with her arts mistress, and she suggested that I might be able to fill in until she was able to resume her duties," he said. "I do hope it's all right that I've come."

Edwina nodded and touched his upper arm. "I'm remarkably pleased to see you all," she said, turning slightly to include Simpkins in her comment. "It's almost like being back at home."

"That was exactly what I hoped you would think," Beryl said. "I know you have found it difficult to be so far from the Beeches."

Simpkins strode back over toward the luggage and opened one of the bags. He lifted a parcel wrapped in newspaper. "That reminds me, I brought you a little something from home." He thrust the lumpy package toward her, and as she lifted it Beryl could see a bit of color emerging from the wrappings. Edwina held it to her nose and inhaled deeply.

"How very sweet of you," Edwina said, peeling the newspaper away from an armful of crimson roses. "Miss DuPont's gardens are lovely, but I confess I was missing our own rather dreadfully."

Even from a distance Beryl could see that Simpkins's large earlobes had turned a shade of red that rivaled the roses. Maybe it was on account of Edwina's heartfelt thanks. Beryl suspected it could also have been caused by the fact that her friend had referred to the gardens at the Beeches as *ours* instead of *hers*.

Ever since Simpkins had moved into a back bedroom on the second floor of Edwina's family home, there had been a significant shift in their relationship. Instead of the previous arrangement of employer and employee, there had developed a warm sense of family, and Beryl thought Edwina the better for it. She was quite certain her friend would not have felt so cheered by someone she only thought of as domestic help.

"I propose that we get you settled directly. After all, Charles will need to be getting straight down to work," Beryl said.

"I suppose you have spoken with Miss DuPont about all this without a word of it to me," Edwina said.

"That's what I was doing when I left you alone in the room earlier today. I suggested to her that Charles would make a fine substitute until Mary could resume her duties, and she readily agreed. After that I telephoned to Charles and to Simpkins, who agreed to come down by the very next train," Beryl said.

Just then Jennings arrived with a young man trailing after him. The boy hurried to the drive and collected the luggage. Simpkins and Charles fell into step behind the butler, who announced he would take them directly to their rooms.

Edwina paused for a moment and turned to Beryl. "Was my homesickness so obvious?" she asked.

"I'm sure it wasn't to anyone but me."

"You must think it quite juvenile. I'm rather ashamed of myself that I haven't outgrown my tendency toward it," Edwina said as she scratched Crumpet behind one of his ears.

"I don't think you should ever feel bad about missing your home or your friends. I think it speaks volumes about how much you love the life you've created for yourself."

"So, you don't think less of me for it?" Edwina asked.

"If anything, I admire you all the more. I've never managed to create such a circumstance for myself, and I'm only glad to be able to be a part of yours. Let's not talk of it any further."

Chapter 33

While Beryl took Charles off to introduce him to Miss DuPont, Edwina went in search of Mrs. Jennings. The housekeeper had a great fondness for dogs, and Edwina was keen to have her make Crumpet's acquaintance. She found her right where she expected to, in the kitchen of the school, rolling out a disk of pastry. Keeping well back from the food preparation area, Edwina waved to Mrs. Jennings, who broke into a broad smile as soon as she spotted the little dog.

"Now who do you have there?" Mrs. Jennings asked, putting down her spoon and wiping her hands upon her well-worn pinny.

"This is my dog, Crumpet, just arrived from Walmsley Parva. Beryl arranged for him to join us, and when I remembered how fond you were of dogs, I thought you might like to meet him," Edwina said.

Mrs. Jennings beckoned her toward the table and then turned to the icebox. She pulled out a bit of cold roast and proceeded to carve off a few small bits. She placed the food in a dish and set it on the floor before whistling for the dog. Edwina set him on the ground, and he made a race for the bowl.

"What a fine little fellow. I can't imagine how you managed to leave him at home in the first place," Mrs. Jennings said. "I've missed having a dog about the place ever since our little spaniel passed on last winter."

Edwina's heart gave a little squeeze. She did not allow herself to imagine a day when she would need to say goodbye to her own dog. It didn't bear thinking about. A lump rose in her throat as she observed Mrs. Jennings looking indulgently down at him.

"Perhaps you might consider acquiring a new one before too long," Edwina said.

"If things become more settled here, that's just what I will do. But as they are now, I am not sure that I would dare to," Mrs. Jennings said.

Edwina pulled out a chair at the kitchen table and sat down in it. Mrs. Jennings fetched a large bowl of rosy-cheeked apples and two paring knives from the counter, then settled herself in the chair opposite Edwina. She slid one knife across the table to Edwina and the two of them companionably began paring the apples, long curls of peel piling up on the table between them. Mrs. Jennings was a dab hand at apple pies, and Edwina felt her stomach begin to rumble at the thought of them.

"Are you very worried about the future of the school?" Edwina asked.

Mrs. Jennings nodded. "Miss DuPont has been asking me for some time if I could find ways to trim the housekeeping budget. I've cut it back as far as I possibly can, but she continues to ask. And that was before this business with Miss DeLisle."

"My friend Charles Jarvis has arrived to fill in for Mary White for the time being. Perhaps that will provide a bit of respite," Edwina said. Crumpet stepped away from the food bowl and came to lie at her feet, stretched out beneath the table. He placed his chin on her foot as if to reassure himself that she was close by.

"Who would have imagined that Miss White's accident would've been the least of our troubles this week?" Mrs. Jennings said, putting out a deep sigh.

"Were you surprised to hear about her fall?" Edwina asked.

Mrs. Jennings looked up sharply. "Why do you ask?"

Edwina paused peeling the apple in her hand. "It just seems curious to me that she would have taken a dangerous tumble at nearly the same time as Veronica was meeting with an accident of her own."

"I hope you're not suggesting that someone had something to do with Miss White falling down the stairs. We certainly don't need that sort of suggestion making the rounds," she said.

"You have to admit it's quite a coincidence," Edwina said.

"I'll have you know that Miss White has been suffering from bouts of sleepwalking ever since she was a student here. As much as it might be unusual in adults, it was not in the least unusual for her," Mrs. Jennings said, reaching for a second apple.

"Have you ever seen her sleepwalking?" Edwina asked.

"On several occasions. As a matter fact, Jennings and I have both seen her doing it. I don't mind telling you it gave us each quite a nasty turn. It's the strangest thing to watch someone move about in that sort of a state," Mrs. Jennings said.

Edwina thought it must have been quite frightening. She remembered having seen Mary do it once or twice when they were girls, and it had been unnerving. On one occasion she herself had helped guide Mary back to bed and had never forgotten how peculiar the entire incident had been. The thing that had struck her at the time was how easily Mary had moved about the dormitory and how she had done so without injuring herself.

"Do you remember her ever coming to harm before whilst doing it?" Edwina asked.

Mrs. Jennings gazed up at the ceiling as if trying to recall. Then she looked back at Edwina. "Now that you come to mention it, I don't. That's one of the things that's so odd about watching a sleepwalker. They tend to be quite graceful, don't they?"

"I suppose it would depend on where on the property they wander. The top of the stairs could be quite precarious, I expect," Edwina said. Perhaps, Mrs. Jennings was one of those people that the more wiggle room one offered, the more likely they were to entertain a wider range of possibilities.

"Yes, I suppose that could be. Although I have seen her in a variety of places both in the house and on the grounds and have never seen her falter, let alone trip or fall," Mrs. Jennings said.

Edwina had not considered the possibility that not only would Mary roam freely about the school in the night but also that she might wander about the grounds as well. A shiver of fear ran up her back. What would become of Mary if she were to make her way out onto the road in the dark? She was lucky she had not been struck down by a passing motorcar. It didn't bear thinking of.

"Have you often seen her out on the grounds?" Edwina asked.

Mrs. Jennings shrugged as she added another long apple peel to the pile. "I wouldn't say often, no. But I have seen her two or three times."

"Two or three times? Do you recall when the last occasion might have been?"

"Perhaps sometime last week. It wasn't more recent than that, I am sure."

"Was she in any danger of wandering into the street?"

"No, as a matter fact on each occasion she was headed back toward the school. I told Jennings we ought to consider some other form of locks for the doors, but he said that he couldn't see bothering since no harm had befallen her."

"Locks, unless they were on her own bedroom door, would not have made much difference considering she fell down a set of stairs inside the school building," Edwina said.

"That's what I told him when he was fretting about it when we found out about her accident this morning. The poor man feels responsible for every little thing that happens here at the school. I don't mind telling you he's been quite overwrought about all the mischief that's been going on. The one bright spot of news today was that there were no odd noises or reported thefts last night."

Edwina had not heard that there were no incidents to report. Surely it could not be a coincidence that on the same night two of the members of the household had experienced an accident, the incidents which had brought herself and Beryl to the school had stopped. Could it be that either Veronica or Mary was involved in the mischief at the school? She had to discuss the possibilities with Beryl. She slid her paring knife toward Mrs. Jennings and pushed back her chair.

"I'm sure that whatever has been going on will not continue for much longer. Please tell Jennings that I think that the school would not be the same without the two of you," Edwina said. Crumpet scrambled to his feet and followed her to the door.

"That's very kind of you to say. Be sure to stop back by with your doggy after dinner. I'll keep something aside for him," Mrs. Jennings said before turning back to her work.

"Before I go, I was wondering, did you or Jennings have a reason to be out on the west lawn last night?"

Mrs. Jennings paused her peeling. "No. Why do you ask?"

"I just thought I saw someone out there after dark."

"Surely it was Miss DeLisle that you saw. After all, we know she was out of doors."

Edwina nodded. "That would explain it." But as she turned to leave, she felt Mrs. Jennings's eyes on her. And she knew it did not explain the fact that she and Beryl had seen two different lights moving across the lawn.

Chapter 34

Beryl could not help but notice the change in Edwina's demeanor. Her friend had a renewed spring in her step, and she looked almost as lively as she did back at home as she hurried into their shared room, Crumpet capering at her heels. From the look on Edwina's face, she thought that her friend had something important to share about the case. As soon as Edwina shut the door firmly behind her, she dropped into the window seat beside Beryl. Crumpet clambered up between them and stretched out next to his mistress.

"Well, you best tell me what it is before you burst," Beryl said.

"I've just been speaking with Mrs. Jennings, and she told me that she and her husband have witnessed Mary sleepwalking on more than one occasion," Edwina said.

Beryl tried not to allow her disappointment to show on her face. "But we heard from several sources that Mary has a habit of sleepwalking. We knew she did from our time here as students. Why should this information have caused such a stir?" Beryl asked.

"Mrs. Jennings said that they have seen her wandering about the grounds," Edwina said, arching an eyebrow significantly.

That made things more interesting. "All that is interesting. Were they quite certain that she was sleepwalking?" Beryl asked.

"She said they believed her to be, but my question is how could they be sure from such a distance? Couldn't they simply have assumed that she was doing so?" Edwina said as she stroked Crumpet's rough coat.

"Well, if she wasn't sleepwalking out on the grounds at night, what was she doing instead?" Beryl asked.

"What indeed. Perhaps we don't know Mary White as well as we thought we did," Edwina said. "After all, we have each seen a good many years and massively unsettling experiences since last we met. She is no less likely than anyone else to have changed in the interim."

Edwina leaned back against the window and tucked her feet beneath her skirt. For a moment, with the sunlight behind her, silhouetting her face, Beryl had an overwhelming sense of déjà vu. She had come across her friend in just such a posture of repose over and over when they had been at the school. In those days Edwina had almost always had a book in her hand as she reclined in a window seat, but other than that she appeared unaltered by time.

She thought the feeling that time had stood still and that the players were as they once had been was enhanced by little memories like the one of Edwina in the window seat. It was far too easy to convince oneself that nothing, and no one, had changed. Perhaps they were fooling themselves about those around them, to a dangerous degree.

Beryl thought back to her conversation with Miss Glover. She was certain they did not know the members of the household as well as they might have thought. After all, people did tend to change over time, and there was no reason to expect

Mary to be the exception. And it was not as though either of them had kept in touch with her to any degree over the years. They had thought fondly of her during their time at school, but that did not necessarily hold much sway in the present.

"I should say that we don't know her well at all. Did Mrs. Jennings say they saw her on the grounds last night?" Beryl asked.

Edwina shook her head. "No. She seemed to think the last incident was some night at least a week ago. But that wasn't the only interesting thing she mentioned."

"Go on," Beryl said encouragingly.

"She said that last night no one reported any disturbances or thefts, for the first time since the term began," Edwina said.

"Adele and Lois reported the same lack of troubles," Beryl said. "You don't think that either Mary or Veronica had something to do with the noises or thefts, do you?"

"I think we have to consider the possibility, although I can't imagine for the life of me what either of them would have had to gain by doing so. After all, Veronica appeared to be eager for her daughter to attend the school and surely Mary would not do something to put herself out of a job, would she?"

At first glance, Beryl could not think of any reason why either of them would take it upon themselves to create such serious problems for the school. There was also something so childish about what had been occurring. As much as she thought of Veronica as quite a petty individual, she would not have considered her to behave against her own interests.

And the notion that Mary White would have jeopardized her employment seemed ludicrous. After all, she had already confided that her need for an income was what had brought her to the school in the first place. Unless something had occurred that they did not know about, it seemed unlikely that her prospects would have changed a great deal since their arrival. Although, it was always possible that there was more to her circumstances than met the eye.

"You don't suppose that Mary had somehow come into some money, do you?" Beryl asked. "If she did, she would no longer need her job."

Edwina leaned back against the cushions lining the window seat. "I haven't heard that she has come into money, but perhaps she has the expectation of doing so."

Beryl looked at her friend with interest. "What sort of expectation?"

"Jennings said he had seen Veronica arguing with Mary, and his impression was that Desmond was the source of the disagreement. When I asked Mary about it later, she said that Jennings was mistaken, and that Veronica had accused her of an inappropriate relationship with the gardener."

"Are you suggesting that perhaps there was some truth to a rumor of a romance brewing between Desmond and Mary?" Beryl asked. If the rumor was true, Beryl would be very pleased for Mary. She thought that they would make a well-suited couple.

"It would explain why she would no longer need her job," Edwina said. "After all, Desmond is a wealthy man and if the two were planning to marry, surely she would not need to remain at the school." Edwina's cheeks flushed and the corners of her mouth turned upward. She always did love any hint of a romance, at least those that involved anyone besides herself.

"It would also explain why she has not committed to accepting the post of deputy head," Beryl said. "If she is still as responsible a person as she was in years past, she would not want to make a commitment to the school that she knew she would renege on shortly."

"It might also explain why Desmond is so eager for Florence to attend the school, even though it is not her cup of tea in the least. It would give him the opportunity to spend time with Mary without making their relationship public," Edwina said.

"But is there any reason why they shouldn't wish for others

to know they were romantically involved? After all, neither of them is married and the relationship would not cause any sort of scandal."

"I think that Veronica would not be best pleased to see Mary becoming the second Mrs. Montrose. I expect she would have been quite vicious about it all, and knowing her, likely would have made an effort to put an end to it before they made it to the altar."

"I hate to say it, but none of these possibilities make Mary look like she is off the hook for the pranks at the school," Beryl said. "If anything, they make her look like a more credible suspect than ever."

"It doesn't explain why she would be motivated toward that sort of maliciousness, though, does it?" Edwina said. "I just cannot see her behaving so childishly."

"No, it doesn't. But I'm afraid it does also make it look more likely that she would want to do away with Veronica," Beryl said.

"I don't think that Mary could have been sleepwalking and taking a tumble down the stairs at the same time as she was supposed to be all the way across the grounds murdering Veronica, do you?"

"No, I suppose not. Besides, when I talked to Miss Glover it occurred to me that she might have had as good a reason as anyone to want Veronica out of the way," Beryl said.

"Miss Glover has moved up on your list of suspects?" Edwina asked.

"She has. When I asked her about the argument Ellen had seen her having with Veronica, she claimed that it was about Florence's suitability for finishing school. When she told Veronica she did not think it was in her daughter's best interest to attend, Veronica became incensed. She told Miss Glover she would report the matter to Miss DuPont and that she did not think she should remain at the school if she saw fit to discourage any girls from attending."

"Surely that would not be enough to cause Miss Glover to wish to harm her, would it?" Edwina said.

"Miss Glover has made the school her life's work. I'm not sure what she would do without a position here. From the way she spoke about Veronica, it was clear there was no love lost between them, and to be honest, she seemed quite determined that Florence not be made to conform to a path she did not choose. She went so far as to say that considering her poor example, perhaps the girl would be better off with her mother dead," Beryl said.

Edwina's eyes widened in surprise. "I suppose we don't know Miss Glover very well either. I never would have credited her with such heartfelt emotions for any of her students."

Beryl thought back to her conversation with Miss Glover and had to agree that there was at least one side to the older woman she would never have imagined. But she decided to keep the rest of the conversation to herself. Beryl was not one who preferred to dwell on the past. She did what came the most naturally and steered the conversation to the present and to the task at hand.

"So, don't you think it's possible that we saw Mary sleepwalking last night? Do you believe there is no possibility that she could have been the source of the light we saw out on the lawn?" she asked.

"I just don't see how she could have been falling down the stairs near her room and out on the lawn the same night, unless she made quite a prolonged journey of it." Edwina swung her feet back out from under her skirts and stretched her legs out in front of her. Crumpet shifted slightly and exposed his underside as if he wished to be scratched. Edwina obliged.

"But who's to say she didn't? Perhaps she found her way out of her room safely the first time, moved about the grounds, returned to the school, and then fell down the stairs. She could have fallen down on her way back up, for that matter," Beryl said.

"Yes, I suppose that one of the lights that we saw could have been her moving about. But was Veronica the source of the other one?"

"I think the main question we need to keep in mind is whether or not anyone reports mischief tonight. If they don't, the case may have solved itself one way or the other."

"If Mary is the source of the pranks, it isn't solved."

"As long as there are no more thefts or strange noises, it is solved enough for our purposes. We cannot move into the school permanently."

Edwina shuddered. "No, we most certainly cannot."

Chapter 35

Up ahead Edwina spotted Miss DuPont turning the corner and strolling into the conservatory. The heady scent of orange blossoms floated on the thick, moist air as she quickened her pace to follow her through the open doorway into the light-filled space. Tendrils of greenery hung from the overhead beams, and she was put in mind of an expedition Beryl had mentioned taking, many years prior, to South America as a guide for a pair of botanists eager to collect tropical plants to send home to collectors.

Edwina had loved the conservatory when she was at the school and had often thought that should she ever have the funds to do so would be eager to add one to the Beeches. She had already picked out the perfect spot for it on the south side of the house overlooking the summerhouse and the koi pond. For now, she contented herself with a Wardian case, complete with an orchid, which she had received as a gift from Charles a few weeks ago.

Miss DuPont paused near a pot of scented geraniums and stopped to rub one of its leaves between her gnarled fingers.

She bent over the moss-covered terra-cotta pot and inhaled deeply. Edwina waited until Miss DuPont straightened to call attention to her presence. Her stomach fluttered with the very notion of confronting Miss DuPont. The temptation to delay for even another moment was too great to resist.

"Miss Davenport, you look like you have something you wish to say to me," Miss DuPont said, catching sight of her standing just inside the doorway to the conservatory.

Edwina took a deep breath and stepped closer. She had no desire for anyone else to overhear their conversation. It would be difficult enough to have in private.

"Beryl and I expect our clients to be completely honest with us. It's the only way that we can accomplish the tasks they set out before us. As a result of our last conversation, I fear that you are withholding information from us," she said.

Miss DuPont pinched off a spent blossom from a nearby angel's trumpet and moved down the brick walkway, brushing her hand across the plants as she walked. When she reached a stone bench beside a splashing fountain she stopped and sat, indicating that Edwina should join her.

"You always were extremely perceptive, which is why I wrote to you for assistance in the first place. I should have known you would pick up on my discomfort concerning Veronica's will," Miss DuPont said.

Edwina felt the nervousness in her stomach grow from a flutter to a raging roll. She was not entirely sure she wished to hear whatever it was that Miss DuPont had to confess. Nevertheless, she prided herself on being a professional, and a personal connection with a potential murderer was not something she could allow to influence the way she proceeded.

"You seemed uncomfortable with the question I had about Veronica's will. Would you care to explain that?" Edwina asked.

"It seems I must, whether I care to or not. It is my opinion that Veronica was someone for whom power and influence mattered more than anything else. Like so many other women before her, she had not found marriage or motherhood to provide her with as much of a feeling of accomplishment as she desired," Miss DuPont said. "In order to feel accomplished, she was forced to look elsewhere."

"How is her ambition connected to her will?"

"All in good time, my dear. I'm not sure how she knew it, probably gossip through the grapevine, but Veronica came to me about a year ago with a great deal of knowledge about my financial difficulties. She offered assistance and I was exceedingly grateful," Miss DuPont said.

Edwina's feelings of unease increased. Veronica had not been the sort of person to give a favor without an expectation of recompense. Edwina expected her gifts would not have come cheap.

"And what exactly did she want in exchange for her generosity?"

Miss DuPont twisted her hands in her lap. "In a nutshell, influence. At first, she didn't couch it just that way. She offered to subsidize specific expenditures, like trips to museums or refurbishments to some of the rooms at the school. She asked for nothing in return for the first two or three donations."

"But it didn't stop there, did it?" Edwina asked.

"Unfortunately, it did not. As soon as I had come to rely on the small but significant influxes of cash she offered, she began to make suggestions as to which girls we ought to accept at the school, and more alarmingly, which employees she felt were worthy of being on staff." Miss DuPont inhaled deeply.

"Were there any staff members in particular she felt should no longer serve here?" Edwina asked.

Miss DuPont nodded. "She was quite adamant that I pension off Miss Glover."

"Did you agree to do so?" Edwina asked.

"I'm ashamed to say that I told her I would take it under consideration," Miss DuPont said. "I felt as though I had to at least consider it. She was offering to underwrite the entire operation if I agreed to her terms."

"Did Veronica give any indication as to why she wished for you to dismiss Miss Glover?"

"Of course I asked her what her complaint was, and she would only say that she thought that Miss Glover had outlived her usefulness. I thought there was something particularly cruel about her demand, but I did not see how I could possibly reject it out of hand," Miss DuPont said.

"Was Miss Glover the only one she wished to see removed from the school?" Edwina asked.

Miss Glover shook her head. "That was a peculiar thing. She brought a fresh demand to me yesterday."

Edwina felt the thrum and buzz that signaled the possibility that a case might be nearing conclusion. "What did she ask of you?"

"Not all that long ago when I suggested that I appoint Mary White as deputy head of the school, she was in complete agreement. But yesterday she insisted that the offer be withdrawn."

"Did you agree?" Edwina asked. Surely that would give Mary a real motive for having done away with Veronica. It would also explain why she claimed that she had not yet decided if she wished to accept the position.

"I told her that I would need to sleep on it. I said that I was not someone who typically went back on her word and that to do so would put my entire character into question."

Edwina imagined that Veronica would not have been pleased to be thwarted. Miss DuPont had been placed in an impossible situation.

"I don't expect she graciously accepted being put off."

"No, she did not. In fact, I would not be surprised if that was one of the reasons that she had indulged so liberally in libations last night," Miss DuPont said.

So, Miss DuPont was not above lying when under duress. Edwina remembered quite clearly that Miss DuPont had stated she did not remember noticing that Veronica had been inebriated on the night of her death. Clearly, she was well aware of the situation. Edwina tucked away the knowledge that her former headmistress was as susceptible to dissembling as an errant parlor maid. How very disconcerting it was to revisit one's past. Having caught Mrs. DuPont in a lie, she felt emboldened to ask her another question, no matter how uncomfortable it might prove.

"I'm sorry to have to ask you this, but you seemed eager to drop the subject of Veronica's will when I asked you about it earlier. I think it would be best for all concerned if you were more forthcoming with me now," Edwina said. She kept her eyes trained on Miss DuPont, willing herself not to blink lest she miss the smallest signal that the older woman was lying.

"I was concerned about anyone knowing the extent to which I was indebted to Veronica. You see, the fact of the matter is she told me that she plans to leave a substantial part of her fortune to the school in the event of her death. It was one of the ways that she convinced me to entertain her demands," Miss DuPont said.

"Do you have any proof that she actually planned to do so, or did you simply take her at her word?" Edwina asked.

"She actually showed it to me while she was here. She waved it right under my nose before demanding that I withdraw the offer I had made to Mary for the deputy head position. I'm not proud of being in a position where I felt compelled to accept the terms of her offer. I did not want you to think less of me."

Edwina thought Miss DuPont's words rang true, but she had to ask herself if that was simply what she wished to hear. Miss DuPont had always been an example of a strong and independent woman in the face of society that did not tend to value such individuals. It occurred to her that without entirely meaning to do so, she had looked up to the older woman and perhaps credited her with her own courage in attempting to enter fields where women traditionally feared to tread. Still, the fact remained that Miss DuPont stood to gain a great deal from Veronica's untimely death. Given the natural order of things, she had no reason to suspect that Veronica would predecease her and that she herself would see any financial gain should Veronica live to a ripe old age. As it stood, all of the school's troubles might have simply disappeared.

Despite this, Edwina had to wonder if Miss DuPont would be foolish enough to invite a pair of sleuths to the school at the very same time she planned to carry out such a reprehensible crime. Or perhaps, that had been her plan all along. Perhaps she thought that their presence would help reinforce the notion that she could not possibly have been involved. Could Miss DuPont herself be the one who had been creating the mischief at the school? Had it all been just an excuse to have private investigators on the premises while she enacted her plan?

Edwina gave herself a slight shake. Could someone as frail and elderly as Miss DuPont actually have managed to harm Veronica? How much strength would it take to cause an inebriated woman to lose her footing on a wet and slippery path next to a pond? Could Miss DuPont have had an accomplice? If she did, who could it be?

"Rest assured, I certainly do not think less of you. If anything, you appear to be a much more complicated person than my remembrance of you."

"I noticed that you did not say that you are certain I could not have been involved in Veronica's accident," Miss DuPont said.

"I would not insult you by telling you an untruth. I sincerely hope you feel the same," Edwina said, getting to her feet. "I would like to take a look at Veronica's room. Do you happen to have a key?"

"I expected you might ask me for this. Miss DuPont reached into her pocket. She pulled out an ornate brass key that appeared to be of the Victorian era with its intricately carved metalwork. She placed it in Edwina's outstretched hand. "I hope that whatever you find in Veronica's room will help you to be convinced of the fact that nothing untoward caused her death. As I said before, I believe the future of the school is riding on it."

Chapter 36

"What did Miss DuPont have to say about Veronica's will? Did she have an explanation for why she seemed so uncomfortable?" Beryl asked.

"Apparently Veronica left a significant part of her estate to the school," Edwina said.

"That was very generous of her," Beryl said. "I should not have thought her someone who is inclined to be a philanthropist."

"You are right about that. She had attached considerable strings to the arrangement. For some reason Veronica had changed her mind about Mary serving as the deputy head and demanded that Miss DuPont withdraw the offer as a condition of her beneficence," Edwina said.

It sounded far more like the Veronica that Beryl remembered from her youth. She had never been one to give something with no thought of return. She also had not been above stretching the truth in order to make things turn out her way.

"Is Miss DuPont quite sure that there was a mention of the school in her will? I wouldn't put it past Veronica to have made the whole thing up," Beryl said.

Edwina hastened her steps along the second floor corridor. "I asked the same thing and Miss DuPont said she had actually seen the will with her own two eyes this very week. Still, I would prefer to see it for myself."

Beryl nodded. "I suppose this means you plan for us to let ourselves into Veronica's room to search for it," she said.

"How well you know me," Edwina said, coming to a stop in front of a room halfway down the hall. She looked over her shoulder as if to verify that no one was observing them and then reached for the door handle. It was locked, and Beryl reached almost automatically into the pocket of her long duster jacket. She held out a pocketknife and nodded to Edwina.

"Shall I?" Beryl asked, flicking open a small set of pliers contained within the knife.

"This may prove a bit faster," Edwina said, retrieving a large brass key from her own pocket and fitting it into the lock.

She tried the knob again and this time it yielded with a soft click. Beryl followed Edwina into a large room that overlooked the west lawn. Light streamed in through the oversized windows and Beryl thought it likely that the room was the best appointed one other than Miss DuPont's. It was spacious and immaculate save for a few of Veronica's belongings strewn about carelessly. It felt disconcertingly unreal that the stack of bracelets left on the dressing table and pair of silk stockings draped over the arm of a nearby chair would never be touched by their owner again. Too little time had passed since Veronica had died for the last space she had inhabited to take on the disused air of a long-vacated place.

The room was sufficiently large to house its own writing desk in addition to a small settee, dressing area complete with an oversized walnut wardrobe, and a bed large enough for two. Beryl stepped toward the wardrobe and pulled open the doors. All of the clothing appeared to belong to Veronica, which led her to suspect that the rumors concerning her intention to divorce Paul were true.

Although, to be fair, people of their social set often preferred separate quarters, so perhaps Paul's apparent absence was not definitive proof of trouble in the marriage. Even Beryl's most agreeable marriages had not involved any permanent setup for shared closet space. In fact, as she considered it, she thought it likely the marriages would have been of even shorter duration should she have needed to make room for a husband's clothing to be housed next to her own.

Edwina had headed straight for the writing desk and had seated herself in the small chair in order to make herself comfortable as she sorted through the copious correspondence and other papers spread out across the desk. Beryl moved about the room as Edwina addressed her attention to the paperwork. As she did so she noted a small table and chair situated not far from a compartment housed in the wall, which appeared to be much like the one she had seen in Mary's room.

She grasped a brass handle attached to the section of wall and discovered that just like in Mary's room, if lifted it revealed a dumbwaiter. She stuck her head inside and noticed how if she listened carefully, she could hear noises from the floor below. Perhaps something like that would be of use at the Beeches. She wondered if Beddoes, the excellent housekeeper, would hold with such an informal arrangement for delivering meals. But before she could consider it further, Edwina called her from across the room.

"Come and take a look at this," she said, waving a handful of papers above her head. Beryl dropped the door to the dumbwaiter and hurried to her side.

"Is that Veronica's will?" she asked, taking them from Edwina's hand.

"Indeed it is, and it does make Miss DuPont's school one of the beneficiaries. In fact, it's quite a generous legacy." Edwina pointed to a figure noted on the document and Beryl's eyes widened with surprise.

"It would be difficult to resist that sort of a sum, no matter how much one might not want Veronica's influence to be felt in one's business," Beryl said. "And that amount would be very useful right about now if the reports on the school's financial health are to be believed."

Beryl would never have thought Miss DuPont capable of causing harm to anyone, let alone one of her own former students, but she had never considered that her former headmistress might be in danger of financial ruin either. How easy would it have been for anyone to resist allowing Veronica a free rein if so much money was at stake? And more importantly, if Veronica had begun to throw her weight around so early on, could Miss DuPont have resisted cashing in on the will unnaturally early? Could Beryl blame her if she did?

"I hate to say it, but that was what I was afraid of too," Edwina said. "Did you happen to notice something else about the will?"

"Paul Deering is left a considerable sum if he is her husband at the time of her death. If they are no longer married, he receives nothing," Beryl said.

"Miss DuPont did say that Veronica had plans to divorce him. But that was just hearsay rather than proof."

"Perhaps there's something more definitive somewhere in the rest of these papers. I suppose she might have kept a journal or mentioned it in a letter to a friend," Beryl said.

They worked their way through more of the stacks of correspondence and paperwork. Invitations to upcoming galas, requests for charitable donations, and solicitations to serve on various boards and committees made up the majority of the correspondence. A green crocodile dispatch case sat on the end of the desk and this time Beryl was able to put her lock-picking skills to use.

The little brass lock on the case was surprisingly sturdy and she was quite pleased with herself when she finally managed to jiggle it open. She popped the latch and lifted the lid, turning it toward Edwina as she did so. They bent their heads over the case and found it contained her passport, a single ticket booked in Veronica's name on a ferry bound from Dover to Calais, and a set of documents drawn up by the same solicitor who had prepared her will.

"I'd say that's the proof," Beryl said. "If there's one thing I'm familiar with it's divorce papers." She tapped the stack of documents with a long, well-manicured fingernail and let out a sigh. Despite how things looked, she was not happy to think of Paul Deering winding up at the end of a rope. While he did not seem the sort likely to set the world on fire, he was a nice enough, if ordinary young man, and in her experience the world had lost far too many of those in recent years.

"Does Paul benefit financially from the divorce?" Edwina asked.

Beryl thumbed through the pages searching for terms of the dissolution. There in black and white was the settlement that Veronica was willing to make to rid herself of her husband. Beryl wondered if Paul knew about the divorce and whether or not he was inclined to accept the money offered or if he had planned to ask for more. Even if he did, Beryl was certain the young man would not have been able to spend more on his legal counsel than Veronica could afford.

Edwina replaced the legal documents, snapped the dispatch case shut and tucked it under her arm. "I think it would be best if we did not leave this here where anyone might come across it."

"Do you really think that either Miss DuPont or Paul might steal it in order to destroy the evidence?" Beryl said.

"Since this will was signed, I'm sure there is a copy at her solicitor's office. Still, it would be much more convenient if this copy did not go astray. Something tells me that Inspector Lloyd would take any obstacles in his path as a sign that he ought not to investigate further," Edwina said.

"Do you think Paul knew about her plans?" Beryl asked.

"I really don't know. But if he did, it looks as though he had a very good reason to want her dead. Surely he was better off financially as a widower than as a former spouse."

"We shall have to question him about it," Beryl said.

Edwina's face fell. "I suppose that we must." Edwina stood and gripped the edge of the writing desk for a moment too long. Edwina found discussions centering around money to be distressing in the extreme, and the notion of such a conversation also involving a divorce likely made her feel light-headed with mortification. Fortunately for them both Beryl had no such qualms.

"I think it might be altogether better if you left this one to me, Ed. Why don't you find out how Charles is doing with the students? I think he is supposed to be leading his first class right about now," Beryl said, patting her on the shoulder.

"Are you certain that you don't mind?" Edwina asked, taking a few hasty steps toward the doorway.

"You know that I am never unhappy to speak with unmarried men," Beryl said, flashing what she was sure was a convincing smile.

"Since you put it that way, I will leave it in your most capable hands," Edwina said before hurrying out the door.

As Beryl watched her retreating back, she wondered if she was in such a rush to avoid the conversation with Paul, or if perhaps Edwina was eager to visit with Charles.

Chapter 37

As sheepish as she felt about leaving Beryl to face Paul Deering on her own, Edwina could not deny feeling enormous relief. With a bit of a bounce to her step she returned to the room she shared with Beryl to stow the dispatch case before heading off in search of Charles. She tucked the handsome leather box in a dresser drawer beneath a wool cardigan for safe keeping.

As she passed the dressing table she glanced in the mirror. She reached up and smoothed a wisp of stray hair that had escaped its pins neatly back into place. Her gaze landed on one of Beryl's lipstick tubes and she surprised herself by plucking it off the table and removing the cap. She twisted the base of the tube to reveal the brilliant red lip color. She looked in the glass once more and leaned forward as if to apply some to her own pale lips.

"Nonsense," she said, carefully but firmly returning the cap to the tube. Whatever had gotten into her? She nodded at her own familiar image looking back at her and brushed an imaginary speck of dust from the bodice of her navy-blue day dress before heading back out through the door.

She had left Crumpet in Simpkins's capable care in order to search Veronica's room without the little dog's dubious assistance. While he was her favorite companion for country walks and cozy evenings by the fire, he was not best suited for surreptitious searches through unfamiliar quarters. She could just imagine him poking his furry little muzzle into nooks and crannies where it most assuredly did not belong. Having completed the task at hand, she was eager to be reunited with him and hoped she might find him as she ventured out to see how Charles was faring as an art instructor.

She slipped out a set of French doors leading onto the rear veranda and made her way across the lawn. She raised a small hand to shield her eyes from the sun and felt a warm glow as Charles's familiar figure came into view. He stood at the front of a group of girls attentively installed at their painting easels. His back was turned to her as he bent over a canvas Lois was holding in her outstretched hands.

She did not wish to disturb him but thought she might hang about for a moment in order to catch his eye when he had occasion to glance her way. She wanted to give him an encouraging nod. He had recently been such a support to her as she had taken on the role of local magistrate, and she wished to return the favor if she could. Surely teaching art to a group of young ladies was well outside his usual purview and she thought it likely that despite his habitual even-tempered demeanor he might benefit from a familiar face and a friendly smile.

She stepped toward Adele, who stood chewing at the end of her long-handled brush. Edwina fretted over the possibility that the girl might poison herself with some noxious substances contained in the paint or at the very least riddle her tongue with splinters from the brush handle. Adele did not seem the sort of girl to be so oblivious to danger.

In fact, she had appeared eminently practical when they had previously met. Adele glanced up at her as she approached. The girl had dark circles under her eyes and her hair was not arranged with the same level of care it had been the day before.

"Is there anything wrong, my dear?" Edwina asked. "You look as though there's something troubling you."

Adele shook her head and bit down even harder on her paintbrush handle. Even someone less skilled than Edwina at identifying falsehoods would have remained unconvinced by Adele's denial. Even the small mounds of paints that she had squeezed out onto her wooden pallet signaled her distress. The colors were somber and wholly unsuited to the landscape scene in front of them. They also had little in common with paint already applied to her partially completed canvas set up on the easel in front of her.

It appeared to Edwina that Adele had simply gone through the motions of setting up a work area without giving any thought to what she was actually doing. Edwina thought it would be best to stop her before she spoiled her painting. It showed great promise, and it would be a shame for her to work on it with little care.

"I must say it is impossible to believe that there is not something on your mind. It would be a great pity if you were to work on your painting in your current state of mind. It has a joyful and lighthearted quality to it that I'm certain you could not possibly maintain at present."

Adele removed the paintbrush handle from between her teeth and laid it down on the tray of her easel. She stepped back from the canvas and squinted. Her slim shoulders under her linen smock lifted slightly and she turned toward Edwina.

"You're right. There is something on my mind but I should not like to get anyone into trouble over it."

"I have rather a lot of experience in assisting ladies in sorting out just such problems," Edwina said. "Perhaps I can help you too."

"You do?" Adele asked.

"Yes. I worked with the Women's Land Army during the war and there were a great many girls with a myriad of troubles that ended up as my responsibility, at least in part," Edwina said.

"What sort of troubles?" Adele asked.

Edwina thought back to the types of mischief young women, many of whom were away from home for the first time, had gotten into. There had been the usual heartbreaks and indiscretions, but one case in particular had bothered Edwina for years. A sensible girl from a good family had gone missing without explanation, and the truth of what had become of her had only recently surfaced. Surely whatever Adele had on her mind was less troublesome than that.

"Many of the young women formed attachments to unsuitable men. One or two turned out to be light-fingered. One of them even went missing," Edwina said. "If your worries are not more serious than that, I might be of assistance."

Adele's eyes widened and she shook her head. "No, it was nothing like that. In fact, it isn't even really my problem that's on my mind."

"It's hardly worth making yourself distressed over something that does not directly involve you, now, is it?" Edwina said.

Adele looked around and lowered her voice slightly. "I suppose not. It's just that I saw something last night that worried me, considering what happened to Florence's mother."

Edwina's heart thumped louder in her chest. "What is it that you saw?" she asked, hoping her voice remained steady and would not betray an excess of eagerness.

Adele released a long, slow breath. "I saw Paul Deering creeping around the lawn after dark."

"Are you sure it was Paul Deering?" Edwina asked, her heart thumping all the more rapidly.

"I am absolutely certain. He was carrying a torch and he

tripped. When he stumbled, the beam flashed up at his face and I recognized his profile."

Perhaps Paul had been the source of one of the lights she and Beryl had seen. And after what they had discovered in Veronica's will, he had good reason to wish to confront her somewhere they were not likely to be overheard. Could he have arranged to meet Veronica at the grotto and an argument had gotten out of hand? It was an easy scenario to imagine.

"You said he seemed as though he were creeping. Was there something in his manner that led you to believe that he did not wish to be observed?" Edwina asked.

"I think he had been shielding the light before he lost his footing. I had been looking out the window of my room since I couldn't fall asleep and saw nothing until there was an erratic flashing of torchlight when his face was illuminated."

"Even if he was out on the lawn last night, why would you be concerned about it?" Edwina said. "There's nothing wrong with taking a stroll around the grounds, is there?"

Adele looked toward the front of the group and her gaze settled on her friend, still deep in conversation with Charles.

"Lois said that she's heard rumors that Veronica DeLisle did not die in an accident. And everyone knows that in the case of murder, the spouse is most likely the one who did it."

Edwina supposed she should have been surprised that it had taken as long as it had before whispers about Veronica's death had begun circulating amongst the students. Miss DuPont had been right to be worried about the school's reputation. Even if it were possible to prove for sure that Veronica had died accidentally, it might be impossible to quell the chatter. And Edwina hardly felt in a position to lead the charge herself as she was so unconvinced that Veronica's death had been an accident. Still, it did no one any good for the students to spend their time speculating, if it could possibly be helped.

"I think it's unlikely that Lois is an expert in such matters.

Perhaps it would be best if you did not give much credence to idle gossip," Edwina said. "I think you would be much better off focusing on your real reasons for being at Miss DuPont's school. After all, you are quite an accomplished artist."

Adele's face brightened. "Do you really think so?"

"I most certainly do. I think you should attend to your painting and let the authorities worry about what happened to Veronica DeLisle," Edwina said. "I hardly think they're going to arrest her husband for taking a midnight stroll."

"That's a relief. I'm sure I was just being silly anyway. No one as handsome as Paul Deering could possibly have hurt his wife." Adele looked toward the front of the group. "Not that he's as handsome as Mr. Jarvis, but still I don't want to think that he did it."

With that Adele began to hum under her breath. She rooted around in her paintbox and pulled out a tube of sunny yellow paint. She squeezed a generous pile of it onto her palette and dipped the bristles of her brush into it. Edwina did not wish to disillusion the girl, so she held her tongue. It had been many years since Edwina had equated looks with virtue.

She glanced away from Adele and toward the front of the group, where Lois stood smiling at something Charles had said. Adele had been right about one thing, however. Charles was a rather handsome man. For some reason, she did not quite like the fact that Adele had noticed.

She gave her head a little shake. She did not wish to think about why that seemed to bother her. Fortunately, ahead she spotted Simpkins seated on a bench beneath a sprawling oak tree with Crumpet sleeping in a sunny spot nearby. Putting thoughts of Charles's good looks out of her mind, she strode toward him.

Chapter 38

It had taken some doing but Beryl finally managed to track Paul down. Jennings had suggested she might find him somewhere on the grounds with his golf club, as he had seen him leaving his room with the implement in hand not even an hour previous.

She would have preferred that he not be holding a potential weapon when she confronted him about the possibility that he had murdered his wife, but it could not be helped. He was hacking away at a bit of underbrush, likely in search of an errant golf ball, when she approached. He looked up at her and it was clear that a missing ball was not the only thing on his mind.

He looked as though he had not slept well the night before, yet another possible piece of evidence pointing toward his guilt. If he already knew about Veronica's plan to divorce him, it was just one more reason why he would have found that sleep was hard to come by.

She had never found it difficult to sleep under most circumstances. Once she had decided to leave a marriage, she gave it absolutely no further thought. In her opinion, there was no use fretting over the past, and all of her ex-husbands were most decidedly left well behind her.

But perhaps Paul was an entirely different sort. Beryl had never made any bones about her interest in passionate love affairs, but she did not consider herself to be a romantic. She had found that the men she became involved with were much more likely to be swayed by such tenderhearted emotions than was she. Paul appeared to her just the sort to take the breakup of the marriage quite badly.

With his weak chin and mild-mannered demeanor, she thought it likely he had been awestruck when Veronica had shown interest in him. Beryl realized that she felt almost sorry for the poor man and not just on account of his less than stellar golfing skills.

Still, it would not keep her from confronting him with their suspicions. And it would be best to get it over with. Paul was not the only one who was interested in getting in a bit of golfing. If they could get the investigation wrapped up quickly, she might still be able to arrange to meet her favorite golfing partner before he checked out of the hotel they had booked. She quickened her pace and swiftly spotted the white gleam of a golf ball in the underbrush. She stooped and picked it up, extending it to him with a smile.

"Is this what you're looking for?" she asked.

"Now how in the world did you find that so quickly?" he asked, taking it from her and stuffing it into his pocket. He lifted his club to his shoulder and Beryl made a quick calculation of how far away she would need to stand to be out of reach of his swing should he have a mind to do so. She stepped slightly farther away while keeping him in her peripheral gaze. If there was one thing she had learned on safari, it was to always remain aware of the position of predators.

"You'd be surprised by the sorts of things that I'm able to discover quickly. For example, I happened to have found out that if you had not become a widower, you would be about to be divorced," she said, stepping nimbly even farther out of reach.

Not that it mattered. Paul had come to a complete and utter standstill. A look of shock washed over his pale face, and the hand holding the golf club trembled slightly.

"How do you know that?" he said, his voice cracking slightly.

"I've seen the divorce papers."

"What business is it of yours if we were about to be divorced?" he said.

"I think the police would be very interested to know that you stood to gain a great deal if you were still married to Veronica at the time of her death."

Paul's pale skin flushed bright red and he opened and closed his mouth several times in rapid succession. He swung his golf club down from his shoulder and Beryl was glad that she had thought to distance herself from him as it crashed through the long grass standing between them.

"Veronica's death was an accident. I won't deny that the divorce settlement would have left me with less money than her will provided for, but that doesn't change the fact that the police don't suspect anyone of causing her death," he said.

"An initial impression is not the conclusion of the case. I think the police would be very interested to know that you might have had good reason to wish her dead," Beryl said. "Especially since you have led everyone to believe that your marriage was a happy one."

Paul swung his golf club back and forth once more, slicing down another swath of grass. Beryl glanced over her shoulder in search of anyone else within view. There was usually someone or other roaming the grounds, but, unfortunately, she was completely alone with him. She gave herself a mental kicking for leaving her pistol in a dresser drawer in her guest room at the school.

"That was Veronica's idea. She didn't want any of the troubles between us to worry Florence. She was having a hard enough time convincing her daughter to come round to her way of thinking about attending, and she didn't want anything to make it more difficult," he said.

"Why would a divorce from you make it more difficult?" Beryl asked.

"Believe it or not, Florence and I get along surprisingly well. I think she looks at me almost as an older brother. Veronica thought that she would take my side and that she would not agree to attend the school, as a way to get back at her mother for hurting me," he said.

Florence certainly had presented herself as an unusual child. Beryl would not have expected most girls to side with their stepfather rather than their own mother, but if anyone could provoke that sort of response from her child, she expected it was Veronica. Still, a desire to keep things quiet did not mean he had not caused his wife to come to harm.

"Even if you had a good reason for lying about the state of your marriage, that doesn't mean you didn't stand to gain a great deal by doing away with her before she could divorce you," Beryl said.

"I was going to do all right out of the divorce," Paul said. "I had no complaints."

"How could you have possibly thought you would make out all right? Your lifestyle was going to take a decided downturn once you lost the use of Veronica's money," Beryl said.

"Believe me, the money wasn't worth it. She had a lot of it, but she didn't hand it out freely. When it came down to disposable income, I think I would have been better off with the divorce settlement than I was with the pittance she allowed me during our marriage," he said.

Beryl imagined that that was a real possibility. She had been married to men in the past who, while wealthy themselves, had given her very little discretionary income. She felt an unexpected level of empathy for the young man standing beside her. He may have been a gold digger, but he certainly had not struck a rich vein.

"So, she was planning on settling some money on you outright as a condition of the divorce?" Beryl asked. Although she was well aware of the answer, she wondered if Paul would respond truthfully.

Paul nodded. "Yes, it was not as much as I would've liked, but I had some plans to make it work for me so that there was no way I would need her money in the future."

"That sounds like the right way to plan ahead. What did you propose to do to make up for the shortfall?"

Paul looked as though he had said too much. He glanced everywhere but at Beryl's face.

"The police are unlikely to leave you alone without a convincing explanation. It's not going to do your case any good when they hear that you were seen wandering the grounds last night in the dark," she said.

Paul shifted from foot to foot like a small boy caught with his hand in the cookie jar. "My reason for being out last night had absolutely nothing to do with Veronica."

"The person who saw you said that you appeared to be trying to sneak about unobserved. Now why would you behave so furtively if you were not up to no good?"

Paul's face had taken on a decidedly green tinge. "Maybe what I was doing wasn't exactly aboveboard, but it had nothing to do with what happened to Veronica."

"You aren't doing a good job of making things look any better for yourself, you do realize that, don't you?" Beryl asked. "If I were you, I would be a little more forthcoming, even if you think that what you were up to casts you in a poor light."

"I was sneaking around because I was meeting someone," he said.

Was Paul involved in an extramarital entanglement? Was

that why Veronica had wanted to divorce him? It would not be unheard of for any man to find companionship outside of his marriage, but especially one who was far younger than his wife. But with whom? The person who sprang immediately to mind was Mary White.

"Who was it that you planned to meet?" Beryl asked.

"Miss Glover," he said, letting out a long sigh.

There was no one at the school Beryl would have been more surprised to hear named as his lover. While she was all for liaisons that pleased both parties no matter how unorthodox they might appear to outsiders, she found it impossible to believe Miss Glover would involve herself in such a sordid matter.

"Miss Glover? Whatever for?" Beryl asked.

"As you mentioned, my divorce settlement was not overly generous. I needed to find a way to make it provide for me going forward. Which is how I hit upon the idea of buying this place."

"Buying Miss DuPont's school? But it's not for sale," Beryl said.

Paul shrugged. "Everything is for sale if you play your cards properly."

"Are you the one who's behind the strange noises and the missing items? Have you been deliberately trying to damage Miss DuPont's reputation in order to force her into a position where she needed to sell the school?"

"You make it sound so reprehensible. Miss DuPont has been in financial trouble for years. Veronica kept yammering on about it and I thought maybe it would be advantageous for both of us in the end."

"Why didn't you just make her an offer if you thought selling the property was in Miss DuPont's best interest?"

"If I came right out and made her an offer, I am sure that the asking price would have been too high for me to afford. As I said, Veronica was not overly generous and I needed to drive the price down as low as possible. This place would need a great deal of work to turn it into the sort of high-end hotel I have imagined it could be. I would need to hold back some of the divorce settlement in order to do the renovations," he said.

"How long have you been sabotaging the school? And why in the world would Miss Glover agree to help you?"

"It's been happening since the beginning of the term. I was able to convince Miss Glover to help, as soon as Veronica told me she had supported Miss DuPont's suggestion that Mary White be offered a position as deputy head."

"Miss Glover was so upset by being passed over that she agreed to help you destroy the reputation of the school?" Beryl asked.

"Of course, she was. Wouldn't you be?" he asked. "She was more than happy to help, and was in a position to do so without much difficulty."

"But why would you decide that this was the property to invest in? Surely there are other places to be picked up at a bargain, considering how difficult the economy is right now," Beryl said.

"The location is perfect for a hotel with the golf course right near the city. Besides, there were two additional reasons for pursuing this opportunity," he said.

"You wanted to get back at Veronica, didn't you?" Beryl said.

"Absolutely. More than anything else, Veronica liked to be in a position of power. Wielding influence at the school was her latest means of doing so. If the school went out of business, she would have no way to exercise that power. And, as an added bonus, she would not be able to force Florence to attend. Like I said, my stepdaughter and I are good friends," he said.

"Did Florence know what you were up to?" Beryl asked.

"Absolutely not. The fewer people involved, the better. Besides, I wouldn't have wanted to put something like that on the poor kid's conscience."

"I suppose Miss Glover will back you up about all this?" Beryl asked.

"I think so," he said, pinching his eyebrows together.

"You'd better hope that she does. She's your best chance of not being implicated if Veronica's death comes under more scrutiny from the police," Beryl said.

"Then you'd best go off and question her about it, hadn't you?" Paul said. He lifted his golf club to his shoulder again and sauntered off as if he didn't have a care in the world.

Beryl, on the other hand, felt like the weight of the world had been placed on her shoulders. Just when she thought she had come to a better understanding with Miss Glover, the rug had been pulled out from under her. But, if what Paul had said was true, at least they had solved the mystery of who was causing the mischief at the school. With any luck she and Edwina would be headed home in no time.

Chapter 39

Crumpet raced toward her pell-mell. Edwina crouched down and scooped the little dog into her arms. Simpkins looked over from his spot on the stone bench and smiled. He got to his feet and swept his hand out to indicate the gardens around him.

"What a fine property this is," he said, tucking his gnarled hands into his pockets and rocking back on his heels. Edwina could not disagree. As much as she adored Beryl's company, it could not be said that her friend showed much enthusiasm for things horticultural. It was a joy to share her enthusiasm with a like-minded person.

"How I wish you could have seen it in its heyday," Edwina said. "I would have to credit my time at the school as the origin of my love of beautiful gardens."

"I will endeavor not to be offended by such a claim," Simpkins said. "I had always thought your exposure to the grounds at the Beeches accounted for your love of gardening," he said, giving her a wink.

She hoped she had not offended him. But the fact of the matter was that one often took for granted those things that were so close to home. It often required something unfamiliar to help one appreciate what one already possessed. She looked up at Simpkins's face and was relieved to see a smile upon it. He really was a remarkably forgiving sort.

"The Beeches is always the closest to my heart, but you must admit the grounds here are at a grander scale and thus more likely to have impressed a naïve girl," Edwina said, hoping to have smoothed over any awkwardness.

"Don't mind me, Edwina," Simpkins said. "You know how much I like to tease."

"Shall I give you a tour?" Edwina asked. Simpkins nodded and she bent to place Crumpet on the ground. The three of them ambled forward and she made sure to point out areas of interest and handsome specimens as they made their way along the gravel path that wound through the grounds.

After they had moved about a hundred yards along, Simpkins bent over a deep herbaceous border and Edwina could see a quizzical look pass across his craggy features. They moved ahead several yards, and he stopped again. He stooped over a mound of greenery at the side of one of the garden beds. He reached out with a practiced hand, intent on searching through the pile. Edwina looked down at what had garnered his notice. He held out a handful of uprooted plants and waggled them in front of her.

"What do you make of this then?" he asked.

"It looks like a perfectly lovely columbine and a healthy daisy," she said. "Those aren't weeds."

"No, missy, they are not," Simpkins said with an excessive degree of familiarity. Edwina had become accustomed to him speaking to her as a friend rather than an employee over the last several months, but generally he only regressed to calling her by a childish endearment when exhibiting an excess of emotion.

"Why should Evans have pulled them up then?" she asked. She inspected the garden for signs of overgrowth but was shocked to see that a large quantity of ragweed had been left to flourish while perfectly good flowering plants had been removed. It made absolutely no sense whatsoever.

"It seems to me that this Evans has no business passing himself off as a gardener. In my day we would've taken someone possessing so little discernment between desirable plants and weeds out behind the potting shed and boxed his ears," he said.

Simpkins knelt down beside the herbaceous border and with his bare hands scooped out a small hollow. He tucked the daisy into it and mounded the soil gently around it. He repeated the procedure with the columbine before stiffly getting to his feet once more.

"The grounds have been looking decidedly shabby despite the fact that they have been fortunate enough to have a gardener on premises," Edwina said. "In fact, the only thing that looks at least as lovely as it did when I was a girl is the grotto."

"That's hardly surprising if the gardener is someone who doesn't know the perennial plants from a bunch of weeds." Simpkins shook his head in disgust as he turned his gaze upon the nearby herbaceous borders. He lifted his hand and gestured toward a nearby shrub. "Look at that poor thing. There is more dead wood clinging to it than greenery."

Edwina looked at the shrub in question and nodded her head in despair. Her mind had been taken up with the case sufficiently that she had not paid attention to how terribly the grounds had suffered. Evans seemed like a nice enough young man, but as she viewed the garden through Simpkins's eyes, she found herself questioning his suitability for the task.

"Perhaps he was the only gardener available," Edwina said.

"There's some help as is no help at all," Simpkins said, a scowl spreading across his face from ear to ear.

Suddenly he straightened and replaced his scowl with a look of interest. Miss DuPont was making slow but steady progress in their direction. Edwina felt a jolt of surprise. Why was Simpkins taking notice of her former headmistress?

He certainly had drawn himself up to his full height and

seemed to be fiddling uncharacteristically with his collar. As she approached, Edwina was surprised to see him shifting awkwardly from one foot to the other.

"Mr. Simpkins, how lovely it is to see you again," Miss DuPont said. "I do hope that my grounds meet with your approval, considering you are such an expert plants man."

Edwina felt she ought to throw herself into the conversational breach, but Simpkins somehow beat her to it.

"You have an enviable location, and the bones of your gardens are impressive," Simpkins said.

"It sounds to me as if you are holding something back. Please do feel free to speak your mind, Mr. Simpkins. I would value your opinion," Miss DuPont said.

Edwina was shocked to see that Simpkins stepped forward and offered the older woman his arm. She was even more surprised to see Miss DuPont take it. She fell into step behind the two of them and strained her ears to capture whichever bits of their conversation she might.

"I should not like to speak out of turn or in any way to give offense," Simpkins said.

"Come now, Mr. Simpkins, we are both of an age not to need to mince words. Who knows how much time we have left ahead of us to waste? Please speak your mind," she said.

"I'm not faulting you, mind, but I would say that your gardener is not worth his wages."

Miss DuPont stopped in her tracks and turned to look up at him. "You seem very sure of your opinion," she said.

"I am. I've been a gardener all my life, both man and boy. I've just returned a columbine and a daisy to one of your perennial borders. Your gardener weeded them out and left stands of ragweed completely untouched."

"Is that so?" Miss DuPont said. "It grieves me to say it, but I have been far too busy with troubles at the school to spend sufficient attention to the grounds."

Simpkins nodded gravely. "Miss Edwina would not have

taken herself off to London if the matter were not an urgent one. I expect if you were able to pry her away from Walmsley Parva there must be a tremendous weight on your shoulders."

"I am afraid that is the case," Miss DuPont said.

"I understand there is no Mr. DuPont," Simpkins said.

Miss DuPont nodded. "Only my dearly departed father," she said.

"I lost my own dear Bess not so very long ago. Managing all that requires doing is difficult on one's own. You mustn't blame yourself if the gardens have slipped a bit."

Edwina could not quite believe her ears. Miss DuPont had always seemed like such a law unto herself. It was almost impossible to imagine her having a father or behaving coquettishly as she was with Simpkins. She could hardly wait to discuss the matter with Beryl.

"How very kind of you to say," Miss DuPont said, wrapping her arm even more tightly around Simpkins's own. "Please accept my condolences on the loss of your wife."

"Thank you, miss. If you don't mind me saying so, you could use a bit of help here. It is certainly no fault of your own. We've had a difficult time at the Beeches finding anyone to assist with the heavy labor. We were lucky recently to find a young Irishman willing to give us a hand," he said.

This comment caused Edwina to form a question in her own mind. "Miss DuPont, how did you come to hire Evans to work here at the school?" she asked.

"It wasn't my idea, I can tell you that," she said.

"Then how did he come to work for you?" Simpkins asked. He looked over his shoulder at Edwina and gave her a surreptitious wink. If she didn't know better, she would have suspected him of using his charms on Miss DuPont to assist with the investigation. She looked at him with new admiration.

"Mary White recommended him. I hired him at her urging," Miss DuPont said.

"Did he come with references?" Edwina asked.

"I didn't call any, if that's what you're asking. Mary's recommendation was enough for me, and I simply agreed. Besides, you must know how difficult it is to find any help whatsoever these days," she said.

"As I was just saying to Miss Edwina, some help is no help at all. If you'd like, I'd be happy to have a word with your young gardener in order to give him the benefit of my many years of experience," Simpkins said.

"Oh, Mr. Simpkins, that's too kind of you," Miss DuPont said, fanning herself with her hand.

As Edwina followed behind them, her mind wandered from their conversation. What occupied her mind instead was a question. Why on earth had Mary White recommended a gardener who was not qualified for the job?

Chapter 40

Beryl forced herself not to break into a trot as she searched the grounds for Edwina. Up ahead she heard the sound of barking and knew she was on the right track. She followed the sound and shortly found herself in front of Miss DuPont arm in arm with Simpkins, a bemused Edwina trailing behind them. She nodded to the elderly pair and hurried to her friend's side.

"I've had the most extraordinary conversation with Paul Deering. We have to speak with Miss Glover."

Beryl slowed her pace and Edwina fell into step beside her. Despite the widening gap between themselves and their elders, Edwina dropped her voice almost to a whisper.

"Whatever for?" Edwina asked.

Edwina stopped in her tracks as Beryl quickly filled her friend in on all that Paul had said about the part Miss Glover had played in the mischief taking place at the school.

"Did you believe him?" Edwina asked.

"It seemed as though it would be foolish for him to lie about it, since it would be easy enough to ask her," Beryl said. "I thought it best to come find you in order for us to confront her together. She might be able to lie to me, but I doubt very much she would get any falsehoods past you."

There were many things that Beryl admired about Edwina, but her ability to ferret out lies had proven exceptionally useful in their business venture. While Beryl herself was handy with a pistol and adept at picking locks, she didn't have a patch on Edwina when it came to sniffing out untruths. Miss Glover did not stand a chance of pulling the wool over Edwina's eyes, of that Beryl was absolutely certain.

"We had best question her straightaway. After all, if that is the solution to the mystery, perhaps we might be able to head home this very evening," Edwina said.

Beryl glanced down at her diminutive friend with affection. Edwina had cheered at Charles and Simpkins's arrival, but nothing would replace returning home. She nodded and veered away from the path and toward the school building, with Edwina following closely behind.

Miss Glover was conveniently closeted in her own rooms. As much as Beryl was disillusioned by her former teacher's involvement in something so underhanded, she had no desire to humiliate her in front of others. Miss Glover invited them into her room, albeit with a quizzical look upon her face. Edwina shut the door firmly behind her and the two of them took the seats Miss Glover offered on a small and slightly shabby sofa near the center of the room.

"What brings the two of you to speak with me, especially with such serious looks on your faces?" Miss Glover said.

"I'm sorry to say there has been an accusation made against you and we wish to verify it," Beryl said. Was she imagining things or had a vein begun to pulse in Miss Glover's forehead?

"An accusation, you say? This should be amusing," Miss Glover said.

"I very much doubt that Miss DuPont will find it amusing in the least," Beryl said.

That did it. Beryl had not imagined Miss Glover's discomfort. She squirmed in her seat like a restless child attending a sermon given by a long-winded minister.

"You'd best come out with it then," Miss Glover said. "It won't be the first time that some silly girl at the school has accused me of something unfounded."

"Paul Deering can hardly be called a silly girl," Edwina said.

Miss Glover's brows drew together. "What has Mr. Deering been saying to you?"

"He accuses you of being the one responsible for the odd noises and thefts here at the school," Beryl said. "Is it true?"

She found herself surprised at herself for holding her breath in the hope that Miss Glover would refute the accusation.

The older woman sagged against the back of her chair; all the color drained out of her already pale face. "He said that, did he?"

"I'm afraid that he did. From the looks of it, Paul told the truth, didn't he?" Beryl said. One would not need Edwina's skills to be able to tell that the accusations were true.

Beryl wasn't quite sure what to say as a tear slid down Miss Glover's papery cheek. The elderly woman nodded.

"He approached me in a moment of weakness," Miss Glover said. Another tear ran down her face and she wiped it away with the back of her hand. Beryl looked over at Edwina, stunned at the sight of her former teacher gripped by sorrow.

"Did you resent Miss DuPont for offering the position of deputy head to Mary rather than to you?" Edwina asked.

Miss Glover shook her head. She retrieved a lace-trimmed handkerchief from her pocket and delicately dabbed at her eyes. "Of course not. The school would be best served by that role being filled by someone with youth and vigor to offer. I had no quarrel whatsoever with the appointment of Mary."

"What was the difficulty then?" Edwina asked.

Miss Glover let out a long sigh. "Miss DuPont and I have been friends for even longer than the two of you. She is my dearest companion and I have been heartsick to watch her crushed with worry about the future of the school. Just before Paul approached me, Miss DuPont had confided that she had consulted a doctor about chest pains she thought were brought on by her concerns about making ends meet. I knew I could never convince her to give up the school voluntarily, but I was worried that if she continued to soldier on it might kill her."

Beryl glanced over at Edwina. As surprising as Miss Glover's reason might seem, she could absolutely imagine doing something similar to save her own dear friend from harm. Edwina was exactly the sort of person who would continue on in the face of extreme difficulty once her mind had been made up. She would be especially inclined to do so if it meant not losing something as dear to her as the school was to Miss DuPont.

"Did you attempt to tell Miss DuPont how concerned you were for her health?" Edwina said.

"I tried to, many times, but to no avail. You may not realize it, but she's a maddeningly stubborn creature. When Paul approached me with this proposal, it seemed like the only way to save Miss DuPont from herself," Miss Glover said.

Edwina looked over at Beryl, her eyes wide in her face. She looked as though she had no idea what else to ask. Beryl had never been one to back away from a difficult task.

"Do you have any idea why the two of us are really here at the school?" Beryl asked.

Miss Glover raised an eyebrow and frowned. "I can only assume that you are here for your stated reason. Don't you have a goddaughter in need of a finishing school?"

"I regret to tell you that that is simply the story Miss DuPont asked us to give out to explain our presence here. In truth, she hired us to get to the bottom of the noises and thefts taking place. I know you were trying to reduce her worries, but in fact you have made them far worse."

"You're here as private enquiry agents?" Miss Glover asked.

"Yes, we are. And I'm sorry to have to tell you that we will be required to tell Miss DuPont that you are the one who has been causing so much distress," Beryl said.

"I never thought it would come to this. I thought that Miss DuPont would be ready to sell the school and to take a well-deserved retirement, perhaps somewhere out in the country or at the seaside. I never imagined that she would come to hear of my involvement. What have I done?" she asked before bursting into heaving sobs.

Edwina got to her feet and moved to Miss Glover's side. She wrapped her slim arm around the older woman's shoulders and did her best to comfort her.

"We are obligated to report to Miss DuPont about our findings, but we make it our mission to leave things better off than we found them. Destroying a lifelong relationship between you and Miss DuPont would serve no purpose. We will do our best to deliver our report whilst still putting you in the best possible light," Edwina said.

Miss Glover slowly calmed. Her shoulders ceased their shaking, and she dabbed her eyes with her handkerchief once again. "You would really do that for me?" she asked.

"Edwina and I owe the school a debt of gratitude. If it weren't for Miss DuPont's, we would never have become friends. If your friendship with Miss DuPont is anything like ours, we would not damage it for the world," Beryl said.

"I don't know how to thank you," Miss Glover said, reaching up and laying a boney hand on Edwina's encircling arm.

Beryl looked over at Edwina before speaking. While she disliked taking advantage of anyone whilst in a vulnerable position, the case was not solved until they understood how the pranks had been accomplished. Miss DuPont deserved to know the whole truth, even if it made her unhappy to hear it.

"I suppose you might start by telling us how you managed to make so much mischief all on your own," Beryl said.

Miss Glover nodded. "It was remarkably easy. Girls of that age are so self-absorbed and so gullible, by and large. They are also remarkably careless with their things."

"So, you simply took advantage of their faults?" Edwina asked, removing her arm from the older woman's shoulders and returning to her spot on the sofa beside Beryl.

"I suppose that I did. Most of the things I purloined were left here, there, and everywhere around the school. The girl who lost the item would swear up and down that it had been in the dormitory with her other things when it went missing, but it almost never was," Miss Glover said, the strength returning to her voice as she remembered the girls' behavior.

Beryl wondered if Miss Glover had felt almost justified in her actions. Did she think she was teaching the students a lesson in responsibility when she helped herself to their things? Was that why she returned them?

"What did you do with them?" Edwina asked. "It must not have seemed like a good idea to keep them in your room. After all, the maid might have seen what you had taken."

"You are correct about that. I simply stashed the items in the nearest disused dumbwaiter. There are so many in the building and with our numbers so diminished, few are actually ever used now. I would place the item into a dumbwaiter and then send it up to the empty wing of the servants' quarters. I'd leave it there until I decided to return it to the dormitory," Miss Glover said.

"The dumbwaiters explain the strange noises too, don't they?" Edwina asked. "They would make the creaking and rattling sounds the household has been hearing."

Miss Glover nodded. "At first, I thought the noises would draw attention to what I was doing. Instead, the girls began telling each other that the school was haunted."

"Just as Paul Deering hoped," Beryl said. "I have to ask, if you were willing to do something as unscrupulous as this, did you have anything to do with Veronica's death?"

Miss Glover drew in a sharp breath. "Of course not. Why would I harm Veronica?" She looked from Beryl to Edwina, her blue eyes wide in her face.

"Veronica told Miss DuPont that she needed to dismiss you if she wanted Veronica to continue to contribute financially to the school," Edwina said.

"If you knew that Veronica planned to leave the school a large sum of money in her will, you might have decided that killing her was a far better way to assist your friend than slowly destroying her school's reputation," Beryl said.

"I didn't have any idea that Veronica had mentioned the school in her will," Miss Glover said. "Or that she asked Miss DuPont to dismiss me. If I had known that, I would have spoken to Miss DuPont about it."

"Can you prove that you didn't know about the money?" Edwina asked.

"I don't suppose that I can, other than to say that if I had killed Veronica, I would not have bothered to take a compact that Bernice left on the hall table yesterday evening," she said. "If my word is not enough for you, I don't know what will be. Now if you will excuse me, I would like to be alone to collect my thoughts before you tell Miss DuPont what I have done."

With that, she rose and crossed the room to open the door. As they passed her on their way out, Beryl's heart squeezed with sadness. At that moment she fervently wished that Miss Glover looked like a dragon once more.

Chapter 41

Edwina was relieved when Beryl suggested that she be the one to deliver unpleasant news to Miss DuPont. Not that she wished to shirk her duties, but one nagging question remained stubbornly on her mind. She was still not satisfied about the question of Mary and Evans the gardener. Why had she suggested him as a groundskeeper when so clearly he had none of the skills required for the job? It was undeniably suspicious and left Edwina with an uncomfortable feeling in the pit of her stomach.

When she reentered the school building, Jennings greeted her with his usual courtesy. She inquired as to Mary's whereabouts, and he said that he thought she might be found in the writing room. Edwina hurried down the hallway as quickly as good manners and a general sense of the decorum expected by Miss DuPont would allow.

As she approached the rear of the building, she slowed her pace and commanded herself to approach with a calm demeanor. No good would come of appearing agitated. As hopeful as she was that Mary could offer a perfectly good excuse for recommending an incompetent gardener, she struggled to think of one and feared that her concern would show.

Edwina had always loved the atmosphere of the writing room when she was a student at Miss DuPont's, and little had changed since those years had passed. The yellow striped wallpaper and heavy furniture with its dark green velvet upholstery appeared the same as it had when she was a girl. The fireplace, not used so early in the year, was filled with the same urn of silk flowers that it had been in years past. A china shepherdess sat on the mantel above the fireplace, its reflection showing in the expanse of mirror hung behind it.

The mirror reflected more than just the shepherdess and other bric-a-brac lined up along the mantelpiece. From her position poised on the doorway's threshold, Edwina could clearly see the recessed alcove at the back of the room where a writing desk sat tucked away. Seeing Mary reflected there, Edwina took a step toward the desk.

But something in the mirror stopped her in her tracks. Mary appeared busy with a mundane and familiar task. Surely, she must have thought herself shielded from view. Edwina held her breath as she watched her former classmate deftly employ both hands in an effort to fill her fountain pen with ink from a bottle placed upon the desk. As Edwina squinted at the reflection, it was clear that Mary had no difficulty in performing the job despite the sling covering her right arm.

Edwina bolted from the door and raced to the side of the desk. Mary glanced up, a look of panic spreading across her face. In her distress she dropped the pen onto the desk blotter and knocked over the bottle of ink. A dark pool of it spread across the surface of the desk and Edwina fought the urge to look for something with which to mop up the spill. She reminded herself that her primary role was that of an investigator, not a student at the school taxed with doing her part to keep it neat and tidy.

"I know this does not look good, but I can explain," Mary said, righting the bottle.

"I think you had better," Edwina said. She took another step forward and took ahold of Mary's sling. She slid it up over Mary's hand and exposed her arm beneath. Sliding her former classmate's sleeve up away from her wrist to reveal her arm, she gasped. Mary's hand and forearm were completely covered with scratches and dark bruises. However, her wrist was not swollen in the least.

"I can think of only one reason why you would feign this sort of an injury. You were involved with Veronica's death, weren't you?"

"I know that it may be difficult to believe, but I do have a very good reason for my deception," Mary said.

"Is that reason that you murdered Veronica?" Edwina asked.

"Certainly not," Mary said. "I am shocked that you don't think more of my character than to accuse me of something so terrible."

"I confess I am shocked to find myself having such suspicions of you. But between your deception about your injury and the fact that you have recommended a completely incompetent gardener to be hired here at the school, things are not looking good for you, Mary," Edwina said.

Mary slumped against her chair back. "No, I'm sure that they don't. But I promise you it's not what you think. If you will allow me to speak with Desmond, I am sure that this entire matter can be cleared up," Mary said.

"Are you saying that Desmond is somehow involved?" Edwina asked.

While she had not been happy to think that Veronica might have met her fate at the hand of her second husband, she was even less pleased to consider that Desmond might have been the guilty party.

"He was vital to the entire affair," Mary said. "Please, let us tell you about it together."

"You aren't just trying to delay things in the hopes of making an escape, are you?" Edwina asked. "Because I will telephone the police immediately."

"I promise I'm not trying to get away with anything. If you will consent to go in search of Desmond together, we will tell you everything."

Edwina searched Mary's face for signs of dishonesty. She wasn't sure if what she saw was sincerity or if she only wanted it to be. Either way, she had to make a decision.

"All right. But first we need to go and find Beryl," Edwina said.

"The two of you are not really here searching for a finishing school for Beryl's goddaughter, are you?" Mary asked.

"You are not the only one with something to hide," Edwina said. "Miss DuPont hired us to get to the bottom of the pranks and thefts here at the school. But while we were at it, we couldn't help suspecting that Veronica's death was not an accident."

"You two were always the noticing kind. Please, let's find Desmond and we will explain," Mary said, getting to her feet.

Edwina nodded and led her out the door.

Chapter 42

As Beryl descended the grand staircase, leaving Miss Glover and Miss DuPont on their own to repair their damaged friendship, she caught sight of her own dearest friend moving swiftly through the foyer below. Edwina glanced up, a look of relief spreading across her face. Mary White stood directly behind her, looking more concerned than Beryl had ever seen, including when they were all so young and Veronica had led a bullying campaign against her. Beryl's hopes for a speedy departure faded with each step she took toward the foyer.

"Beryl, have you seen Desmond?" Edwina called up to her.

"Were you looking for me?" A man's voice floated toward them from along the corridor.

Beryl quickened her pace and joined Edwina at the base of the stairs. Desmond hurried from the far side of the building and Beryl felt certain that she caught a look of grave concern flash across his face as he spotted Mary and Edwina together.

"Yes, we were," Mary said. There was definitely a tremor in her voice and Beryl looked at Edwina questioningly. Her friend arched an eyebrow and inclined her head toward the drawing room.

"Why don't we all see if the drawing room is empty," Edwina said. "I think we could do with a bit of privacy."

As they entered the grand room, Beryl was relieved to see that it was devoid of any other occupants. Even the servants were absent. Edwina led them to the seating area nearest the drinks tray and Beryl wondered what the chances were that she might fix them all a stiff gin fizz. From the look on Edwina's face, it was not particularly likely.

Without her usual attention to social niceties, Edwina launched directly into her question. "Mary, would you be willing to show Beryl your arm?" she asked.

Mary nodded and removed her sling. She pulled her sleeve up over her forearm, exposing a series of raw, red scratches and inky bruises. Whatever Beryl had imagined was about to be revealed, she would not have imagined that.

"I take it you did not actually sprain your wrist while sleepwalking, did you?" Beryl asked.

Mary shook her head as she sank into a sturdy armchair. "My injuries occurred during a confrontation with Veronica."

Beryl looked from Mary to Desmond, who nodded slowly.

"It's true," he said.

"So, you did know about this?" Edwina asked Desmond.

Beryl looked at Edwina with admiration. Somehow, she had managed to keep any note of criticism from her tone of voice. Beryl was not sure that she could have done the same.

"I did. In fact, the sling was my idea," he said.

"There wasn't really any doctor that you called, was there?" Beryl asked.

"No, there wasn't," Desmond said.

"Mary, you claimed that if we spoke with you both, it would prove that you did not kill Veronica," Edwina said. "But so far what you've admitted leaves me less convinced than ever of your innocence."

"Before I say any more, I must have your assurance that you

will not make public what I'm about to share with you," Mary said.

There was something in Mary's tone that Beryl recognized. She looked over at Edwina and gave her a slight nod. Edwina pursed her lips as if trying to decide what to do. After a moment's pause, she nodded.

"We will not be the ones to speak with the public. I cannot promise that we will not speak with the authorities."

Mary and Desmond exchanged a look of their own.

"That will have to be good enough for us," Desmond said.

Mary looked down at her arm and gently ran a slim finger over the angry, red marks. "I was at the grotto when Veronica died, but I did not murder her," Mary said. "It truly was an accident."

"We're listening," Beryl said.

She looked over at Edwina, who had drawn her usually impeccable posture into an even more upright pose. Mary had better be convincing or Beryl knew that her friend would be telephoning to the authorities immediately. Knowing Edwina, even if she could not convince Inspector Lloyd to take her seriously, she would be sure to find someone who would. As a local magistrate and a trusted member of her community, she tended to make a favorable impression on those in positions of power.

"Edwina asked why I hired Evans the gardener when he so clearly has no skills for the job. The fact of the matter is that my position here at Miss DuPont's is not what I led you to believe earlier," Mary said. "I am not here as a result of any financial woes."

Beryl's suspicions seemed confirmed. "You're involved with intelligence work, aren't you?"

Mary lifted an eyebrow and looked over at Desmond before nodding. "You sound like someone in the know about such things," she said.

"Perhaps I am. But what does that have to do with what happened to Veronica?" Beryl asked.

"Evans is an operative for the Germans. You may be aware that there are rumblings that they are looking to rearm." Mary paused and waited for Beryl to nod. When she did so, she continued. "He thinks that I am sympathetic to his views, but I assure you I'm not."

Beryl was well aware of rumors in certain circles that the world might once more be headed for war. She hoped with all her being that such chatter was entirely unfounded, but she knew in her heart of hearts that such hope was likely futile. The aftermath of the first conflict had been bungled, in her opinion, and it had left the German people even worse off than when it all began. They were unsurprisingly looking for some sort of hope of their own, and it would take only the right sort of leader to light a fire that would burn them all.

"What's that have to do with Veronica—or Desmond, for that matter?" Edwina asked.

Beryl heard a tremor in Edwina's voice that she could not disguise. Beryl knew that a second outbreak of hostilities was amongst Edwina's darkest fears, and she wished there was one way to shield her from the notion. But under such circumstances no one's feelings were likely to be spared.

"I told Evans that I had secured a job at Miss DuPont's school for the sole purpose of placing myself in the path of people with important connections. The girls who attend a school like this have fathers in important government positions and mothers with social influence. It was easy to convince him that I would have access to secrets he would wish to pass along to his handlers," Mary said.

"And so, you procured a job for him here as well?" Edwina asked.

"I did. I told him that it would be easy to pass on information if we were both on the spot," Mary said. "He took to the suggestion with enthusiasm."

Beryl heard Edwina draw in a breath as if she was shocked at Mary's admission.

"I assume that you did pass on information whenever the opportunity arose," Beryl said.

"Yes, I did. As I'm sure you suspect, that information was misleading, to say the least," Mary said.

Edwina slowly exhaled. "So, you were acting as a double agent?" she asked.

Mary nodded. "That's it exactly. Over the last several weeks I've been doling out believable but manifestly untrue pieces of information that the Germans are eager to acquire. Unfortunately, the latest of these transactions went woefully awry."

Beryl looked over at Desmond, who had shifted in his seat. He cleared his throat.

"Early in the term, Mary approached me and asked if I would be willing to provide her with altered plans and schematics for aircraft supposedly being created by Montrose Aeronautics for the Royal Air Force. Naturally I agreed. When Veronica insisted that Florence attend Miss DuPont's school, it made it all the easier for Mary to convince Evans that she had taken the documents without my knowledge."

"But what does any of this have to do with Veronica?" Edwina asked.

"Veronica was never one to mind her own business. I'm afraid that I lied to you when I said that she had not actually seen me with the gardener. But she had completely misinterpreted what she witnessed. She assumed that I was conducting a romantic affair with him and she was determined to catch me out about it."

"I am guessing that she saw something she should not have," Beryl said.

"On the night of her death she had been drinking heavily,

just as Desmond indicated," Mary said, looking from Beryl to Edwina. "I had arranged to meet Evans at the grotto in order to give him a convincing, yet false, set of plans for a new airplane designed by Montrose Aeronautics and destined for the Royal Air Force. Unfortunately, Veronica followed me, hoping to catch me in flagrante."

"But that's not what she saw, was it?" Beryl asked.

"No. She saw me handing a file to Evans and she recognized the logo for Montrose Aeronautics printed on the outside of it. She flew at me and accused me of treason. She grabbed my wrists and scratched me. The marks on my forearm are from her. But she really did slip on the moss-covered rocks. She hit her head as soon as she lost her footing. She didn't drown in the pool. The blow to her head killed her instantly," Mary said.

The color had drained from Mary's face and despite the fact that she was clearly a seasoned operative, it was plain to see that retelling of the experience had rattled her. Beryl knew just how she felt. She had found herself in shocking and perilous situations more times than she cared to recall, especially in service to her own country or one of its allies.

"Did you turn her over in order to make it look as though she drowned?" Edwina asked.

"Evans was the one who did that. He thought it would be more convincing somehow," Mary said. "I told him that we both had to deny all knowledge of the incident in order to preserve our secrecy about the documents. I handed him the file folder and we each hurried back to the school."

"So, he still has no idea that you have been passing him false documents?" Edwina asked.

"No, he hasn't. And no one else has either, thanks to Desmond," Mary said. "I would go so far as to say that Veronica's reaction to seeing the file made him all the more convinced that I was on his side."

"Were you the one who thought of disguising Mary's injuries in the sling?" Edwina asked, turning to Desmond.

Desmond nodded. "It seemed like a practical way to hide the evidence of their confrontation. But I assure you, I took Inspector Lloyd into my confidence, which is why he has made so little effort to investigate Veronica's death. We really were only trying to look out for the country's best interest."

Edwina's posture relaxed slightly. Her hands fidgeted in her lap and Beryl imagined that her friend desperately craved her knitting needles.

"I'm pleased to hear that the constabulary is no less professional here than it is in Walmsley Parva," Edwina said. "I have been rather worried about what might have happened to a reputable institution."

"Can we count on you to keep our secret?" Mary asked.

Beryl looked over at Edwina, who nodded slightly. "We were not hired to look into Veronica's murder. We are simply here to get to the bottom of strange noises and petty thefts that were damaging the school's reputation. I'm happy to say we've gotten to the bottom of that, so there's nothing else for us to look into," Beryl said.

"You've solved that too, have you?" Mary asked.

"We have, but you are not the only ones bound to secrecy," Beryl said. She looked over at Edwina and winked. "Now if you'll excuse us, Edwina and I are eager to head for home." She stood and waited for Edwina to get to her feet. As they reached the door she looked back once more. "Desmond, I'm going to hold you to your promise to let me take a ride in your plane sooner or later." With that, they headed out the door.

Chapter 43

Edwina doubted that her legs would hold her as they exited the drawing room. Her knees felt weak, and her skin had grown both hot and clammy. If it were not for Beryl's sturdy arm helping to support her, she was not sure she would have made it down the hall.

It was not just the reality of spies and counterspies ensconced beneath Miss DuPont's respectable roof that had rattled her so terribly. No, it was the idea that more trouble with the Germans very well might be brewing. Enduring the Great War had been bad enough.

The very thought that hostilities might not have come decisively to an end left her feeling chilled through and through. She looked over at Beryl as if to assure herself that the whole thing had simply been a mistake. From the grave expression on her friend's face, she knew she was wrong to hope for that.

"You knew that it was possible we might be headed for more trouble, didn't you?" Edwina asked.

Beryl stopped and looked at her friend. "I had hoped very much that I was wrong."

"I suppose there's no harm in continuing to hope that you were, is there?" Edwina asked.

"There's never any harm in hoping for the best," Beryl said, giving her a warm smile. "You know what I'm hoping for right now?"

"Knowing you, it's that we'll be able to return to the village in time for you to still squeeze in a bit of your golfing vacation," Edwina said, feeling her spirits lift.

Even when so much seemed to have changed, some things stayed comfortingly predictable.

"You read my mind. Shall we see if we can convince Simpkins and Charles to join us?" she asked.

"Since it appears that Mary does not actually need any assistance with the art class, I think it would be best to load them into the motorcar and head for home straightaway," Edwina said. "I am sure that Mary will be able to come up with a convincing explanation of how her wrist has healed so quickly."

"Then let's see if we can find them," Beryl said.

Edwina looked through the French doors out onto the veranda and spotted Crumpet capering toward her across the lawn.

"We shall have to take our leave of Miss DuPont as well. We can't have her thinking she neglected to teach us how to behave as proper houseguests," Edwina said.

As she spoke, Simpkins and Miss DuPont appeared, closely following on Crumpet's heels. The two older people had their heads bent toward each other companionably, and Edwina wondered what they possibly could have found to discuss for so long. As she and Beryl met them on the veranda, Miss DuPont looked up, her face covered in an enormous smile.

"Your Mr. Simpkins has just made me the most unexpected proposal," Miss DuPont said with a tinkling laugh.

Two bright spots of color decorated the elderly woman's papery cheeks. Edwina felt her heart clutch in her chest. While she had needed time to become accustomed to Simpkins becoming a very real part of her household, ensconced as he was in a back bedroom on the second floor, she had come to truly enjoy having him there. In fact, she had come to depend on him being close at hand and underfoot, hobnailed boots and all. If he had made a proposal to Miss DuPont, what would that mean to their living arrangements?

It had been a most distressing afternoon. She felt her knees begin to wobble once more. Again, Beryl seemed to sense her distress and reached out a steadying arm. Edwina forced herself to breathe in slowly.

"And what sort of proposal might that be, Miss DuPont?" Beryl asked.

"Would you care to tell them about it yourself, Mr. Simpkins? After all, it was your idea," Miss DuPont said, beaming up at him.

"It would be my pleasure," he said, giving them a mischievous grin. "It occurred to me that Miss DuPont's difficulties at the school might be easily solved if she looked at her objectives with fresh eyes."

He winked at Edwina as if to let her in on the jest. She squinted at him, not sure she wished to look at anything else with fresh eyes.

"What exactly does that mean?" she asked.

"I suggested to her that the world had changed a great deal in recent years. I told her all about how Colonel Kimberly's Condiment Company is committed to changing with the times by trying new things, like developing new products such as convenience foods, on account of all the working women such as yourselves."

"That's right, he did," Miss DuPont said. "I feel rather foolish not to have considered his proposal myself. It's such an obvious solution."

She smiled up at Simpkins again with obvious delight. Edwina did not feel the least bit better or more enlightened.

"What new proposal has he asked you to consider?" Edwina asked.

"As you well know, I do enjoy investing in a variety of businesses. I suggested to Miss DuPont that if she would take it upon herself to offer a whole new sort of program, one for modern young career women to prepare themselves to participate in the business world, much as you two have done, it would be my pleasure to provide her with financial backing while she did so."

Edwina felt her jaw drop most unbecomingly. She snapped it shut and looked over at Beryl.

"That promises to be a perfect solution to the challenges you face here," Beryl said. "It sounds like the sort of thing that even Florence Montrose might find appealing. I expect Miss Glover might even be persuaded to see its merits."

Miss DuPont nodded vigorously. "I thought that Miss Glover could continue to assist me with the traditional finishing school students and that Mary White would be perfect to help launch this new endeavor. What do you think?" she asked.

"I can't imagine anything that I would like more than to see you succeed with something so forward-thinking," Edwina said.

"If it weren't for the two of you, I don't know that I would have believed Mr. Simpkins that such a thing was possible. You are the very picture of independent modern women."

Edwina looked over Miss DuPont's shoulder to where the familiar figure of Charles was making his way toward them. Over the last few months, she had grown quite comfortable in considering herself to be a modern sort of woman, but she wasn't sure how entirely independent she wished to be. After all, there was nothing she loved more than sharing her life and her triumphs with her friends.